J. S. Fletcher
Scarhaven Keep

Abridged Edition

journeyforth®

Greenville, South Carolina

Library of Congress Cataloging-in-Publication Data

Fletcher, J. S. (Joseph Smith), 1863–1935.
  Scarhaven Keep / J.S. Fletcher.—Abridged ed.
    p. cm.
  Summary: When famed actor Bassett Oliver fails to show for a
rehearsal, aspiring playwright Richard Copplestone uncovers a mys-
tery when he is sent to the small village of Scarhaven on the northern
coast of England to track down the actor's movements.
  ISBN 978–1–60682–173–2 (perfect bound pbk. : alk. paper)
  [1. Mystery and detective stories. 2. Missing persons—Fiction. 3.
Great Britain—History—George V, 1910–1936—Fiction.] I. Title.
  PZ7.F631Sc 2011
  [Fic]—dc22

                                                   2011001906

Design and page layout by Nathan Hutcheon

© 2012 by BJU Press
Greenville, South Carolina 29614
JourneyForth Books is a division of BJU Press

ISBN 978–1–60682–173–2

15 14 13 12 11 10 9 8 7 6 5 4 3 2 1

Publisher's Note

British author J.S. Fletcher (1863–1935) studied law, but he ultimately turned his interests to journalism. His first published books were poetry, and he went on to pen over two hundred books, both fiction and non-fiction, on a wide range of topics. He was one of the leading writers of detective fiction, a genre which presents the mystery early in the book and features a gifted, but amateur, investigator who unravels the clues to reveal a clear solution.

Originally published in 1922, *Scarhaven Keep* features the search for a missing person . . . and perhaps a crime. Playwright Richard Copplestone's keen observations and ability to link cause to effect aid him in his search for the missing actor Bassett Oliver.

Every true mystery has at its heart a crime that needs to be resolved, and this Fingerprint Classic edition of *Scarhaven Keep* delivers to mystery lovers an intriguing problem with an interesting, if unexpected conclusion.

Contents

Chapter 1

Wanted at Rehearsal

Jerramy had been for thirty years the stage doorkeeper at the Theatre Royal, Norcaster, where theatrical companies came and went with unfailing regularity. Sometimes new faces came along, but as a rule the same old favorites showed themselves for a good many years in succession.

And every actor and actress who came to Norcaster knew Jerramy. He was the first official person encountered; he handed them little bundles of letters and papers, he answered inquiries made of him, and he gave satisfactory advice about lodgings and landladies. His genial greeting always culminated in a hearty handshake.

At a quarter past one on a Monday afternoon in a sunny October, Jerramy leaned over the half door of his chamber. He spoke with an anxious man who had hung about restlessly for the past ten minutes obviously waiting for somebody. The man had looked up the street and down a dozen times; almost as often he had pulled out his watch and compared it with the clock of a neighboring church; he had several times gone up the dark passage which led to the dressing rooms, returning more perplexed than ever. He was, in fact, the business manager of the great Mr. Bassett Oliver, who was opening for the week at the Theatre Royal. Mr. Oliver, not quite satisfied with the way the play was coming along, had called a special rehearsal for a quarter to one. Everything and everybody was ready for that rehearsal. But the great man himself had not arrived.

Mr. Bassett Oliver was neither irregular nor unpunctual, as many a man would attest. On the contrary, he was very strict, precise, and systematic. Moreover, he always did himself what he expected each member of his company to do. Therefore his half hour of tardiness seemed all the more extraordinary.

"Never knew him to be late before. Never!" exclaimed the business manager, impatiently pulling out his watch for the twentieth time. "Not in all my ten years' experience of him. Not once."

"You've seen him this morning, Mr. Stafford?" inquired Jerramy. "He's in the town?"

"I suppose he's in the town," answered Mr. Stafford. "I suppose he's at his old quarters, the Angel. But *I* haven't seen him. Been too busy to call there."

Jerramy opened the half door and, going out to the end of the passage, looked up and down the street.

"There's a taxicab coming quick around the corner now," he announced presently. "I should think he's in it."

The business manager bustled out to the pavement as the cab came to a halt. But instead of the fine face and distinguished presence of Mr. Bassett Oliver, he found himself confronting a young man, somewhat shy and rather nervous. The young man immediately produced a card case and presented his card.

"Mr. Bassett Oliver?" he said inquiringly. "Is he here? I . . . I've got an appointment with him for one o'clock, and I'm sorry I'm late . . . my train—"

"Mr. Oliver is not here yet," broke in Stafford. "He's late too. Unaccountably late. An appointment, you say?"

He was looking the stranger over as he spoke, taking him for some stage-struck youth who had probably persuaded the good-natured actor to give him an interview. His expression changed, however, as he read the card which the young man handed over. He started a little and held out his hand with a smile.

"Oh, Mr. Copplestone!" he exclaimed. "How do you do? My name's Stafford. I'm Mr. Oliver's business manager. He must want to see you about your play, of course."

He looked at the newcomer with renewed interest, thinking secretly that he was a very youthful innocent to have written a play which Bassett Oliver, a shrewd critic and by no means easy to please, had been eager to accept and was about to produce.

"I got a wire from Mr. Oliver yesterday," replied Mr. Copplestone. "I ought to have received it in the morning, I suppose, but I'd gone out for the day. You know—gone out early, so I didn't find it until I got back to my rooms late at night. I got on the very next train I could from King's Cross, and it was late getting in here."

"Then you've practically been traveling all night," remarked Stafford. "Well, Mr. Oliver hasn't turned up. Most unusual for him."

Just then another man came hurrying down the passage from the dressing rooms. "I say, Stafford!" he exclaimed as he emerged on the street. "This is bizarre! I've just rung up the Angel, and Oliver's rooms were all ready for him as usual yesterday, but he never came. They've neither seen nor heard of him. Did you see him yesterday?"

"No," replied Stafford. "I didn't. He ordered this rehearsal a quarter to one—here, today. But *somebody* must have seen him yesterday. Where's his dresser? Where's Hackett?"

"Inside," said the other man. "But he hasn't seen him either since Saturday night. Hackett has friends living in these parts, and he went off to see them early yesterday morning, He's only just now returned. He expected to find Oliver here."

"So did this gentleman." Stafford turned with a wave of the hand towards Copplestone. "Mr. Copplestone, this is our stage manager, Mr. Rothwell. Rothwell, this is Mr. Richard Copplestone, author of the new play that Mr. Oliver's going to produce next month. Mr. Copplestone got a wire yesterday, asking him to come here, and he's traveled all night to get here."

"A wire sent from where?" asked Rothwell. "And when?"

Copplestone drew some letters and papers from his pocket and selected one. "That's it," he said. "There you are. Sent off from Northborough at nine-thirty, yesterday morning. Sunday."

"Look here, Stafford, we'd better telephone to Northborough to his hotel," remarked Rothwell. "The Golden Apple, wasn't it?"

"Then it's no good," replied Stafford. "The Golden Apple has no phone. Old-fashioned place. We'd better wire."

"Too slow," said Rothwell. "Let's telephone the theater there and ask them to step across and make inquiries. I'll do it at once."

He hurried inside again, and Stafford turned to Copplestone.

"Come inside until we get some news," he said. "Let Jerramy take your things into his chamber; he'll keep an eye on them till you want them. Look here," he turned to the cab driver, "just you wait a bit. Ten minutes anyway. Come in, Mr. Copplestone."

Copplestone followed the business manager up the passage to a dressing room in which an elderly man was engaged in unpacking trunks and cases. He looked up expectantly at the sound of footsteps, then looked down again at the work in hand and went silently on with it.

"This is Hackett, Mr. Oliver's dresser," said Stafford. "Been with him . . . how long, Hackett?"

"Twenty years next January, Mr. Stafford," answered the dresser quietly.

"Ever known Mr. Oliver to be late like this?" inquired Stafford.

"Never, sir. There's something wrong," replied Hackett. "I'm sure of it. I feel it. You ought to go and look for him, some of you gentlemen."

"Where?" asked Stafford. "He's not come to the Angel, as he ought to have done yesterday. I believe you're the last person who saw him, Hackett. Aren't you now?"

"I saw him at the Golden Apple at Northborough at twelve o'clock Saturday night, sir," answered Hackett. "I took a bag of his to his rooms there. He knew I was going off first thing next morning to see an uncle of mine, who's a farmer on the coast between here and Northborough. And he told me he shouldn't want me until one o'clock today, so I came straight here to the theater. I didn't call in at the Angel at all this morning."

"Did he say anything about himself yesterday?" asked Stafford. "Was he going anywhere?"

"Not a word, Mr. Stafford," replied Hackett. "But you know his habits as well as I do."

"Just so. Mr. Oliver," Stafford continued, turning to Copplestone, "is a great lover of outdoor life. On days when we're traveling from one town to another, he likes to journey by motorcar—alone. When the two towns are not very far apart like this, it's his practice to find a particular spot of beauty or a place of interest between them and to spend his day there. I daresay that's what he did yesterday. All last week we were at Northborough, which is, like Norcaster, a coast town. There's fifty miles between them. If he followed his usual plan, he'd hire a motorcar and follow the coast road. And if he came to any place that was of special interest, he'd stop there. But in the usual way of things, he would have turned up at his rooms at the Angel Hotel here last night. He didn't, and he hasn't turned up here either. So where is he?"

"Have you made inquiries of the company, Mr. Stafford?" asked Hackett. "Most of 'em wander about a bit of a Sunday. They might have seen him."

"Good idea," agreed Stafford. He steered Copplestone through a maze of scenery and stepped out onto the stage, where the members of the company sat or stood about in groups, each conscious that something unusual had occurred.

"I say! Have any of you seen Mr. Oliver anywhere since Saturday night? Can anybody tell anything about him? Anything at all? Because he's not come here, and he's not come to town at all, so far as we know."

Rothwell came hurrying onto the stage from the opposite wings. He hastened across to Stafford and drew him and Copplestone a little aside.

"I've just heard from Northborough," he said. "I phoned Waters, the manager there, to run across to the Golden Apple and make inquiries. The Golden Apple people say that Oliver left there at eleven o'clock yesterday morning. He was alone. He simply walked out of the hotel. And they know nothing more."

Chapter 2

Gray Rock and Gray Sea

The three men stood for a while silently looking at each other. Copplestone secretly wondered why the two managers seemed so concerned; to him a delay of half an hour did not seem as serious as they evidently considered it. But he had never met Bassett Oliver and knew nothing of his ways; he began to comprehend matters only when Rothwell turned to Stafford with an air of decision and spoke.

"Look here," said Rothwell, "You'd better go yourself and make inquiry at Northborough. See if you can track him. Something must be wrong—seriously wrong."

"One minute," said Stafford. He turned again to the groups behind him. "We've just heard that Mr. Oliver left his hotel at Northborough yesterday morning at eleven o'clock, alone, walking. Has anybody any idea of any project, any excursion, that he had in mind? Has anybody anything to tell?" he asked anxiously.

An elderly man who had been in conversation with the leading lady stepped forward.

"I was talking to Oliver about the coast scenery between here and Northborough the other day. Friday. He'd never seen the coast and said he'd try and see something of it on Sunday. Yesterday, you know." Here he came closer to the two managers and lowered his voice. "I used to know that coast pretty well. It is very wild, lonely, and a good bit dangerous. Sharp and precipitous cliffs. Eh?"

Rothwell clapped a hand on Stafford's arm.

"You'd really better be off to Northborough," he said with decision. "You're sure to come across him. Go to the Golden Apple, then the station. Wire or telephone me here. Of course, this rehearsal's off. About this evening—well, a lot may happen before then. But go at once. I believe you can get expresses from here to Northborough pretty often."

"I'll go with you, if I may," said Copplestone suddenly. "I might be of use. There's that cab still at the door, you know."

"Good!" said Stafford. "Yes, come by all means." He turned to Rothwell for a moment. "If he should turn up here, phone Waters at the theater in Northborough," he said. "We'll look in there as soon as we arrive."

He hurried out with Copplestone, and together they drove up to the station where an express was just leaving for the south. Once on their way to Northborough, Stafford turned to his companion with a grave shake of the head.

"I daresay you still don't quite see the reason of our anxiety," he observed. "But if he's been exploring some spot on this coast yesterday, and it's as wild and dangerous as that chap Rutherford said, why, then—"

"You think he may have had an accident? Fallen over the cliffs or something?" asked Copplestone.

"I don't like to think anything," replied Stafford. "But I shall be a good deal relieved if we can get some definite news about him."

The first half-hour at Northborough yielded nothing definite. A telephone message from Rothwell had just come to the theater when they drove up to it. Nothing had so far been heard of the missing man at Norcaster, either at the theater or the hotel. Stafford and Copplestone hurried across to the Golden Apple and interviewed its proprietor; he could tell no more than that Mr. Bassett Oliver, having sent his luggage forward to Norcaster, had left the house on foot at eleven o'clock the previous morning, and had been seen to walk across the marketplace in the direction of the railway station. But an old headwaiter, who had served the famous actor's breakfast, was able to give some information. Mr. Oliver, he said, had talked a little to him about the coast scenery between Northborough and Norcaster and had asked him which stretch of it was worth seeing.

It was his impression that Mr. Oliver meant to journey somewhere along the coast.

"Then that's it," said Stafford, as he and Copplestone drove off again. "He's gone to some place between the two towns. But where? Anyhow, nobody's likely to forget Oliver if they've once seen him. And wherever he went, he'd have to have a ticket. Therefore . . . the booking office."

Here at last was light. One of the clerks in the booking office came forward at once with news of Mr. Bassett Oliver. He had come there the previous morning and had taken a first-class single ticket for Scarhaven on the 11:35 train, which arrived at Scarhaven at 12:10. Where was Scarhaven? On the coast twenty miles off on the way to Norcaster, and a train was leaving for Scarhaven in five minutes.

Stafford and Copplestone soon found themselves traveling back along the main line. A run of twenty minutes brought them to the junction, where at an adjacent siding they found a miniature train which ran over a narrow gauge railway towards the sea. Its course lay through a romantic valley hidden between high heather-clad moorland. They saw nothing of their destination nor of the coast until they came to a stop in a little station perched high on the side of a hill above the shore and sea lying far beneath them. They passed outside the gray walls of the station to take in the view.

"Just the place to attract Oliver," muttered Stafford, as he gazed around him. "He'd revel in it. Fairly revel!"

Copplestone gazed at the scene in silence. It was the first time he had ever seen the northern coast, and the strange glamour and romance of this stretch of it appealed strongly to his artistic senses. From high above, the landward extremity of a narrow bay resembled a Norwegian fjord running in from the sea between high shelving cliffs. The thickly wooded slopes were interrupted in intervals by great, gaunt outcroppings of gray rock. On the edge of either side of the bay were lines of ancient houses and cottages, built and grouped with the irregularity of individual liking. On the north side rose the square tower and low nave of an ancient church; on the opposite side stood a great Norman keep, half in ruins. Quays ran between the old cottages and the water's edge where small crafts nestled against the worn timbers. And at the end of the quays and the wooded promontories lay the North Sea, cold, gray, and mysterious in the waning October light.

"Just the place," repeated Stafford. "He'd have cheerfully traveled a thousand miles to see this. Now we know that he came here. What we next want to know is what he did when he got here."

Copplestone pointed to a house of many gables which stood a little way beneath them at the point where the waters of a narrow stream ran into the bay.

"That looks like an inn," he said. "Let's go down there and inquire. He would get here just about time for lunch, so he'd probably turn in there. And if they have a telephone there, you can call the theater at Norcaster and find out if anything else has been heard yet."

Stafford smiled approvingly and started out in the direction of the buildings towards which Copplestone had pointed.

"Excellent notion," he said. "Come on, then. You're quite a business man. An unusual thing in authors. Ah, look. I can make out the sign now: The Admiral's Arms, Mary Wooler. Let's hope landlady Mary Wooler can give us some useful news."

The Admiral's Arms proved to be an old-fashioned, spacious hostelry, comfortable in appearance. It stood on the edge of a broad shelf of headland and commanded a fine view of the little village and the bay. Stafford and Copplestone, turning in at the front door, found themselves in a deep, stone-paved hall. On one side behind a bar window, a pleasant-faced woman, silk-aproned and smartly-capped, was engaged in adding up columns of figures in a big account book. At the sight of strangers she threw open a door and invited them into a snugly furnished parlor, where a bright fire burned in an open hearth. Stafford gave his companion a look. This, again, was just the sort of old-world place which would appeal to Basset Oliver, supposing he had come across it.

"I wonder if you can give me some information?" he asked presently, when the attractive landlady had attended to their requests for refreshment. "Well, now, Mrs. Wooler, did you have a tall, hand-some, slightly gray-haired gentleman in here to lunch yesterday? Say about one o'clock?"

The landlady turned on her questioner with an intelligent smile.

"You mean Mr. Oliver, the actor?" she said.

"Good!" exclaimed Stafford, with a hearty sigh of relief. "I do! You know him then?"

"I've often seen him both at Northborough and at Norcaster," replied Mrs. Wooler. "But I never saw him *here* before yesterday. Yes, I knew him as soon as he walked in, and I had a bit of chat with him before he went out. He remarked that though he'd been coming into these parts for some years, he'd never been to Scarhaven before. He said he'd usually gone inland amongst the hills. Oh, yes, he was here. He had lunch here."

"We're seeking him," said Stafford, going directly to the question. "He ought to have turned up at the Angel Hotel at Norcaster last night and at the theater today at noon, but he did neither. I'm his business manager, Mrs. Wooler. Now can you tell us anything? More than you've already told, I mean."

The landlady, whose face expressed more and more concern as Stafford spoke, shook her head.

"I can't," she answered. "I don't know any more. He was here per-haps an hour or so. Then he went away, saying he was going to have a look round the place. I expected he'd come in again on his way to the station, but he never did. Dear, dear! I hope nothing's happened to him. Such a fine, pleasant man. And—"

"And what?" asked Stafford.

"These cliffs and rocks are so dangerous," murmured Mrs. Wooler. "I often say that no stranger ought to go alone here. They aren't safe, these cliffs."

Stafford set down his glass and rose.

"I think you've got a telephone in your hall," he said. "I'll just call up Norcaster and find out if they've heard anything. If they haven't—"

He shook his head and went out, and Copplestone glanced at the landlady.

"You are sure the cliffs are dangerous?" he said.

"To people who don't know them, yes," she replied. "They ought to be protected, but we don't get many tourists here, and the Scarhaven people know the danger spots well enough. Then again at the end of the south promontory there, beyond the Keep—"

"Is the Keep that high square tower amongst the woods?" asked Copplestone.

"That's it. It's all that's left of the old castle," answered Mrs. Wooler. "Well, off the point beneath that, there's a group of rocks. You'd perhaps noticed them as you came down from the station? They've various names. There's the King, the Queen, the Sugar Loaf, and so on. At low tide you can walk across to them. And some people like to climb them. But they are particularly dangerous. On the Queen rock there's a great hole called the Devil's Spout up which the sea rushes. Everybody wants to look over it, you know. If a man was there alone, and his foot slipped, and he fell, why—"

Stafford came back, looking more cast down than ever.

"They've heard nothing there," he announced. "Come on. We'll go down and see if we can learn anything from any of the people. We'll call in and see you later, Mrs. Wooler, and if you can make any inquiries in the meantime, do."

"Look here," he went on, when he and Copplestone had got outside, "you take this south side of the bay, and I'll take the north. Ask anybody you see, any likely person, fishermen and so on. Then come back here. And if we've heard nothing—"

He shook his head significantly and turned away. Copplestone, taking the other direction, felt that the manager's despondency was influencing himself. A disappearance of this sort was surely not to be explained easily. Nothing but exceptional happenings could have kept Bassett Oliver from the scene of his week's labors. There must have been an accident; it needed little imagination to conjure up its easy occurrence: a too careless step, a too near approach, a loose stone, a sudden giving way of crumbling soil, the shifting of an already detached rock. Any of these things might happen. And the thought of what might follow cast a gray tint over the already cold and gray sea.

He went on among the old cottages and fishing huts which lay at the foot of the wooded heights on the tops of whose pines and firs the gaunt ruins of the old Keep seemed to stand sentinel. He made inquiry at open doors and of little groups of men gathered on the quay and by the drawn-up boats. Nobody knew anything. According to what they told him, most of these people had been out and about all the previous afternoon; it had been a particularly fine day that Sunday, and they had all been out of doors on the quay and the shore in the sunshine. But nobody had any recollection of the man described, and Copplestone came to the conclusion that Oliver had not chosen that side of the bay. There was, however, one objection to that theory. So far as he could judge, that side was certainly the more attractive. And he himself went on to the end of it, on until he had left quay and village far behind and had come to a spit of sand which ran out into the sea exactly opposite the group of rocks of which Mrs. Wooler had spoken. There they lay, rising out of the surf like great monsters, a half-mile from where he stood. The tide was out at that time, and between him and them stretched a shining expanse of glittering wet sand. And, coming straight towards him across it, Copplestone saw the slim and graceful figure of a girl.

Chapter 3

The Man Who Knew Something

I t was not from any idle curiosity that Copplestone made up his mind to await the girl's nearer approach. There was no other human being in view, and he was anxious to get some information about the rocks whose grim outlines were rapidly becoming faint and indistinct in the gathering darkness. And so as the girl came towards him, picking her way across the pools which lay amidst the brown ribs of sand, he went forward, throwing away all formality and reserve in his eagerness.

"Forgive me for speaking so unceremoniously," he said as they met. "I'm looking for a friend who has disappeared mysteriously. Can you tell me if any time yesterday afternoon or evening you saw anywhere about here a tall, distinguished-looking man? The actor type. In fact, he is an actor. Perhaps you've heard of him? Mr. Bassett Oliver."

He was looking narrowly at the girl as he spoke, and she, too, looked narrowly at him out of a pair of gray eyes of more than ordinary intelligence and perception. At the famous actor's name she started a little and a faint color stole over her cheeks.

"Mr. Bassett Oliver!" she exclaimed in a clear, cultured voice. "My mother and I saw Mr. Oliver at the Northborough Theatre on Friday evening. Do you mean that he—"

"I mean, to put it bluntly, that Bassett Oliver is lost," answered Copplestone. "He came to this place yesterday to look round, he lunched at the Admiral's Arms, he went out after a chat with the landlady, and he's never been seen since. He should have turned up at the Angel at Norcaster last night and at a rehearsal at the Theatre Royal there today at noon, but he didn't. His manager and I have tracked him here. I've asked people all through the village, this side anyway. Nobody knows anything."

He and the girl still looked attentively at each other. Copplestone, indeed, was quietly inspecting her while he talked. He judged her to be twenty-one or two; she was a little above medium height, slim, graceful, pretty; and he was quick to notice that her entire air and appearance suggested their present surroundings. Her fair hair escaped from a knitted cap such as fisherfolk wear, she wore a rough blue jersey, her blue serge skirt was short and practical, and she was shod in brogues which seemed more acquainted with sand and salt water than with polish. Her face was tanned with the strong northern winds, and her ungloved hands, small and shapely as they were, were brown as the beach across which she had come.

"I have not seen nor heard of Mr. Bassett Oliver here," she answered. "I was out and about all yesterday afternoon and evening too, not on this side of the bay though. Have you been to the police station?"

"The manager may have been there," replied Copplestone. "He's gone along the other shore. But I don't think he'll get any help there. I'm afraid Mr. Oliver must have met with an accident. I saw you coming from the direction of those rocks just now. Could he have got out there across those sands yesterday afternoon?"

"Between three o'clock and evening, yes," said the girl.

"And is it dangerous out there?"

"Very dangerous. Especially to one who doesn't know them."

"There's something there called the Devil's Spout?"

"Yes. A deep fissure up which the sea boils. I hope he didn't fall in there. It seems dreadful to think of. If he did—"

"Well?" asked Copplestone bluntly, "what if he did?"

"Nothing ever came out that once went in," she answered. "It's a sort of whirlpool that's sucked right away into the sea. The people hereabouts say it's bottomless."

Copplestone turned his face towards the village.

"Well," he said, with a hint of hopelessness. "I can do no more here since it's growing dusk. I must go back and meet the manager."

The girl walked along at his side as he turned towards the village. "I suppose you are one of Mr. Oliver's company?" she observed presently. "You must all be much concerned."

"They're all greatly concerned," answered Copplestone. "But I don't belong to the company. No, I came to Norcaster this morning to meet Mr. Oliver. He is going—I hope I needn't say *was* going—to produce a play of mine next month, and he wanted to talk about the rehearsals. Everything was at a standstill when I reached Norcaster at one o'clock, so I came with Stafford, the business manager, to see what we could do about tracking Mr. Oliver. And I'm afraid. I'm very much afraid."

He paused as a gate set in the thick hedge of a garden suddenly opened to let out a man who at sight of the girl stopped, hesitated, and then waited for her approach. He was a tall, well-built man of apparently thirty years, dressed in a rough tweed knickerbocker suit. But the dusk had now deepened so that Copplestone could only gather an impression of ordinary good-lookingness from the face that was turned inquiringly on his companion. The girl turned and spoke hurriedly.

"This is my cousin, Mr. Greyle, of Scarhaven Keep," she murmured. "He may be able to help. Marston!" she went on, raising her voice, "can you give any help here? This gentleman," she paused, looking at Copplestone.

"My name is Richard Copplestone," he said.

"Mr. Copplestone is looking for Mr. Bassett Oliver, the famous actor," she continued, as the three met. "Mr. Oliver has mysteriously disappeared. Mr. Copplestone has traced him here to Scarhaven. He was here yesterday lunching at the inn, but there is no further news. Did you see anything, or hear anything of him?"

Marston Greyle, who had been inspecting the stranger narrowly in the fading light, shook his head.

"Bassett Oliver, the actor," he said. "Oh, yes, I saw his name on the bills in Norcaster the other day. Came here and has disappeared, you say? Under what circumstances?"

15

Scarhaven Keep

Copplestone had listened carefully to the newcomer's voice, more particularly to his accent. He had already gathered sufficient knowledge of Scarhaven to know that this man was the Squire, the master of the old house and gray ruin in the wood above the cliff. He also happened to know, being something of an archaeologist and well acquainted with family histories, that there had been Greyles of Scarhaven for many hundred years. And he wondered how it was that though this Greyle's voice was pleasant and cultured enough, its accent was decidedly American.

"Perhaps I'd better explain," said Copplestone. "I've already told most of it to this lady, but you will both understand more fully if I tell you more. It's this way," and he went on to tell everything that had come to light since one o'clock that day. "So you see," he concluded. "We're absolutely certain that Oliver went out of the Admiral's Arms up there about half-past two yesterday. But where? From that moment, no one seems to have seen him. Yet how could he come along this village street, this quay, without being seen?"

"He need not have come along the quayside," interrupted the girl. "There is a cliff path just below the inn which leads up to the Keep."

"Also, he mayn't have taken this side of the bay either." remarked Greyle. "He may have chosen the other. You didn't see or hear of him on your side, Audrey?"

"Nothing," replied the girl. "Nothing!"

Marston Greyle had fallen into line with the other two, and they were now walking along the quay in the direction of the Admiral's Arms. And presently Stafford, accompanied by a policeman, came hurriedly around a corner and quickened his steps at sight of Copplestone. The policeman, evidently much puzzled and interested, saluted the Squire as the two groups met.

"No news at all!" exclaimed Stafford, glancing at Copplestone's companions. "You got any?"

"None," replied Copplestone. "Not a word. This is Mr. Greyle, of the Keep. He has heard nothing. This lady, Miss Greyle, was out a good deal yesterday afternoon; she knows Oliver quite well by sight, but she did not see him. So if you've no news—"

Marston Greyle interrupted, turning to the policeman.

"What ought to be done?" he asked. "You've had cases of disappearance to deal with before, eh?"

"Can't say as I have, sir, in my time," answered the policeman. "Leastways, not of this sort. Of course, we can get search parties together, and one of 'em can go along the coast north'ards, and the other can go south'ards. And we might have a look round the rocks out yonder tomorrow, as soon as it's light. But if the gentleman went out there and had the bad luck to fall into that Devil's Spout, why, then, sir, I'm afraid all the searching in the world'll do no good. The odd thing is, gentlemen, if I may express an opinion, that nobody ever saw the gentleman after he had left Mrs. Wooler's!"

A fisherman came lounging across the quay from the shadow of one of the neighboring cottages. He touched his cap to Marston Greyle and looked inquiringly at the two strangers.

"Are you the gentlemen as is asking after another gentleman?" he said. "Cause if so, I make no doubt as how I had a word or two with him yesterday afternoon."

Stafford and Copplestone turned sharply on the newcomer. He was an elderly man, plain and homely, who responded frankly to their questioning glances. He went on at once, before they could put their questions into words.

"It 'ud be about half-past two, or maybe a bit nearer three o'clock," he said. "Up yonder it was, about a hundred yards this side of the Admiral's Arms. I was sitting on a baulk o' timber there, doing nothing, when he comes along. A tall, fine-looking man. He gives me a pleasant sort o' nod and said it was a grand day, and we got talking a bit about the scenery and such-like, and he said he'd never been here before. Then he pointed up to the big house and the old Keep yonder and asked whose place that might be, and I said that was the Squire's. 'And who may the Squire be?' says he. 'Mr. Marston Greyle,' says I. 'Recent come into the property.' 'Marston Greyle?' he says, sharp like. 'Why, I used to know a young man of that very name in America!' he says. 'Very like,' says I. 'I have heard as how the Squire had been in them parts before he came here.'

'Bless me!' he says, 'I've a good mind to call on him. How do you get up there?' he says. So I showed him that side path that runs up through the plantation to near the top, and I told him that if he followed that till he came to the Keep, he'd find another path there as would take him to the door of the house. And he gave me a shilling for my trouble, and off he went, the way as I'd pointed out. D'ye think that'll be the same gentleman now?"

Nobody answered this question. Everybody there was looking at Marston Greyle. The little group had drawn near to the light of one of the gas lamps which feebly illuminated the quay. It seemed to Copplestone that the Squire's face had paled when the fisherman arrived at the middle of his story, and he laughed a little uneasily.

"Said he knew me? In America?" he exclaimed. "I don't remember meeting Mr. Bassett Oliver out there. But then I met so many Englishmen in one place or another that I may have been introduced to him somewhere at some time and forgotten all about it."

Stafford spoke, with unnecessary abruptness in Copplestone's opinion.

"Bassett Oliver isn't—or wasn't—the sort of man anybody could forget once they'd met him," he said. "Anyhow, *did* he come to your house yesterday afternoon as this man suggests?"

Marston Greyle drew himself up. He looked Stafford up and down. Then he made a slight gesture to the girl, whose face had already assumed a troubled expression.

"If I had seen Mr. Bassett Oliver yesterday, sir," said Greyle, icily, "We would not be discussing his possible whereabouts now. Are you coming, Audrey?"

The girl hesitated, glanced at Copplestone, and then walked away with her cousin. Stafford sniffed contemptuously.

"Dolt," he muttered. "Couldn't he see that what I meant was that Oliver must either have been mistaken or have referred to some other Greyle whom he met? Foolish pride. Well, now," he went on, turning to the fisherman, "you're dead certain about what you've told us?"

"As certain as mortal man can be of aught there is," answered the informant. "Sure certain, mister."

"Make a note of it, constable," said Stafford. "Mr. Oliver was last seen going up the path to the Keep, having said he meant to call on Mr. Marston Greyle. I'll call on you again tomorrow morning. Copplestone," he went on, drawing his companion away, "I'm off to Norcaster. I shall see the police there and get detectives. There's something seriously wrong here, and we've got to get to the bottom of it! Now, look here. Will you stay here for the night, so as to be on the spot? I'll come back first thing in the morning and bring your luggage. Keep your eyes and ears open, Copplestone. It's my firm belief that there's been foul play. *Foul play*!"

Stafford hurried away up hill to the station, and Copplestone, after waiting a minute or two, turned along the quay on the north of the bay. He was following Audrey Greyle who was in front, alone.

Chapter 4

The Estate Agent

Copplestone had kept a sharp watch on Marston Greyle and his cousin when they walked off. He had seen that they had parted at a point a little farther along the shore road, the man turning up into the wood, the girl going forward along the quay which led to the other half of the village. He quickened his pace and followed her, catching up to her as she came to a path which led towards the old church. At the sound of his hurrying steps she turned and faced him, and he saw in the light of a cottage lamp that she still looked troubled and perplexed.

"Forgive me for running after you," said Copplestone as he went up to her. "I just wanted to say that I'm sorry about . . . about that little scene down there, you know. Your cousin misunderstood Mr. Stafford. What Stafford meant was that—"

"I saw what Mr. Stafford meant," she broke in quickly. "I'm sorry my cousin didn't see it. It was obvious."

"All the same, Stafford put it rather, shall we say, brusquely," remarked Copplestone. "He's terribly upset about Oliver's disappearance, and he didn't consider the effect of his words. And it was rather a surprise to hear that Oliver had known some man of your cousin's name over there in America, wasn't it?"

"And that Mr. Oliver should mysteriously disappear just after making such an announcement," said Audrey. "That certainly seems very surprising."

The two looked at each other, a question in the eyes of each, and Copplestone knew that the trouble in the girl's eyes arose from the inability to understand what was already a suspicious circumstance.

"But after all, that may have been a mere coincidence," he hastened to say. "Let's hope things may be cleared. I only hope that Oliver hasn't met with an accident and is lying somewhere without help. I'm going to remain here for the night, however, and Stafford will come back early in the morning and go more thoroughly into things. I suppose there will have to be a search of the neighborhood."

They had walked slowly up a path on the side of the cliff as they talked, and now the girl stopped before a small cottage which stood at the end of the churchyard, set in a tree-shaded garden and looking out on the bay. She laid her hand on the gate, glancing at Copplestone, and suddenly she spoke, a little impulsively.

"Will you come in and speak to my mother?" she said. "She was a great admirer of Mr. Oliver's acting, and she knew him at one time. She will be interested . . . and grieved."

Copplestone followed her up the garden and into the house, where she led the way into a small old-fashioned parlor in which a gray-haired woman sat writing at a bureau. Though the woman had once been strikingly handsome, her face seemed to bear traces of great trouble. She turned in surprise as her daughter led Copplestone in, but her manner became remarkably calm and collected as Audrey explained who he was and why he was there. And Copplestone, watching her narrowly, fancied that he saw interest flash into her eyes when she heard of Bassett Oliver's remark to the fisherman. But she made no comment, and when Audrey had finished the story, she turned to Copplestone as if she had already summed up the situation.

"We know this place so well, having lived here so long, you know," she said, "that we can make a fairly accurate guess at what Mr. Oliver might do. There seems no doubt that he went up the path to the Keep. According to Mr. Marston Greyle's statement, he certainly did not go to the house. So he might have done one of two other things. There is a path which leads from the Keep down to the beach immediately opposite the big rocks which you have no doubt seen. There is another path which turns out of the woods and follows the cliffs towards Lenwick, a village along the coast, a mile

21

away. But at that time, on a Sunday afternoon, both paths would be frequented. Speaking from knowledge, I would say that Mr. Oliver cannot have left the woods; he would have been seen had he done so. It's impossible that he could have gone down to the shore or along the cliffs without being seen too. Impossible!"

There was a certain amount of insistence in the last few words which puzzled Copplestone; it was almost as if the speaker was appealing to him to use his own common sense about a difficult question. And before he could make any reply, Mrs. Greyle put a direct inquiry to him.

"What is going to be done?"

"I don't know exactly," answered Copplestone. "I'm going to stay here for the night anyway on the chance of hearing something. Stafford is coming back in the morning; he spoke of detectives."

He looked a little doubtfully at his questioner as he uttered the last word, and again he saw the sudden strange flash of unusual interest in her eyes, and she nodded her head emphatically.

"Precisely. The proper thing to do," she said. "There must have been foul play. Must!"

"Mother!" exclaimed Audrey, half doubtfully. "Do you really think that?"

"I don't think anything else," replied Mrs. Greyle. "I certainly don't believe that Bassett Oliver would put himself into any position of danger which would result in his breaking his neck. Bassett Oliver never left Scarhaven Wood."

Copplestone made no comment on this direct assertion.

Instead, after a brief silence, he asked Mrs. Greyle a question.

"You knew Mr. Oliver personally?"

"Five and twenty years ago, yes," she answered. "I was on the stage myself before my marriage. But I have never met him since then; I've only seen him at the local theaters."

"He—you won't mind my asking?" said Copplestone, hesitantly, "he didn't know that you lived here?"

Mrs. Greyle smiled, somewhat mysteriously.

"Not at all. My name wouldn't have conveyed anything to him," she answered. "He never knew whom I married. Otherwise, if he met some one named Marston Greyle in America, he would have connected him with me and have made inquiry about me. And had he known I lived here, he would have called. On the other hand, Marston Greyle is not a common name. Did you ever hear the name before, Mr. Copplestone?"

"Only in connection with your own family. I have read of the Greyles of Scarhaven," replied Copplestone. "But, after all, I suppose the name is not confined to your family. There may be Greyles in America. It's all very curious," he went on, as he rose to leave. "May I come in tomorrow and tell you what's being done? I'm sure Stafford means to leave no stone unturned. He's tremendously keen about it."

"Do," said Mrs. Greyle heartily. "But the probability is that you'll see us out and about in the morning; we spend most of our time out of doors, having little else to do."

Copplestone went away feeling more puzzled than ever.

Now that he was alone for the first time since meeting Audrey Greyle on the beach, he was able to reflect on certain events of the afternoon in uninterrupted fashion. He thought over them as he walked back towards the Admiral's Arms. It was certainly a strange thing that Bassett Oliver, after remarking to the fisherman that he had known a Mr. Marston Greyle in America and hearing that the Squire of Scarhaven had been in that country, would have gone up to the house saying that he would call on the Squire and would never have been seen again.

That was one problem closely affecting Oliver's disappearance. The other had nothing to do with Oliver's disappearance; nevertheless, it interested Richard Copplestone. He was a young man of accurate observation, and he had noted that the Squire of Scarhaven occupied a position that suggested power and wealth. The house which stood beneath the old Keep was one of size and importance. Copplestone's glances at its grounds, its gardens, its entrance lodge, its entire surroundings had shown him that only a well-to-do man could live there. How was it, then, that the Squire's cousin and her mother lived in a small and unpretentious cottage and were obviously not well off with regard to material goods?

Copplestone saw at a glance that refined and cultivated as the atmosphere of Mrs. Greyle's parlor was, she was in what some folk call genteel poverty. Mrs. Greyle's black attire had done duty for a long time; the carpet was threadbare; there was an absence of those little touches of comfort with which refined women of even modest means love to surround themselves. Here were two women who had to carefully count their pence and lay out their shillings with caution, and yet on the other side of the little bay was a near kinsman whose rental income must bring him a few thousands a year!

And there was yet one more curious occasion of perplexity to add to the other two. Copplestone had felt instinctively attracted to Audrey Greyle when he met her on the sands, and the attraction increased as he walked at her side towards the village. In his quiet unobtrusive fashion he had watched her closely when they encountered the man whom she introduced as her cousin, and he had fancied that her manner underwent a curious change when Marston Greyle came on the scene. She had seemed to become constrained, chilled, aloof—not with himself, but with her kinsman. This notion had become assurance during the conversation which had abruptly ended when Greyle took offense at Stafford's brusque remark. Copplestone had seen a sudden look in the girl's eyes when the fisherman repeated what Oliver had said about meeting a Mr. Marston Greyle in America. It was a look of . . . what? Suspicion? Apprehension? He could not decide. But it was the same look which had come into her mother's eyes later on.

Moreover, when the Squire turned huffily away, taking his cousin with him, Copplestone had noticed that there was a sharp passage of words between them after leaving the little group on the quay, and they had parted unceremoniously, the man turning on his heel up a side path into his own grounds and the girl going forward with a sudden acceleration of pace. All of this made Copplestone draw a conclusion.

"There's no great love lost between the gentleman at the big house and his lady relatives in the little cottage," he mused. "Around the gentleman there appears to be some cloud of mystery. But what? And has it anything to do with the Oliver mystery?"

He went back to the inn and made his arrangements with its landlady, who by that time was full to overflowing with interest and amazement at the strange affair which had brought her this guest. But Mrs. Wooler had eyes as well as ears, and noticing that Copplestone was already looking weary and harassed, she hastened to provide a hot dinner for him, which in her opinion possessed remarkable revivifying qualities. Copplestone, who had eaten nothing for several hours, accepted her hospitable attentions with gratitude; and he was enjoying himself greatly in a quaint old-world parlor in close proximity to a bright fire when Mrs. Wooler entered with a countenance which betokened mystery in every feature.

"There's the estate agent, Mr. Chatfield, outside, very anxious to have a word with you about this affair," she said. "Would you be for having him in? He's the sort of man," she went on, sinking her tones to a whisper, "who must know everything that's going on, and, of course, having the position he has, he might be useful. Mr. Peter Chatfield, Mr. Greyle's agent and his uncle's before him. That's who he is. Peeping Peter, they call him hereabouts, because he's fond of knowing everybody's business."

"Bring him in," said Copplestone. He was by no means averse to having a companion, and Mrs. Wooler's graphic characterization had awakened his curiosity. "Tell him I shall be glad to see him."

Mrs. Wooler presently ushered in a figure which Copplestone's dramatic sense immediately seized on. He saw before him a tall, heavily built man with a large, solemn, deeply lined face out of which looked a pair of the smallest and slyest eyes ever seen in a human being, strange, almost hidden eyes set beneath thick bushy eyebrows above which rose the dome of an unusually high forehead and a bald head. As for the rest of him, Mr. Peter Chatfield had a snub nose, a wide slit of a mouth, and a flabby hand; his garments were of a Quaker kind in cut and hue; and he wore an old-fashioned stand-up collar and a voluminous black scarf. In one hand he carried a stout oaken staff, in the other a square-crowned beaver hat. Altogether, his mere outward appearance would have gained notice for him anywhere, and Copplestone rejoiced in him as a character. He rose, greeted his visitor cordially, and invited him to a seat by the fire. The estate agent settled his heavy figure comfortably and made a careful inspection of the young stranger before he spoke. At last he leaned forward.

"Sir," he whispered in a confidential tone. "Do you consider this here a matter of murder?"

Chapter 5

The Greyle History

If Copplestone had followed his first natural impulse, he would have laughed aloud at this solemnly propounded question. As it was, he found it difficult to content himself with a smile.

"Isn't it a little early to arrive at any conclusion of any sort, Mr. Chatfield?" he asked. "You haven't made up your own mind surely?"

Chatfield pursed up his long thin lips and shook his head, continuing to stare fixedly at Copplestone.

"Now I may have, and I may not have, mister," he said at last, suddenly relaxing. "What I was asking of was, what might you consider?"

"You are upset, Mr. Chatfield?" he remarked. "Now, why?"

"Things like this here are not pleasant to have in a quiet, respectable community like ours," he said. "There's very wicked people in this world, mister, and they will talk. You'll excuse me, but I'm a good deal more than twice your age, and I've learnt experience. My experience, sir, is that a wise man holds his tongue until he's called upon to use it. Now, in my opinion, it was a very unwise thing of yon there sea-going man to say that this unfortunate play-actor told him that he'd met our Squire in America."

Copplestone pricked his ears. Had the estate agent come there to tell him that? And if so, why? "You've heard that, have you? Who told you, Mr. Chatfield? For I don't think that's generally known."

"If you knew this here village, mister, as well as what I do," replied Chatfield coolly, "you'd know that there is known all over the place by this time. The constable told me, and of course that Ewbank, he'll have told it all round since his bit of talk with you and your friend. He'll have been to every public place there is in Scarhaven, repeating it. And a very, very serious complexion, of course, could be put on them words, sir."

"How so?" asked Copplestone.

"Put it to yourself, sir," replied Chatfield. "The unfortunate man comes here, tells Ewbank he knew Mr. Greyle in that faraway land, says he'll call on him, is seen going towards the big house . . . and is never seen no more! Why, sir, what does human nature—which is wicked—say?"

"What does *your* human nature—which I'm sure is not wicked— say?" suggested Copplestone. "Come, now."

"What *I* say, sir, is neither here nor there," answered the agent. "It's what evil-disposed tongues says."

"But they haven't said anything yet," said Copplestone.

"I should say they've said a deal, sir," responded Chatfield, mournfully. "I know Scarhaven tongues. They'll have thrown out a deal of suspicious talk about the Squire."

"Have you seen Mr. Greyle?" asked Copplestone. He was sure that Chatfield was there with a purpose, and he wanted to know its precise nature. "Is he concerned about this?"

"I have seen Mr. Greyle, mister," replied Chatfield. "Mr. Greyle, sir, came straight to me where I reside in a residence within the park. Mr. Greyle, mister, says that he has no recollection whatever of meeting this play-actor person in America; he may have and he mayn't. But he doesn't remember him. Him, an English landlord and a gentleman, wouldn't be very like to remember a play-actor person that's here today and gone tomorrow! I mean no offense, sir. Maybe you're a play-actor yourself."

"I am not," answered Copplestone. He sat staring at his visitor for awhile, and when he spoke again his voice had lost its cordial tone. "Well," he said, "then what have you called on me about?"

Chatfield looked up sharply, noticing the altered tone.

"To tell you—and them as you no doubt represent—that Mr. Greyle will be glad to help in any possible way towards finding out something in this here affair," he answered. "He'll welcome any in-quiry that's opened."

"I see," said Copplestone. "But you're making a mistake, Mr. Chatfield. I don't represent anybody. I'm not even a relation of Mr. Bassett Oliver. In fact, I never met Mr. Oliver in my life. Never spoke to him. So I'm not here in any representative or official sense."

Chatfield's small eyes grew smaller with suspicious curiosity.

"Oh?" he said questioningly. "Then what might you be here for, mister?"

Copplestone stood up and rang the bell.

"That's my business." he answered. "Sorry I can't give you any more time," he went on as Mrs. Wooler opened the door. "I'm engaged now. If you or Mr. Greyle want to see Mr. Oliver's friends, I believe his brother, Sir Cresswell Oliver, will be here tomorrow. He's been wired for anyhow."

Chatfield's mouth opened as he picked up his hat. He stared at this self-assured young man as if he were something quite new to him.

"Sir Cresswell Oliver!" he exclaimed. "Did you say, sir?"

"I said Sir Cresswell Oliver . . . quite plainly," answered Copplestone.

Chatfield's mouth grew wider.

"You don't mean to tell me that a play-actor is brother to a titled gentleman!" he said.

"Good night," replied Copplestone, motioning his visitor towards the door. "I can't give you any more time, really. However, as you seem anxious, Mr. Bassett Oliver is the younger brother of Rear Admiral Sir Cresswell Oliver, and I should imagine that Sir Cresswell will want to know a lot about what's become of him. So you'd better—or Mr. Greyle had better—speak to him. Now once more, good night."

When Chatfield had gone, Copplestone laughed and flung himself into an easy chair before the fire. The stupid, ignorant, self-sufficient old fool had come fishing for news. He and his master wanted to know what was going to be done in the way of making inquiry. But why? Why so much anxiety if they knew nothing whatever about Bassett Oliver's strange disappearance? Why this profession of eager willingness to welcome any inquiry that might be made? Nobody had accused Marston Greyle of having anything to do with Bassett Oliver's strange exit—if it *was* an exit. Why, then?

"But it's useless speculating," he mused. "I can't do anything, and here I am with nothing to do!"

He had pleaded an engagement, but he had none, of course. There was a shelf of old books in the room, but he did not care to read. And presently, hands in pockets, he lounged out into the hall and saw Mrs. Wooler standing at the door of the little parlor into which she had shown him and Stafford earlier in the day.

"There's nobody in here, sir," she said, invitingly; "if you'd like to sit here."

"Thank you," answered Copplestone. "I got rid of that old fellow," he observed confidentially when he had followed the landlady within and had dropped into a chair near her own. "I think he had come fishing."

"That's his usual occupation," said Mrs. Wooler with a meaning smile. "I told you he was called Peeping Peter. He's the sort of man who will have his nose in everybody's affairs. But," she added, with a shake of the head which seemed to say a good deal more than the smile, "he doesn't often come here. This is almost the only house in Scarhaven that doesn't belong to the Greyle estate. This house and the land round it have belonged to the Wooler family as long as the rest of the place has belonged to the Greyles. Many a Greyle has wanted to buy it, and every Wooler has refused to sell it. And always will!"

"That's very interesting," said Copplestone. "Does the present Greyle want to buy?"

The landlady picked up a piece of sewing and sat down in a chair which seemed to be purposely placed so that she could keep an eye on the adjacent parlor on one side and the hall on the other.

"I don't know much about what the present Squire would like," she said. "Nobody does. He's a newcomer, and nobody knows anything about him. You saw him this afternoon?"

"I met a young lady on the sands who turned out to be his cousin, and he came up while I was talking to her," replied Copplestone. "Yes, I saw him. I'm afraid Mr. Stafford, who came in here with me, you know, offended him," he continued, and gave Mrs. Wooler an account of what had happened. "Is he rather touchy?" he concluded.

"I don't know," she said. "He's a stranger. Although he's a Greyle, he's not a Scarhaven man. I know all his family history. I'm Scarhaven born and bred. In my time there have been three generations of Greyles. The first one I knew was this Squire's grandfather, old Mr. Stephen Greyle; he died when I was a girl in my teens. He had three sons and no daughters. The three sons were all different in their tastes and ideas; the eldest, Stephen John, who came into the estates on his father's death, was a real home bird. He never left Scarhaven for more than a day or two at a time all his life. And he never married; he was a real old bachelor, almost a woman-hater. The next one, Marcus, went out to America and settled there. He was the father of this present Squire, Mr. Marston Greyle. Then there was the third son, Valentine, who went to live in London. And years after he came back here, very poor, and settled down in a little house near Scarhaven Church with his wife and daughter. That was the daughter you met this afternoon, Miss Audrey. I don't know why, and nobody else knows either, but the last Squire, Stephen John, never had anything to do with Valentine and his family. What's more, when Valentine died and left the widow and daughter very poorly off, Stephen John did nothing for them. He died very soon after Valentine, and then, as Marcus had already died in America, everything came to this Mr. Marston. As I said, he's a stranger to Scarhaven folk and Scarhaven ways. Indeed, you might say a stranger to England and English ways, for I understand he'd never been in England until he came to take up the family property."

"Is he more friendly with the mother and daughter than the last Squire was?" asked Copplestone, who had been much interested in this chapter of family history.

Mrs. Wooler made several stitches in her sewing before she answered this direct question, and when she spoke it was in lower tones and with a glance of caution.

"He would be, if he could," she said. "There are those in the village who say that he wants to marry his cousin. But the truth is that for some reason or other, neither Mrs. Valentine Greyle nor Miss Audrey can bear him. They took some odd dislike to the young man when he first came, and they've kept it up. They're outwardly friendly, and he occasionally goes to the cottage; but they rarely go to the big house, and they're seldom ever seen together. I have heard—one does hear things in villages—that he'd be very glad to do something handsome for them, but they're both as proud as they are poor and not the sort to accept anything from anybody. I believe they've just enough to live on, but it can't be a great deal. There it is. However much the new Squire wants to marry his cousin, it's very flat she'll not have anything to say to him. It's my private opinion that Miss Audrey dislikes that young man just about as heartily as she possibly could!"

"What does Mr. Marston Greyle find to do with himself in this place?" asked Copplestone, turning the conversation. "Can't be very lively for him, if he's a man of any activity."

"Oh, I don't know," replied Mrs. Wooler. "I think he's a good deal like his uncle, the last squire. He certainly never goes anywhere, except out to sea in his yacht. He shoots a bit and fishes a bit and so on, and spends a lot of time with Peeping Peter. He's a widower, is Chatfield, and lives alone, except when his daughter runs down to see him. And that daughter, by the way, Mr. Copplestone, is on the stage."

"That is surprising," said Copplestone. "Her father made several contemptuous references to play-actors when he was talking to me."

"Oh, he hates them and all connected with them," replied Mrs. Wooler, laughing. "All the same, his own daughter has been on the stage for a good five years, and I fancy she's doing well. A fine, handsome girl she is too. She's been down here a good deal lately, and—"

The landlady suddenly paused, hearing a light step in the hall. She glanced through the window and then turned to Copplestone with an arch smile.

"Talk of the— Well, you know," she exclaimed. "Here's Addie Chatfield herself!"

Chapter 6

The Leading Lady

Copplestone looked up with interest as the door of the private parlor was thrown open, and a tall, handsome young woman burst in with a briskness of movement which spoke of unusual energy. He got an impression of the old estate agent's daughter in one glance and wondered how Chatfield came to have such a good-looking girl as his progeny. The impression was of dark, sparkling eyes, a mass of darker, highly burnished hair, bright color, a flashing vivacious smile, a general air of sprightliness, and glowing health. This was certainly the sort of personality that would appeal to theater goers, and Copplestone, budding playwright, immediately began to cast Addie Chatfield for an appropriate part.

The newcomer stopped short on the threshold as she caught sight of a stranger, and she glanced with sharp inquisitiveness at Copplestone as he rose from his chair.

"Oh! I supposed you were alone, Mrs. Wooler," she exclaimed. "You usually are, you know, so I came in anyhow. Sorry!"

"Come in," said the landlady. "Don't go, Mr. Copplestone. This is Miss Adela Chatfield. Your father has just been to see this gentleman, Addie. Perhaps he told you?"

Addie Chatfield dropped into a chair at Mrs. Wooler's side and looked the stranger over slowly and carefully.

"No," she answered. "My father didn't tell me. He doesn't tell me anything about his own affairs. All his talk is about mine—the iniquity of them."

She showed a fine set of even white teeth as she made this remark, and her eyes sought Copplestone's again with a direct challenge. Copplestone looked calmly at her, half-smiling; he was beginning, in his youthful innocence, to think that he already understood this type of young woman. And seeing him smile, Addie also smiled.

"Now I wonder whatever my father wanted to see *you* about?" she said, with a strong accent on the personal pronoun. "For you don't look his sort, and he certainly isn't yours. Unless you're deceptive."

"Perhaps I am," responded Copplestone, still keeping his eyes on her. "Your father wanted to see me about the strange disappearance of Mr. Bassett Oliver. That was all."

The girl's glance, bold and challenging, suddenly shifted before Copplestone's steady look. She half turned to Mrs. Wooler, and her color rose a little.

"I've heard of that," she said, with an affectation of indifference. "And as I happen to know a bit of Bassett Oliver, I don't see what all this fuss is about. I should say Bassett Oliver took it into his head to go off somewhere yesterday on a little game of his own, and that he's turned up at Norcaster by this time and is safe in his dressing room or on the stage. That's my notion."

"I wish I could think it the correct one," replied Copplestone. "But Mr. Bassett Oliver has disappeared here."

"Are you a member of his company?" asked Addie, again looking Copplestone over with speculative glances.

"Not at all. I'm a humble person whose play Mr. Oliver was about to produce next month. I came down to see him and found this state of affairs. I'm now here to help to find him . . . alive or dead."

"So you're a writer?" said Addie.

"You are an actress?" responded Copplestone. "I wonder if I've ever seen you anywhere?"

Addie tipped her head and gave him a sharp glance.

"Evidently not," she retorted. "Or you wouldn't wonder! As if anybody could forget me once they'd seen me. Do you live in town?"

"I live," replied Copplestone slowly and with affected solemnity, "in chambers in Jermyn Street."

"And do you mean to tell me that you didn't see me last year in *The Clever Lady Hartletop*?" she exclaimed.

Copplestone put the tips of his fingers together and his head on one side and regarded her critically.

"What part did you play?" he asked innocently.

"Part? Why, *the* part, of course!" she retorted. "Goodness! Why, I created it! And played it to crowded houses for nearly two hundred nights too!"

"Ah," said Copplestone. "But I'll make a confession to you. I rarely visit the theater. I never saw *Lady Hartletop*. I haven't been in a theater of any sort for two years. So you must forgive me. I congratulate you on your success."

Addie received this tribute with a mollified smile, which changed to a glance of surprised curiosity.

"You never go to the theater, and yet you write plays," she exclaimed. "That's curious, isn't it? But I believe writing people are odd. All the same, you don't look like a writer. What does he look like, Mrs. Wooler? I know—a sort of nice little officer boy, just washed and tidied up!"

The landlady, who had evidently enjoyed this passage at arms, laughed as she gave Copplestone a significant glance.

"And when did you come down home, Addie?" she asked quietly. "I didn't know you were here again."

"Came down Saturday night on my way to Edinburgh," said Addie. "I've business there on Wednesday. So I broke the journey here, just to pay my respects to my worshipful parent."

"I heard you say that you knew Mr. Bassett Oliver?" asked Copplestone. "You've met him?"

"Met him in this country and in America," replied Addie calmly. "He was on tour over there when I was. Three years ago. We were in two or three towns together at the same time. Different houses, of course. I never saw much of him in London though."

"You didn't see anything of him yesterday, here?" suggested Copplestone.

Addie stared and glanced at the landlady.

"Here?" she exclaimed. "Goodness, no! You really think this disappearance is serious?"

"Oliver's managers think it most serious," replied Copplestone, "that nothing but an accident of a really serious nature would have kept him from his engagements."

"Then that settles it," said Addie. "He's fallen down the Devil's Spout. Plain as plain can be. He's made his way there, been a bit too daring, and slipped over the edge. And whoever falls in there never comes out again! Isn't that it, Mrs. Wooler?"

"That's what they say," answered the landlady. "But I don't remember any accident at the Devil's Spout in my time."

"Well, there's been one now, anyway. That's certain," remarked Addie. "Poor old Bassett. I'm sorry for him! Well, I'm off. Good night, Mr. Copplestone, and perhaps you'll so far overcome your repugnance to the theater as to come and see me in one some day."

"Supposing I escort you homeward instead, now," suggested Copplestone. "That will at least show that I am ready to become your devoted . . ."

"Admirer, I suppose," said Addie. "I'm afraid he's not quite as innocent as he looks, Mrs. Wooler. Well, you can escort me as far as the gates of the park, then I daren't take you further, because it's so dark in there that you'd surely lose your way, and then there'd be a second disappearance and all sorts of complications."

She went out of the inn, laughing and chattering, but once outside she suddenly became serious, and she laid her hand on Copplestone's arm as they turned down the hillside towards the quay.

"I wasn't going to ask questions in there," she said in a low voice, "but what's going to be done about this Oliver affair? You're stopping here to do something. What?"

Copplestone hesitated before answering this direct question. He had not seen anything which would lead him to suppose that Miss Adela Chatfield was a disingenuous and designing young woman, but she was certainly Peeping Peter's daughter; and the old man, having failed to get anything out of Copplestone himself, might possibly have sent her to see what she could accomplish. He replied noncommittally.

"I'm not in a position to do anything," he said. "I'm not a relative, not even a personal friend. I daresay you know that Bassett Oliver was—already talking of him in the past tense!—the brother of Rear Admiral Sir Cresswell Oliver, the famous seaman?"

"I knew he was a man of what they call family, but I didn't know that," she answered. "What of it?"

"Stafford's wired to Sir Cresswell," replied Copplestone. "He'll be down here some time tomorrow, no doubt. And of course he'll take everything into his own hands."

"And he'll do what?" she asked.

"I don't know," replied Copplestone. "Set the police to work, I should think. They'll want to find out where Bassett Oliver went, where he got to, when he turned up to the Keep saying he'd go and call on the Squire, as he'd met some man of that name in America. By the bye, you said you'd been in America. Did you meet anybody of the Squire's name there?"

They were passing along the quay by that time, and in the light of one of its feeble gas lamps he turned and looked narrowly at his companion. He fancied that he saw her face change in expression at his question; if there was any change, however, it was so quick that it was gone in a second. She shook her head with emphatic decision.

"I?" she exclaimed. "Never! It's a most uncommon name, that. I never heard of anybody called Greyle except at Scarhaven."

"The present Mr. Greyle came from America," said Copplestone.

"I know, of course," she answered. "But I never met any Greyles out there. Bassett Oliver may have though. I know he toured in a lot of American towns. I only went to three: New York, Chicago, St. Louis. I suppose," she continued, turning to Copplestone with a suggestion of confidence in her manner, "I suppose you consider it a very damning thing that Bassett Oliver should disappear, after saying what he did to Ewbank."

It was very evident to Copplestone that whether Miss Chatfield had spoken the truth or not when she said that her father had not told her of his visit to the Admiral's Arms, she was thoroughly conversant with all the facts relating to the Oliver mystery, and he had no doubt that she was seeking information.

"Does it matter at all what I think?" he answered evasively. "I have no part in this affair. I'm a mere spectator. I don't know how what you refer to might be considered by people who are accustomed to sizing things up. They might say all that was a mere coincidence."

"But what do *you* think?" she said with feminine persistence. "Come, now, between ourselves?"

Copplestone laughed. They had come to the edge of the wooded park in which the estate agent's house stood, and at a gate which led into it, he paused.

"Between ourselves then, I don't think at all . . . yet," he answered. "I haven't sized anything up. All I should say at present is that if—or *as*, for I'm sure the fisherman repeated accurately what he heard—as Oliver said he met somebody called Marston Greyle in America, why . . . I conclude he did. That's all. Now, won't you please let me see you through these dark woods?"

But Addie said her farewell and left him somewhat abruptly, and he watched her until she had passed out of the circle of light from the lamp which swung over the gate. She passed on into the shadows; and Copplestone, who had already memorized the chief geographical points of his new surroundings, noticed what she probably thought no stranger would notice, that instead of going towards her father's house, she turned up the drive to the Squire's.

Chapter 7

Left on Guard

Stafford was back at Scarhaven before breakfast time next morning, bringing with him copies of the *Norcaster Daily Chronicle*, one of which he immediately displayed to Copplestone and Mrs. Wooler, who met him at the inn door. He pointed with great pride to certain staring headlines.

"I engineered that!" he exclaimed. "Went round to the newspaper office last night and put them up to everything. Nothing like publicity in these cases. There you are! 'MYSTERIOUS DISAPPEARANCE OF FAMOUS ACTOR! BASSETT OLIVER MISSING! INTERVIEW WITH MAN WHO SAW HIM LAST!' That's the style, Copplestone! Every human being along this coast'll be reading that by now!"

"So there was no news of him last night?" asked Copplestone.

"Neither last night nor this morning, my boy," replied Stafford. "Of course not! No, he never left here. Not he. Now then, let Mrs. Wooler serve us that nice breakfast which I'm sure she has in readiness, and then we're going to plunge into business, hot and strong. There's a couple of detectives coming on by the nine o'clock train, and we're going to do the whole thing thoroughly."

"What about his brother?" inquired Copplestone.

"I wired him last night to his London address and got a reply first thing this morning," said Stafford. "He's coming along by the 5:15 from King's Cross. He'll be here before noon. I want to get to work before he arrives though. And the first thing to do is to make sympathetic inquiry and to search the shore and the cliffs and these woods and that Keep. All that, we'll attend to at once."

But on going around to the village police station they found that Stafford's ideas had already been largely anticipated. The news of the gentleman's mysterious disappearance had spread like wildfire through Scarhaven and the immediate district during the previous evening, and at daybreak parties of fisherfolk had begun a systematic search. These parties kept coming in to report progress all the morning. By noon they had all returned. They had searched the famous rocks, the woods, the park, the Keep and its adjacent ruins, the cliffs, and the shore for some considerable distance north and south of the bay. And there was no result. Not a trace, not a sign of the missing man was to be found anywhere. And when Stafford and Copplestone walked up to the little station to meet Sir Cresswell Oliver, it was with the disappointing consciousness that they had no news to give him.

Copplestone, who nourished a natural taste for celebrities of any sort, had looked forward with interest to meeting Sir Cresswell Oliver, who, only a few months previously, had made himself famous by a remarkable feat of seamanship in which great personal bravery and courage had been displayed. Copplestone had a vague expectation of seeing a bluff, stalwart, sea-dog type of man; instead he found himself shaking hands with a very quiet-looking, elderly gentleman, who might have been a barrister or a doctor of pleasant and kindly manners. With him was another gentleman of a similar type and of about the same age, whom he introduced as the family solicitor, Mr. Petherton. And in a private sitting room at the Admiral's Arms, Stafford, as Bassett Oliver's business representative, and Copplestone, as having remained on the spot since the day before, told these two every detail of what had transpired since it was established that the famous actor was missing. Both listened in silence and with deep attention, and when all the facts had been put before them, they went aside and talked together; then they returned and Sir Cresswell asked for Stafford and Copplestone's attention.

"I want to tell you young gentlemen precisely what Mr. Petherton and I think it best to do," he said in mild and bland accents which astonished Copplestone. "We have listened, as you will acknowledge, with our best attention. Mr. Petherton, as you know, is a man of law; I myself, when I have the good luck to be ashore, am a

Chairman of Quarter Sessions, so I'm accustomed to periodic courts where I hear and weigh evidence. We don't think there's any doubt that my poor brother has met with some curious mishap which has resulted in his death. It seems impossible, going on what you tell us from the evidence you've collected, that he could ever have approached that Devil's Spout place unseen; it also seems impossible that he could have had a fatal fall over the cliffs, since his body has not been found. We think something befell him in the neighborhood of Scarhaven Keep. But what? Foul play? Possibly. If it was, why? And there are three people Mr. Petherton and I would like to speak to privately: the fisherman Ewbank, Mr. Marston Greyle, and Mrs. Valentine Greyle. We should like to hear Ewbank's story for ourselves; we certainly want to see the Squire; and I, personally, wish to see Mrs. Greyle, because—from what Mr. Copplestone there has told us—I am quite sure that I, too, knew her a good many years ago when she was acquainted with my brother Bassett. So we propose, Mr. Stafford, to go and see these three people. And when we have seen them, I will tell you and Mr. Copplestone exactly what I, as my brother's representative, wish to be done."

The two younger men waited impatiently in and about the hotel while their elders went on their self-appointed mission. Stafford, essentially a man of activity, speculated on their reasons for seeing the three people whom Sir Cresswell Oliver had specifically mentioned; Copplestone was meanwhile wondering if he could with propriety pay another visit to Mrs. Greyle's cottage that night. It was drawing near to dusk when the two elderly gentlemen returned and summoned the younger ones to another conference. Both looked as reserved and bland as when they had set out, and the old seaman's voice was just as suave as ever when he addressed them.

"Well, gentlemen," he said, "we have paid our visits, and I suppose I had better tell you at once that we are no wiser as to actual facts than we were when we left you earlier in the afternoon. The man Ewbank stands emphatically by his story; Mr. Marston Greyle says that he cannot remember any meeting with my brother in America, and that he certainly did not call on him here on Sunday; Mrs.

Valentine Greyle has not met Bassett for a great many years. There the matter stands. Of course, it cannot rest there. Further inquiries will have to be made. Mr. Petherton and I are going on to Norcaster this evening, and we shall have a very substantial reward offered to any person who can give any information about my brother. That may result in something or in nothing. As to my brother's business arrangements, I will go fully into that matter with you, Mr. Stafford, at Norcaster tomorrow. Now Mr. Copplestone, will you have a word or two with me in private?"

Copplestone followed the old seaman into a quiet corner of the room, where Sir Cresswell turned on him with a smile.

"I take it," he said, "that you are a young gentleman of leisure, and that you can abide wherever you like, eh?"

"Yes, you may take that as granted," answered Copplestone, wondering what was coming.

"Doesn't much matter if you write your plays in Jermyn Street or anywhere else, eh?" questioned Sir Cresswell with a humorous smile.

"Practically, no," replied Copplestone.

Sir Cresswell tapped him on the shoulder.

"I want you to do me a favor," he said. "I shall take it as a kindness if you will. I don't want to talk about this affair . . . yet, anyway. Not even to you. But do you think you could manage to stay where you are for a week or two?"

"Here?" exclaimed Copplestone.

"This seems very comfortable," said Sir Cresswell, looking around. "The landlady is a nice, motherly person; she gave me a very well-cooked lunch; this is a quiet room in which to do your writing, eh?"

"Well, of course I can stay here," answered Copplestone, who was a good deal bewildered. "But mayn't I know why and in what capacity?"

"Just to keep your eyes and your ears open," said Sir Cresswell. "Don't make any inquiry. Do nothing. No private detective work. Just stop here a bit, amuse yourself, write, read, and watch things quietly. And don't be cross; I've an elderly man's privilege, you know. You'll send your bills to me."

"No need of that," said Copplestone, hurriedly. "I'm pretty well off as regards this world's goods."

"So I guessed when I found that you lived in the expensive atmosphere of Jermyn Street," said Sir Cresswell with a sly laugh. "But all the same, you'll let me be paymaster here. That's only fair."

"All right. If you wish it," agreed Copplestone. "But look here, won't you trust me? I assure you I am to be trusted. You suspect somebody. Hadn't you better give me your confidence? I won't tell a soul."

Sir Cresswell waited a moment or two, looking quietly at Copplestone. Then he clapped a hand on the young man's shoulder.

"All right, my lad," he said. "Yes, we do suspect somebody. Marston Greyle. Now you know it."

"I expected that," answered Copplestone. "All right, sir. And my orders are just what you said."

"Just what I said," agreed Sir Cresswell. "Carry on at that. Eyes and ears open; no fuss; everything quiet, unobtrusive, silent. Meanwhile Petherton will be at work. And I say, if you want company, I think you'll find it across the bay there at Mrs. Greyle's, eh?"

"I was there last night," said Copplestone. "I liked both of the ladies very much. You knew Mrs. Greyle once upon a time, I think, you and your brother?"

"We did," replied Sir Cresswell with a sigh. "The fact is that both Bassett and I were in love with her at that time. And she married another man instead. That's all."

He gave Copplestone a squeeze of the elbow, laughed, and went across to the solicitor, who was chatting with Stafford in one of the bow windows. Ten minutes later all three were off to Norcaster, and Copplestone was alone, ruminating over this sudden and extraordinary change in his life. Little more than twenty-four hours ago, all he had been concerned about was the production of his play by Bassett Oliver. Here he was now, mixed up in a drama of real life with Bassett Oliver as its main figure and the plot as yet unrevealed. He himself was committed to play in it, but what part?

Now that the others had gone, Copplestone began to feel strangely alone. He had accepted Sir Cresswell Oliver's commission readily, feeling genuinely interested in the affair. But now that he considered things quietly, he began to see that his position was a somewhat curious and possibly unpleasant one. He was to watch . . . and to seem *not* to watch. He was to listen . . . and appear not to listen. The task would be difficult and perhaps unpleasant, for he was very certain that Marston Greyle would resent his presence in the village, and that Chatfield would be suspicious of it. What reason could he, an utter stranger, have for taking up residence at the Admiral's Arms? The tourist season was over. These people would say that he was left there to peep and pry, and they would all know that the Squire was the object of suspicion. It was all very well, his telling Mrs. Wooler that being an idle man he had taken a fancy to Scarhaven and would stay in her inn for a few weeks; but Mrs. Wooler, like everybody else, would see through that. However, the promise had been given, and he would keep it. He would do nothing in the way of active detective work; he would just wait and see what, if anything, turned up.

But upon one thing Copplestone had made up his mind determinedly before that second evening came, he would make no pretense to Audrey Greyle and her mother. And availing himself of their permission to call again, he went around to the cottage, and before he had been in it five minutes told them bluntly that he was going to stay at Scarhaven awhile on the chance of learning any further news of Bassett Oliver.

"Which," he added, with a grim smile, "seems about as likely as that I should hear that I am to be Lord Chancellor when the Woolsack is next vacant!"

"You don't know," remarked Mrs. Greyle. "A reward for information is to be offered, isn't it?"

"Do you think that will do much good?" asked Copplestone.

"It depends upon the amount," replied Mrs. Greyle. "We know these people. They are close and reserved; no people could keep secrets better. For all one knows, somebody in this village may know something and may at present feel it wisest to keep the knowledge to himself. But if money—what would seem a lot of money—comes into question . . . ah!"

"Especially if the information could be given in secret," said Audrey. "Scarhaven folk love secrecy; it's the salt of life to them; it's in their very blood. Chatfield is an excellent specimen. He'll watch you as a cat watches a mouse when he finds you're going to stay here."

"I shall be quite open," said Copplestone. "I'm not going to indulge in any secret investigations. But I mean to have a thorough look round the place. That Keep, now, may one look round that?"

"There's a path which leads close by the Keep from which you can get a good outside view of it," replied Audrey. "But the Keep itself and the rest of the ruins round about it are in private ground."

"But you have a key, Audrey, and you can take Mr. Copplestone in there," said Mrs. Greyle. "And you could show him more than he would find out for himself. Audrey," she continued, turning to Copplestone, "knows every inch of the place and every stone of the walls."

Copplestone made no attempt to conceal his delight at this suggestion. He turned to the girl with almost boyish eagerness.

"Will you?" he exclaimed. "When?"

"Tomorrow morning, if you like," replied Audrey. "Meet me on the south quay soon after ten."

Copplestone was down on the quay by ten o'clock. He became aware as he descended the road from the inn that the fisherfolk, who were always lounging about the seafront, were keenly interested in something that was going on there. Drawing nearer he found that an energetic bill poster was attaching his bills to various walls and doors. Sir Cresswell and his solicitor had evidently lost no time and had set a Norcaster printer to work immediately on their arrival the previous evening. And there the bill was. It offered a thousand pounds reward to any person who should give information which would lead to the finding of Bassett Oliver, alive or dead.

Copplestone purposely refrained from mingling with the groups of men and lads who thronged about the bills, eagerly discussing the great affair of the moment. He sauntered along the quay, waiting for Audrey. She came at last with a mysterious smile on her lips.

"Our particular excursion is off, Mr. Copplestone," she said. "Extraordinary events seem to be happening. Mr. Chatfield called on us an hour ago, took my key away from me, and solemnly informed us that Scarhaven Keep is strictly closed until further notice."

Chapter 8

Right of Way

The look of blank astonishment which spread over Copplestone's face on hearing this announcement seemed to afford his companion great amusement, and she laughed merrily as she signed to him to turn back towards the woods.

"All the same," she observed, "I know how to steal a countermarch on Master Chatfield. Come along! You shan't be disappointed."

"Does your cousin know of that?" asked Copplestone. "Are those his orders?"

Audrey's lips curled a little, and she laughed again, but this time the laughter was cynical.

"I don't think it much matters whether my cousin knows or not," she said. "He's the nominal Squire of Scarhaven, but everybody knows that the real overlord is Peter Chatfield. Peter Chatfield does everything. And he hates me! He won't have had such a pleasant moment for a long time as he had this morning when he took my key away from me and warned me off."

"But why you?" asked Copplestone.

"Oh, Peter is deep," she said. "Peter, no doubt, knew that you came to see us last night. Peter knows all that goes on in Scarhaven, and he put things together and decided that I might act as your guide over the Keep and the ruins. And so, there you are."

"Why should he object to my visiting the Keep?" demanded Copplestone.

"That's obvious. He considers you a spy," replied Audrey. "And there may be reasons why he doesn't desire your presence in those ancient regions. But we'll go there all the same, if you don't mind breaking rules and defying Peter."

"Not I!" said Copplestone. "Hang Peter!"

"There are people who firmly believe that Peter Chatfield should have been hanged long since," she remarked quietly. "I'm one of them. Chatfield is a bad old man—thoroughly bad. But I'll circumvent him in this anyhow. I know how to get into the Keep in spite of him and of his locks and bolts. There's a big curtain wall, twenty feet high, all round the Keep, but I know where there's a hole in it behind some bushes, and we'll get in there. Come along!"

She led him up the same path through the woods along which Bassett Oliver had gone, according to Ewbank's account. It wound through groves of fir and pine until it came out on a plateau in the midst of which, surrounded by a high irregular wall, stood Scarhaven Keep. And there, at the head of a path which evidently led up from the big house, stood Chatfield, angry and threatening. Beyond him distributed at intervals about the other paths which converged on the plateau were other men, obviously estate laborers, who appeared to be mounting guard over the forbidden spot.

"Now there's going to be a row between me and Chatfield," murmured Audrey. "You play spectator. Don't say a word. Leave it to me. We are on our rights along this path. Take no notice of Peter."

But Chatfield was already bearing down on them, his solemn-featured face dark with displeasure. He raised his voice while he was yet a dozen yards away.

"I thought I'd told you as you wasn't to come near these here ruins!" he said, addressing Audrey in a fashion which Copplestone's fingers itch to snatch the oak staff from the agent and lay it freely about his person. "My orders was to that there effect! And when I give orders I mean 'em to be obeyed. You'll turn straight back where you came from, miss, and in the future do as I instruct. D'ye hear that now?"

"If you expect me to keep quiet under that sort of thing," whispered Copplestone, bending towards Audrey, "you're very much mistaken in me! I shall give this fellow a lesson in another minute if—"

"Wait another minute then," said Audrey, who had continued to walk forward, steadily regarding the agent's threatening figure. "Let me talk a little first. I'm enjoying it. Are you addressing me, Mr. Chatfield?" she went on in her sweetest accents. "I hear you speaking, but I don't know if you are speaking to me. If so, you needn't shout."

"You know very well who I'm a-speaking to," growled Chatfield. "I told you you wasn't to come near these ruins. It's forbidden by order. You'll take yourself off and that there young man with you. We want no paid spies hereabouts!"

"If you speak to me like that again, I'll knock you down!" exclaimed Copplestone, stepping forward before Audrey could stop him. "Or to this lady either. Stand aside, will you?"

Chatfield twisted on his heel with a surprising agility, not to stand aside, but to wave his arm to the men who stood here and there behind him.

"Here, you!" he shouted. "Here, this way, all of you! This here fellow's threatening me with assault. You lay a finger on me, you young snapper, and I'll have you in the lockup in ten minutes. Stand between us, you men! He's for knocking me down. Now then," he went on, as the bodyguard got between him and Copplestone, "off you go, out o' these grounds, both of you—quick! I'll have no defiance of my orders from neither girl nor boy, man nor woman. Out you go, now, or you'll be put out."

But Audrey continued to advance, still watching the agent. "You're mistaken, Mr. Chatfield," she said calmly. "You will observe that Mr. Copplestone and I are on this path. You know very well that this is a public footpath with a proper and legal right-of-way from time immemorial. You can't turn us off it, you know, without exposing yourself to all sorts of pains and penalties. You men know that too," she continued, turning to the laborers and dropping her bantering tone. "You all know this is a public footpath. So stand out of our way, or I'll summon every one of you!"

The last words were spoken with so much force and decision that the three laborers involuntarily moved aside. But Chatfield hastened to oppose Audrey's progress, planting himself in front of a gate which stood across the path, and he laughed sneeringly.

"And where would you find money to take summonses out?" he said with a look of contempt. "I should think you and your mother's something better to do with your bit o' money than that. Now then, no more words! Back you turn!"

Copplestone's temper had been gradually rising during the last few minutes. Now, at the man's carefully measured taunts, he let it go. Before Chatfield or the laborers saw what he was at, he sprang on the agent's big form, grasped him by the neck with one hand, twisted his oak staff away from him with the other, flung him headlong on the turf, and raised the staff threateningly.

"Now!" he said, "beg Miss Greyle's pardon instantly, or I'll split your wicked old head for you. Quick, man! I mean it!"

Before Chatfield, moaning and groaning, could find his voice capable of words, Marston Greyle, pale and excited, came around a corner of the ruins.

"What's this? What's all this?" he demanded. "Here, here, sir. What are you doing with that stick! What—"

"I'm about to chastise your agent for his scoundrelly insolence to your cousin," retorted Copplestone with cheerful determination. "Now then, my man, quick! I always keep my word!"

"Hand the stick to Mr. Marston Greyle, Mr. Copplestone," said Audrey in her demurest manner. "I'm sure he would beat Chatfield soundly if he had heard what he said to me his cousin."

"Thank you, but I'm in possession," said Copplestone grimly. "Mr. Marston Greyle can kick him when I've thrashed him. Now, then, are you going to beg Miss Greyle's pardon, you ancient sinner?"

"What on earth is it all about?" exclaimed Greyle, obviously upset and afraid. "Chatfield, what have you been saying? Go away, you men. Go away, all of you, at once. Mr. Copplestone, don't hit him. Audrey, what is it? I seem to have nothing but bother. It's most annoying. What is it, I say?"

"It is merely, Marston, that your agent there, after trying to turn Mr. Copplestone and myself off this public footpath, insulted me with shameful taunts about my mother's poverty," replied Audrey. "That's all. Whereupon—as you were not here to do it—Mr. Copplestone promptly and very properly knocked him down. And now, is Mr. Copplestone to punish him or will you?"

Copplestone, keeping a sharp eye on the groaning and sputtering agent, contrived at the same time to turn a corner of it on Marston Greyle. That momentary glance showed him much. The Squire was mortally afraid of his man. That was certain, as certain as that they were there. He stood, a picture of vexation and indecision, glancing furtively at Chatfield, then at Audrey, and evidently hating to be asked to take a side.

"Confound it all, Chatfield!" he suddenly burst out. "Why don't you mind what you're saying? It's all very well, Audrey, but you shouldn't have come here, especially with strangers. The fact is, I'm so upset about this Oliver affair that I'm going to have a thorough search and examination of the Keep and the ruins, and I won't allow anyone inside the grounds while it's going on. You should have kept to Chatfield's orders."

"And since when has a Greyle of Scarhaven kept to a servant's orders?" interrupted Audrey, with a sneer that sent the blood rushing to the Squire's face. "Never until this present régime, I should think. Orders, indeed. From an agent! I wonder what the last Squire of Scarhaven would have said to a proposition like that? Mr. Copplestone, you've punished that bad old man quite sufficiently. Will you open the gate for me? We'll go on our way."

The girl spoke with so much decision that Copplestone moved away from Chatfield, who struggled to his feet, muttering words that sounded very much like smothered curses.

"I'll have the law on you," he growled, shaking his fist at Copplestone. "Before this day's out, I'll have the law!"

"Sooner the better," retorted Copplestone. "Nothing will please me so much as to tell the local magistrates precisely what you said to your master's kinswoman. You know where I'm to be found, and there," he added, throwing a card at the agent's feet, "there you'll find my permanent address."

"Give me my walking stick!" demanded Chatfield.

"Not I!" exclaimed Copplestone. "That's mine, my good man, by right of conquest. You can summon me or arrest me, if you like, for stealing it."

He opened the gate for Audrey, and together they passed through, skirted the walls of the ruins, and went away into the higher portion of the woods. Once there the girl laughed.

"Now there'll be another row," she said, "Between master and man this time."

"I think not," observed Copplestone with unusual emphasis. "For the master is afraid of the man."

"Ah, but which is master and which is man?" asked Audrey in a low voice.

Copplestone stopped and looked narrowly at her.

"Oh?" he said quietly, "so you've seen that?"

"Does it need much observation?" she replied. "My mother and I have known for some time that Marston Greyle is entirely under Peter Chatfield's thumb. He daren't do anything, save by Chatfield's permission."

Copplestone walked on a few yards, ruminating.

"Why?" he asked suddenly.

"How do we know?" retorted Audrey.

"Well, in cases like that," said Copplestone, "it generally means that one man has a hold on the other. What hold can Chatfield have on your cousin? I understand Mr. Marston Greyle came straight to his inheritance from America. So what could Chatfield know of him in order to have such a hold?"

"I don't know, and I don't care much," replied Audrey, as they passed out of the woods. "Never mind all that; here's the sea and the open sky. Forget Chatfield and Marston too! Since we cannot see the Keep, let's enjoy ourselves some other way. What shall we do?"

"You're the guide, conductress," answered Copplestone. "Shall I suggest something that sounds very material? Can we go along these cliffs to some village where we can find a nice old fishing inn and get a simple lunch of some sort?"

"That's certainly material and eminently practical," laughed Audrey. "We can. How about that place along there to the south? Lenwick. Come on, and no more talk of Squire and agent. I've a remarkable facility in throwing away unpleasant things."

"It's a grand skill, and I'll try to imitate you," said Copplestone. "So today's our own, eh? Is that it?"

"Until the middle of this afternoon," responded Audrey. "Don't forget that I have a mother at home."

It was well past the middle of the afternoon, however, when these two returned to Scarhaven, very well satisfied with themselves. They had found plenty to talk about without falling back on Marston Greyle or Peter Chatfield or the event of the morning, and Copplestone suddenly remembered, almost with compunction, that he had been so engrossed in his companion that he had almost forgotten the Oliver mystery. But that was sharply recalled to him as he entered the Admiral's Arms. Mrs. Wooler came forward from her parlor with a mysterious smile on her good-looking face.

"Here's a love letter for you, Mr. Copplestone," she said. "But I can't tell you who left it. One of the girls found it lying on the hall table an hour ago." With that she handed Copplestone a much thumbed, very grimy, heavily-sealed envelope.

Chapter 9

Hobkin's Hole

C opplestone carried the strange-looking missive into his private sitting room and carefully examined it, back and front, before slitting it open. The envelope was of the cheapest kind; the big splotch of red wax at the flap had been pressed into flatness by forcing a coarse-grained thumb upon it; the address was inscribed in ill-formed characters evidently made with difficulty by a bad pen, which seemed to have been dipped into watery ink at every third or fourth letter. And it read thus: "The Young Gentleman Staying at 'The Admiral'—Private."

The envelope contained nothing but a scrap of paper obviously torn from a penny cash book. No ink had been used in writing the two or three lines which were scrawled across this scrap. The vehicle this time was an indelible pencil, which the writer appeared to have moistened with his tongue every now and then, some letters being thicker and darker than others. The message, if mysterious, was straightforward enough. "Sir," it ran, "if so be as you'd like to have a bit of news from one as has it, take a walk through Hobkin's Hole tomorrow morning and look out for yours truly." It was signed, "Him as writes this."

Like most young men, when Copplestone had arrived at what he called manhood (by which he meant the age of twenty-one years), he had drawn up for himself a code of ethics—certain things to be done and certain things not to be done. One of the things which he had firmly resolved never to do was to take any notice of an anonymous letter. Yet here was an anonymous letter, and with it a conflict between his principles and his inclinations. In plain English, he made up his mind to visit Hobkin's Hole next morning and find out who the unknown correspondent was.

He was half tempted to go around to the cottage and show the quaint scrawl to Audrey Greyle, but he was still young enough to have some bashfulness about him, and he did not want to seem too pushy or forward. Regardless, it seemed to him that the anonymous letter conveyed in subtle fashion a hint—one to be regarded as sacred and secret. And as Copplestone had a strong sense of honor, he took care not to mention the contents to Mrs. Wooler. Instead he quietly consulted a map of the district which hung framed in the hall of the inn. He discovered that Hobkin's Hole was a mile or two out of Scarhaven on the inland side, and next morning after breakfast he set out in its direction without a word to anyone as to where he was going. And that he might not be entirely defenseless, he carried Peter Chatfield's oaken staff with him. That would certainly serve to crack any ordinary skull, if need arose for a measure of defense.

The road which Copplestone followed out of the village soon turned off into the heart of the moorlands that lay, rising and falling in irregular undulations, between the sea and the hills. He was quickly out of sight of Scarhaven. All around him stretched wide expanses of heather and gorse, broken up by great masses of rock. From a rise in the road he looked about him and saw only solitude. There was no sign of a human habitation and no sound save the rush of the wind across the moors and the plaintive cry of the sea birds flapping their way to the cultivated land beyond the barrier of hills. And from that point he saw no sign of any depression in the landscape to suggest the place which he sought. But at the next turn he found himself at the mouth of a narrow ravine, which cut deep into the heart of the hill and was dark and somber enough to seem a likely place for secret meetings. It wound away from a little bridge which carried the road over a brawling stream; along the side of that stream were faint indications of a path which might have been made by human feet, but was more likely to have been trodden out by the mountain sheep. This path was quickly obscured by dwarf oaks and alder bushes which completely roofed in the narrow valley. Any timid or suspicious soul might have turned back. But Copplestone was neither timid nor suspicious, and he was intensely curious about this adventure; wherefore, grasping Peter Chatfield's oaken cudgel firmly in his right hand, he jumped over the bridge and followed the narrow path into the gloom of the trees.

He soon found that the valley resolved itself in a narrow and rocky gorge. The stream, level at first, soon came tumbling down amongst huge boulders; the path disappeared; high cliffs of limestones began to lift themselves. The morning was unusually dark and gray, even for October; and leaves, brown and withered, still clustered thickly on the trees. Copplestone quickly found himself in a gloom that would have made a nervous person frightened, and his forward progress became increasingly difficult. At the foot of a tall cliff which suddenly rose up before him he was obliged to pause; it seemed impossible to go further. But as he hesitated, peering here and there under the branches of the dwarf oaks, he heard a voice, so suddenly, that he started in spite of himself.

"Guv'nor!"

Copplestone looked around and saw nothing. Then came a low laugh, as if the unseen person was enjoying his perplexity.

"Look overhead, guv'nor," said the voice. "Look aloft!"

Copplestone glanced upward and saw a man's head and face, framed in a screen of bushes which grew on a shelf of the limestone cliff. The head was crowned by a much worn fur cap; the face, very brown and wrinkled, was ornamented by a short, well-blackened clay pipe from the bowl of which a wisp of blue smoke curled upward. And as he grew accustomed to the gloom, he was aware of a pair of shrewd, twinkling eyes, and a set of very white teeth which gleamed like an animal's.

"Hullo!" said Copplestone. "Come down from there!"

The white teeth showed themselves still more; their owner laughed again.

"You come up, guv'nor," he said. "There's a natural staircase round the corner. Come up and make yourself at home. I've a nice little parlor here and a matter of refreshment in it too."

"Not till you show yourself," answered Copplestone. "I want to see what I'm dealing with. Come out now!"

The unseen laughed again, moved away from his screen, and presently showed himself on the edge of the shelf of rock. And Copplestone found himself staring at an outlandish figure of a man—an under-sized, quaint-looking fellow, clad in dirty velveteens, a once red waistcoat, and leather breeches and gaiters, a sort of compound between a poacher, a gamekeeper, and a hostler. But quainter than figure or garments was the man's face, a gnarled, weather-beaten, sea-and-wind stained face, which, in Copplestone's opinion, was fair enough and not without abundant traces of a sense of humor.

Copplestone at once trusted that face. He swung himself up by the nooks and crannies of the rock, and joined the man on his ledge.

"Well?" he said. "You're the chap who sent me that letter? Why?"

"Come this way, guv'nor," replied the brown-faced one. "We'll talk more comfortable-like in my parlor. Here you are."

He led Copplestone along the ridge behind the bushes and presently revealed a cave in the face of the overhanging limestone, mostly natural, but partly due to ingenuity. Therein were rude seats covered over with old sacking, a box or two which evidently served for pantry and larder, and a shelf on which stood a wicker-covered jug in company with a row of bottles of ale.

The lord of this retreat waved a hospitable hand towards his cellar.

"You'll not refuse a poor man's hospitality, guv'nor?" he said politely. "I can give you a clean glass, and there's fresh water from the stream—good as you'll find in England. Or maybe, though it's early in the day, you'd prefer ale? Say the word!"

"Water's fine, thank you," responded Copplestone, who saw that he had to deal with an original. "And whom am I going to drink with, may I ask?"

The man carefully drew the cork from the jug, poured out its contents, handed the glass to his visitor with a bow, helped himself to a measure of ale, and bowed again as he drank.

"My best respects to you, guv'nor," he said. "Glad to see you in Hobkin's Hole Castle. That's here. Strange place for gentlemen to meet in, ain't it? Who are you talking to, says you? My name, guv'nor—well-known hereabouts—is Zachary Spurge!"

"You sent me that note last night?" asked Copplestone, taking a seat. "How did you get it there unseen?"

"Got a cousin as is odd-job man at the Admiral's Arms," replied Spurge. "He slipped it in for me. You may ha' seen him there, guv'nor—chap with one eye and odd-looking, but to be trusted. As I am! Down to the ground."

"And what do you want to see me about?" inquired Copplestone. "What's this bit of news you've got to tell?"

Zachary Spurge thrust a hand inside his velveteen jacket and drew out a much folded and creased paper, which proved to be the bill which offered a reward for the finding of Bassett Oliver. He held it up before his visitor.

"This!" he said. "A thousand pound is a vast lot o' money, guv'nor! Now, if I was to tell something as I knows of, what chances should I have of getting that there money?"

"That depends," replied Copplestone. "The reward is to be given to . . . but you see the plain wording of it. Can you give information of that sort?"

"I can give a certain piece of information, guv'nor," said Spurge. "Whether it'll lead to the finding of that there gentleman or not I can't say. But something I do know. Certain sure!"

Copplestone reflected awhile.

"I'll tell you what, Spurge," he said. "I'll promise you this much. If you can give any information, I'll give you my word that, whether what you can tell is worth much or little, you shall be well paid. That do?"

"That'll do, guv'nor," responded Spurge. "I take your word as between gentlemen. Well, now, it's this here. You see me as I am, here in a cave like one o' them old hermits. Why am I here? Cause just now it ain't quite convenient for me to show my face in Scarhaven. I'm wanted for poaching, guv'nor. That's the fact!

This here is a safe retreat. If I was tracked here, I could make my way out at the back of this hole—there's a passage here—before anybody could climb that rock. However, nobody suspects I'm here. They think—that is, that old devil Chatfield and the police—they think I'm off to sea. However, here I am, and last Sunday afternoon I was in Scarhaven. In the wood I was, guv'nor, at the back of the Keep. Never mind what for. I was there. And at precisely ten minutes to three o'clock I saw Bassett Oliver."

"How did you know him?" demanded Copplestone.

"Cause I've seen him a dozen times, I have, at both Northborough and Norcaster," answered Spurge. "I knew him well enough, even if I'd only viewed him from the thee-ayter gallery. Well, he come along up the path from the south quay. He passed within a dozen yards of me and went up to the door in the wall of the ruins right opposite where I was hidin' in amongst some bushes. He poked the door with the point of his stick. It was ajar, that door, and it went open. And so he walks in . . . and disappears. Guv'nor! I reckon that 'ud be the last time as he was seen alive! Unless . . . unless."

"Unless what?" asked Copplestone eagerly.

"Unless one other man saw him. For there was another man there, guv'nor." said Spurge solemnly. "Squire Greyle!"

Copplestone looked hard at Spurge; Spurge returned the stare, and nodded two or three times.

"Truth," he said. "I kept where I was. I'd reasons of my own. Maybe eight minutes or so—certainly not ten—after Bassett Oliver walked in there, Squire Greyle walked out. In a hurry, guv'nor. He come out quick. He looked a bit dazed like. You know how quick a man can think, guv'nor, under certain circumstances? I thought quicker'n lightning. I says to myself 'Squire's seen somebody or something he hadn't no taste for!' Why, you could read it on his face! Plain as print."

"And then?" said Copplestone.

"Then," continued Spurge, "then he stood for just a second or two, looking right and left, up and down. There wasn't a soul in sight. Nobody. But he slunk off—sneaked off—same as a fox sneaks away from a farmyard. He went down the side of the curtain wall that shuts in the ruins, taking as much cover as ever he could find. At the end of the wall, he popped into the wood that stands between the ruins and his house. And then, of course, I lost all sight of him."

"And Mr. Oliver?" said Copplestone. "Did you see him again?"

Spurge relighted his pipe.

"I did not," he answered. "I was there until a quarter-past three, and then I went away. And no Oliver had come out o' that door when I left."

Chapter 10

The Invalid Curate

S purge and his visitor sat staring at each other in silence for a few minutes; the silence was eventually broken by Copplestone.

"Of course," he said reflectively, "if Mr. Oliver was looking round those ruins, he could easily spend half an hour there."

"Just so," agreed Spurge. "He could spend an hour, and if so be as he was one of these here antiquarian-minded gents as loves to potter about old places like that, he could spend two hours, three hours, profitable-like. But he'd have come out in the end; and the evidence is, guv'nor, that he never did come out! After Bassett Oliver went up that there path, subsequent to his bit of talk with Ewbank, he was never seen no more 'cepting by me and possibly by Squire Greyle. Them as lives a good deal alone like me, guv'nor, develops what you may call logical faculties. They thinks, and thinks deep. I've thought B.O.—that's Oliver—didn't go back by the way he'd come, or he'd ha' been seen; B.O. didn't go forward or through the woods to the headlands, or he'd ha' been seen; B.O. didn't go down to the shore, or he'd ha' been seen. 'Twixt you and me, guv'nor, B.O.'s dead body is in that there Keep!"

"What are you suggesting?" asked Copplestone.

"Nothing, guv'nor. No more than that," answered Spurge. "I'm making no suggestion and no accusation against nobody. Appearances is all very well, but appearances may be against a man to the very last degree, and yet him be as innocent as a newborn baby! No, I make no suggestions, 'cepting this here, which has no doubt occurred to you or to B.O.'s brother. If I were the missing gentleman's friends, I should want to know a lot! I should want to know precisely what he meant when he said to Dan'l Ewbank as how he'd known a man called Marston Greyle in America. 'Taint a common name, that, guv'nor."

Copplestone made no answer to these observations. His own train of thought was somewhat similar to his host's, and presently he turned to a different track.

"You saw no one else about there that afternoon?" he asked.

"No one, guv'nor," replied Spurge.

"And where did you go when you left the place?" inquired Copplestone.

"To tell you the truth, guv'nor, I was waiting there for that cousin o' mine, him as carried you the letter," answered Spurge. "It was a fixture between us; he was to meet me there about three o'clock that day. If he wasn't there or in sight by a quarter-past three, I was to know he wasn't able to get away. So as he didn't come, I slipped back into the woods and made my way back here round by the moors."

"Are you going to stay in this place?" asked Copplestone.

"For a bit, guv'nor. Till I see how things are," replied Spurge. "As I say, I'm wanted for poaching, and Chatfield's been watching to get his knife into me this long while. All the same, if more serious things drew his attention off, he might let me be. What do you ask for, guv'nor?"

"I wanted to know where you could be found in case you were required to give evidence about seeing Mr. Oliver," replied Copplestone. "That evidence may be wanted."

"I've thought of that," observed Spurge. "And you can always find that much out from my cousin at the Admiral. He keeps in touch with me. If it got too hot for me here, I should clear out to Norcaster. There's a spot there where I've laid low many a time. You can trust my cousin—Jim Spurge, that's his name. One eye, no mistaking of him. He's always about the yard there at Mrs. Wooler's."

"All right," said Copplestone. "If I want you, I'll tell him. Have you told this to anybody?"

"Not to a soul, guv'nor," replied Spurge. "Not even to Jim. No, I kept it dark till I could see you. Considering, of course, that you are left in charge of things, like."

Copplestone presently went away and returned slowly to Scarhaven, meditating deeply on what he had heard. He saw no reason to doubt the truth of Zachary Spurge's tale; it bore the marks of credibility. But what did it amount to? That Spurge saw Bassett Oliver enter the ruins of the Keep by the one point of ingress; that a few moments later he saw Marston Greyle come away from the same place, evidently considerably upset, and sneak off in a manner which showed that he dreaded observation. That was all very suspicious to say the least of it. But it was only suspicion; it afforded no direct proof to Oliver's undoubted disappearance. However, it gave material for a report to Sir Cresswell Oliver, and he determined to write out an account of his dealings with Spurge that afternoon and to send it off at once by registered letter.

He was busily engaged in this task when Mrs. Wooler came into his sitting room to lay the table for his lunch. Copplestone saw at once that she was full of news.

"Never rains but it pours," she said with a smile. "Though, to be sure, it isn't a very heavy shower. I've got another visitor now, Mr. Copplestone."

"Oh?" responded Copplestone, seeming not particularly interested. "Indeed."

"A young clergyman from London, the Reverend Gilling," continued the landlady. "Been ill for some time, and his doctor has recommended him to try the north coast air. So he came down here, and he's going to stop awhile to see how it suits him."

"I should have thought the air of the north coast a bit strong for an invalid," remarked Copplestone. "I'm not delicate, but I find it quite strong enough for me."

"I daresay it's a case of kill or cure," replied Mrs. Wooler. "Chest complaint, I should think. Not that the young gentleman looks particularly delicate, and he tells me that he has a good appetite and that his doctor says he's to live well and to eat as much as ever he can."

Copplestone got a view of the visitor that afternoon in the hall of the inn and agreed with the landlady that he showed no evident signs of delicate health. He had a rather pale, good-humored face set between his round curate's collar and a wide brimmed hat, and he glanced at Copplestone with friendly curiosity and something of a question in his eyes. And Copplestone, out of neighborliness, stopped and spoke to him.

"Mrs. Wooler tells me you're come here to pick up," he remarked. "Pretty strong air round this quarter of the globe."

"Oh, that's all right," said the new arrival. "The air of Scarhaven will do me good. It's full of just what I want." He gave Copplestone another look and then glanced at the letters which he held in his hand. "Are you going to the post office?" he asked. "May I come? I want to go there too."

The two young men walked out of the inn, and Copplestone led the way down the road towards the northern quay. Once they were well out of earshot of the Admiral's Arms and the two or three men who lounged near the wall in front of it, the curate turned to his companion with a sly look.

"Of course you're Mr. Copplestone?" he remarked. "You can't be anybody else. Besides, I heard the landlady call you so."

"Yes," replied Copplestone, distinctly puzzled by the other's manner. "What then?"

The curate laughed quietly, and putting his fingers inside his heavy overcoat, produced a card which he handed over.

"My credentials," he said.

Copplestone glanced at the card and read "Sir Cresswell Oliver." He turned wonderingly to his companion, who laughed again.

"Sir Cresswell told me to give you that as soon as I conveniently could," he said. "The fact is, I'm not a clergyman at all. Not I! I'm a private detective, sent down here by him and Petherton. See?"

Copplestone stared for a moment at the wide-brimmed hat, the round collar, the eminently clerical countenance. Then he burst into laughter. "I congratulate you on your getup anyway!" he exclaimed. "Capital!"

"Oh, I've been on the stage in my time," responded the private detective. "I'm a good hand at fitting myself to various parts. I don't think anybody would see through me, and I'm very particular to avoid the clergy."

"And you left the stage for this?" asked Copplestone. "Why?"

"Pays better, heaps better," replied the other calmly. "Also, it's more exciting. There's much more variety in it. Well, now you know who I am. My name is Gilling, though I'm not the Reverend Gilling, as Mrs. Wooler will call me. And so, as I've made things plain, how's this matter going so far?"

Copplestone shook his head.

"My orders," he said with a significant look, "are to say nothing to anyone."

"Except to me," responded Gilling. "Sir Cresswell Oliver's card is my passport. You can tell me anything."

"Tell me something first," replied Copplestone. "Precisely what are you here for? If I'm to talk confidentially to you, you must talk in the same fashion to me."

He stopped at a deserted stretch of the quay and leaning against the wall which separated it from the sand, signed to Gilling to stop also.

"If we're going to have a quiet talk," he went on, "we'd better have it now; no one's about, and if anyone sees us from a distance, they'll only think we are what we look to be—casual acquaintances. Now, what is your job?"

Gilling looked about him and then perched himself on the wall.

"To watch Marston Greyle," he replied.

"They suspect him?" asked Copplestone.

"Undoubtedly!"

"Sir Cresswell Oliver said as much to me, but no more. What have they said to you?"

"The suspicion seemed to have originated with Petherton. Petherton, in spite of his meek old-fashioned manners, is as sharp an old bird as you'll find in London. He fastened at once on what Bassett Oliver said to that fisherman, Ewbank. A keen nose for a scent, Petherton's. And he's determined to find out who it was that Bassett Oliver met in the United States under the name of Marston

Greyle. He's already set the machinery in motion. In the meantime, I'm to keep my eye on this Squire, as I shall!"

"Why watch him particularly?"

"To see that he doesn't depart for unknown regions or, if he does, to follow in his track. He's not to be lost sight of until this mystery is cleared, because something is wrong."

Copplestone considered matters in silence for a few moments and decided not to reveal the story of Zachary Spurge to Gilling, not yet at any rate. However, he had news which there was no harm in communicating.

"Marston Greyle," he said, presently, "or his agent, Peter Chatfield, or both in common agreement, are already doing something to solve the mystery, so far as Greyle's property is concerned. They've closed the Keep and its surrounding ruins to the people who used to be permitted to go in, and they're conducting an exhaustive search. . . for Bassett Oliver, of course."

Gilling made a grimace.

"Of course," he said, cynically. "Just so. I expected something of that sort. That's all part of a clever scheme."

"I don't understand you," remarked Copplestone. "How a clever scheme?"

"Whitewash," answered Gilling. "Sheer whitewash! You don't suppose that either Greyle or Chatfield are fools? I should say they're far from it from what little I've heard of 'em. Well, don't they know very well that Marston Greyle is under suspicion? All right. They want to clear him, so they close their ruins and make a search—a private search, mind you—and at the end they announce that nothing's been found. And there you are! And supposing they did find something, supposing they found Bassett Oliver's body—What is it?" he asked suddenly, seeing Copplestone staring hard across the sands at the opposite quay. "Something happened?"

"I believe something has happened!" exclaimed Copplestone. "Look there. Men running down the hillside from the Keep. And listen. They're shouting to those fellows on the other quay. Come on! Will it be out of keeping with your invalid pose if you run?"

Gilling answered that question by lightly vaulting the wall and dropping to the sands beneath.

"I'm not an invalid in my legs anyway," he answered, as they began to splash across the pools left by the recently retreated tide. "Why, I do believe something has happened! Look at those people, running out of their cottages!"

All along the south quay the fisher folk, men, women, and children, were crowding eagerly towards the gate of the path by which Bassett Oliver had gone up towards the Keep. When Copplestone and his companion gained the quay and climbed up its wall, they were pouring in at this gate and swarming up to the woods, all talking at the top of their voices. Copplestone suddenly recognized Ewbank on the fringe of the crowd and called to him.

"What is it?" he demanded. "What's happened?"

Ewbank, a man of leisurely movement, paused and waited for the two young men to come up. At their approach he took his pipe out of his mouth and inclined his head towards the Keep.

"They're saying something's been found up there," he replied. "I don't know what. But Chatfield, he's sent two men down here to the village. One of 'em's gone for the police and the doctor, and t'other's gone to the Admiral, looking for you. You're wanted up there—partiklar!"

Chapter 11

Beneath the Brambles

By the time Copplestone and the pseudocurate had reached the plateau of open ground surrounding the ruins, it seemed as if half the population of Scarhaven had gathered there. Men, women, and children were swarming about the door in the curtain wall, all wanting to pass through. But the door was strictly guarded. Chatfield, armed with a new oak cudgel, stood there, masterful and lowering; behind him were several estate laborers, all keeping the people back. And within the door stood Marston Greyle, considerably restless and perturbed, and every now and then looking out on the mob which the fast-spreading rumor had called together. In one of these inspections he caught sight of Copplestone and spoke to Chatfield, who immediately sent one of his bodyguards through the throng.

"Mr. Greyle says will you go forward, sir?" said the man. "Your friend can go in too, if he likes."

"That's your clerical garb," whispered Copplestone as he and Gilling made their way to the door. "But why this sudden politeness?"

"Oh, that's easy to reckon," answered Gilling. "I see through it. They want respectable witnesses to something. This big, heavy-jowled man is Chatfield?"

"That's Chatfield," responded Copplestone. "What's he after?"

As the two young men approached, the agent turned away from them, moving a few steps from the door. He muttered a word or two to the men who guarded it, and they stood aside and allowed Copplestone and the curate to enter. Marston Greyle came forward, eyeing Gilling with a sharp glance of inspection. He turned from him to Copplestone.

"Will you come in?" he asked, not impolitely and with a certain anxiety of manner. "I want you to . . . to be present, in fact. This gentleman is a friend of yours?"

"An acquaintance of an hour," interposed Gilling with ready wit. "I have just come to stay at the inn for my health's sake."

"Perhaps you'll be kind enough to accompany us?" said Greyle. "The fact is, Mr. Copplestone, we've found Mr. Bassett Oliver's body."

"I thought so," remarked Copplestone.

"And as soon as the police come up," continued Greyle, "I want you all to see exactly where it is. No one's touched it; no one's been near it. Of course, he's dead."

He lifted his hand with a nervous gesture, and the two others, who were watching him closely, saw that he was trembling a good deal, and that his face was very pale.

"Dead, of course," he went on. "He . . . he must have been killed instantaneously. And you'll see in a minute or two why the body wasn't found before when we made that first search. It's quite explainable. The fact is—"

A sudden bustle at the door in the wall heralded the entrance of two policemen. The Squire went forward to meet them. The prospect of immediate action seemed to pull him together, and his manner changed to one of assertive superintendence of things.

"Now, Mr. Chatfield!" he called out. "Keep all these people away! Close the door and let no one enter for any reason. Stay there yourself and see that we are not interrupted. Come this way now," he went on, addressing the policemen and the two favored spectators.

"You've found him, then, sir?" asked the police sergeant in a thick whisper, as Greyle led his party across the grass to the foot of the Keep. "The doctor, he wasn't in, but they'll send him up as soon—"

"Mr. Bassett Oliver is dead," interrupted Greyle, almost harshly. "No doctors can do any good. Now, look here," he continued, pulling them to a sudden halt, "I want all of you to take particular notice of this old Keep. I believe you have not been in here before, Mr. Copplestone. Pay particular attention to this place. The Keep stands in the middle of what I suppose was the courtyard of the old castle. It's a square tower with a stair turret at one angle. The stair in that turret is in a very good state of preservation. In fact, it is quite easy to climb to the top, and from the top there's a fine view of land and sea. The Keep itself is nearly a hundred feet in height. Now the inside of the Keep is completely gutted, as you'll presently see. There isn't a floor left of the five or six which were once there. And I'm sorry to say there's very little protection when one's at the top, merely a narrow ledge with a very low parapet, which is badly broken in places. Consequently, anyone who climbs to the top must be very careful or there's the danger of slipping off that ledge and falling to the bottom. And in my opinion, that's precisely what happened on Sunday afternoon. Oliver evidently got in here, climbed the stairs in the turret to enjoy the view, and fell from the parapet. And why his body hasn't been found before I'll now show you."

He led the way to the extreme foot of the Keep and to a very low-arched door. There stood a couple of the estate laborers, one of whom carried a lighted lantern. To this man the Squire made a sign.

"Show the way," he said in a low voice.

The man turned and descended several steps of worn and moss-covered stone which led through the archway into a dark, cellar-like place smelling strongly of damp and age. Greyle drew the attention of his companions to a heap of earth and rubbish at the entrance.

"We had to clear all that out before we could get in here," he said. "This archway hadn't been opened for ages. This is the very lowest story of the Keep, and it is half beneath the level of the ground outside. Its roof has gone like all the rest, but as you see, something else has supplied its place. Hold up your lantern, Marris."

The other men looked up and saw what the Squire meant. Across the tower at a height of some fifteen or twenty feet from the floor, nature, left unchecked, had grown a ceiling of green. Bramble, ivy, and other spreading and climbing plants had, in the course of years, made a complete network from wall to wall. In places it was so thick that no light could be seen through from beneath; in other thin places glimpses of the sky could be seen from above the gray, tunnel-like walls. And in one of those places close to the walls, there was a distinct gap, jagged and irregular, as if some heavy mass had recently plunged through the screen of leaf and branch from the heights above. And beneath this, the startled searchers saw the body, lying beside a heap of stones and earth in the unmistakable stillness of death.

"You see how it must have happened," whispered Greyle as they all bent round the dead man. "He must have fallen from the very top of the Keep—from the parapet, in fact—and plunged through this mass of green stuff above us. If he had hit where it's thick—there!—it might have broken his fall; but, you see, he struck it at the very thinnest part, and being a large man, of course, he'd crash right through it. When we examined the Keep on Monday morning, it never struck us that there might be something down here. If you go up the turret stairs to the top and look down on this mass of green stuff from the very top, you'll see that it looks undisturbed; there's scarcely anything to show from up there that he fell through it. But he did."

"Whose notion was it that he might be found here?" asked Copplestone.

"Chatfield's," replied the Squire. "Chatfield's. He and I were up at the top there, and he suddenly suggested that Oliver might have fallen from the parapet and be lying beneath that mass of green stuff. We didn't know then—even Chatfield didn't know—that there was this empty space beneath the green stuff. But when we found there was, we had that archway cleared of all the stone and rubbish, and we found him."

"The body'll have to be removed, sir," whispered the police sergeant. "It'll have to be taken down to the inn to wait the inquest."

Marston Greyle started.

"Inquest!" he said. "Will that have to be held? Yes, I suppose so. But we'd better wait until the doctor comes, hadn't we? I want him—"

The doctor came into the gloomy vault at that moment. He was an elderly, old-fashioned person, who evidently attached much more importance to the living Squire than to the dead man. He listened to all Marston Greyle's explanations and theories with great deference and accepted each without demur. "Ah yes, to be sure," he said, after a perfunctory examination of the body. "The affair is easily understood. It is precisely as you suggest, Squire. The unfortunate man evidently climbed to the top of the tower, missed his footing, and fell headlong. That slight mass of branch and leaf would make little difference. He was, you see, a heavy man—some two hundred pounds, I should think. Oh, instantaneous death without a doubt! Well, well, these constables must see to the removal of the body, and we must let my friend the coroner know. He will hold the inquest tomorrow, no doubt. A mere formality, my dear sir! The whole thing is as plain as a pikestaff. It will be a relief to know that the mystery is now satisfactorily solved."

Outside in the welcome freshness, Copplestone turned to the doctor.

"You say the inquest will be held tomorrow?" he asked. The doctor looked his questioner up and down with an inquiry which signified doubt as to Copplestone's right to demand information.

"In the usual course," he replied stiffly.

"Then his brother, Sir Cresswell Oliver, and his solicitor, Mr. Petherton, must be wired for from London," observed Copplestone, turning to Greyle. "I'll communicate with them at once. May we go up the tower?" he continued as Greyle nodded his assent. "I'd like to see the stairs and the parapet."

Greyle looked a little doubtful and uneasy.

"Well, I had meant that no one should go up until all this was gone into," he answered. "I don't want any more accidents. You'll be careful?"

"We're both young and agile," responded Copplestone. "There's no need for alarm. Do you care to go up, Mr. Gilling?"

The pseudocurate accepted the invitation readily, and he and Copplestone entered the turret. They had climbed half its height before Copplestone spoke.

"Well?" he whispered. "What do you think?"

"It may be an accident," muttered Gilling. "It may not."

"You think he might have been—what?—thrown down?"

"Might have been caught unawares and pushed over. Let's see what there is up above anyway."

The stair in the turret was much worn, but comparatively safe and lighted by loopholes and arrow slits. It terminated in a low arched doorway to a parapet which ran completely around the inner wall of the Keep. It was no more than a yard wide; the balustrading which fenced it in was in some places completely gone. A mere glance was sufficient to show that only an extremely sure-footed person ought to traverse it. Copplestone contented himself with an inspection from the archway; he looked down and saw at once that a fall from that height would mean sure and swift death; he saw, too, that Greyle had been quite right in saying that the sudden plunge of Oliver's body through the leafy screen far beneath had made little difference to the appearance of that screen as seen from above. And now that he saw everything, it seemed to him that the real truth might well lie in one word: accident.

"Coming round this parapet?" asked Gilling, who was looking narrowly about him.

"No," replied Copplestone. "I can't stand looking down from great heights. It makes my head swim. Are you?"

"Sure!" answered Gilling. He took off his heavy overcoat and handed it to his companion. "Mind holding it?" he asked. "I want to have a good look at the exact spot from which Oliver must have fallen. There's the gap in the green stuff down below, such as it is. It doesn't look much from here, does it? So he must have been here on the parapet exactly above it. My! It's very narrow and a bit risky, this, when all's said and done."

Copplestone watched his companion make his way around to the place from which it was only too evident Oliver must have fallen. Gilling went slowly, carefully inspecting every yard of the moss and lichen-covered stones. Once he paused and seemed to be examining a part of the parapet with unusual attention. When he reached the precise spot at which he had aimed, he instantly called across to Copplestone.

"There's no doubt about his having fallen from here!" he said. "Some of the masonry on the very edge of this parapet is loose. I could dislodge it with a touch."

"Then be careful," answered Copplestone. "Don't cross that bit."

But Gilling quietly continued his progress and returned to his companion by the opposite side from which he had set out, having thus accomplished the entire around. He quietly reassumed his overcoat.

"No doubt about the fall," he said as they turned down the stair. "The next thing is, was it accidental?"

"And as regards that, what's to be done next?" asked Copplestone.

"That's easy. We must go at once and wire for Sir Cresswell and old Petherton," replied Gilling. "It's now four-thirty. If they catch an evening express at King's Cross, they'll get here early in the morning. Or they can motor from Norcaster and get here in the small hours. But they must be here for that inquest."

Greyle was talking to Chatfield at the foot of the Keep when they got down. The agent turned arrogantly away, but the Squire looked at both with an unmistakable eagerness.

"There's no doubt whatever that Oliver fell from the parapet," said Copplestone. "The marks of a fall are there quite unmistakably."

Greyle nodded, but made no remark, and the two made their way through the still eager crowd and went down to the village post office. Both were wondering about the same thing, the evident anxiety and mental uneasiness of Marston Greyle.

Chapter 12

Good Men and True

C opplestone saw little of his bed that night. At seven o'clock in the evening came a telegram from Sir Cresswell Oliver, saying that he and Petherton were leaving at once, would reach Norcaster soon after midnight, and would motor out to Scarhaven immediately on arrival. Copplestone made all the arrangements for their reception, and, after snatching a couple of hours' sleep, was up to receive them. By two o'clock in the morning Sir Cresswell and the old solicitor and Gilling were smuggled into his sitting room and heard all he had to tell about Zachary Spurge and his story.

"We must have that fellow at the inquest," said Petherton. "At any cost we must have him! That's sure and certain!"

"You think it wise?" asked Sir Cresswell. "Won't it be a bit premature? Wouldn't it be better to wait until we know more?"

"No, we must have his evidence," declared Petherton. "It will serve as an opening. Spurge must be produced."

"If Spurge comes into Scarhaven," observed Copplestone, "he'll be promptly collared by the police. They want him for poaching."

"Then they can get him when the proceedings are over," retorted the old lawyer dryly. "They daren't touch him while he's giving evidence, and that's all we want. Perhaps he won't come? Oh, he'll come all right if we make it worth his while. A month in Norcaster jail will mean nothing to him if he knows there's a chance of that reward or something substantial out of it at the end of his sentence. You must go out to this retreat of his and bring him in; we must have him. Better go very early in the morning."

"I'll go now," said Copplestone. "It's as easy to go by night as by day." He left the other three to seek their beds, slipped quietly out of the hotel by one of the ground-floor windows, and set off in a pitch-black night to seek Spurge in his lair. And after sundry barkings of his shins against the rocks and scratchings of his hands and cheeks by the undergrowth of Hobkin's Hole, he rounded the poacher out and delivered his message.

Spurge, blinking at his visitor in the pale light of a guttering candle, nodded his head.

"I'll come, guv'nor," he said. "And I'll trust to luck to get away, but it don't matter if the luck's agen me. I've done a month in Norcaster before today, and it ain't half a bad rest, if you only take it that way. But guv'nor, that old lawyer's making a mistake. You shouldn't ought to have my bit of evidence at this stage. It's too soon. You want to work up the case a bit. There's such a thing, guv'nor, as being a bit previous, and this here's too previous. You want to be surer of your facts. Because you know, guv'nor, nobody'll believe my word agen Squire Greyle's. Guv'nor, this here inquest'll be naught but a blooming farce! You ain't a native o' this part; I am. D'you think a Scarhaven jury's going to say aught agen its own Squire and landlord? No sir! Mark my words."

"All the same, you'll come?" asked Copplestone, who was secretly of Spurge's opinion. "You won't lose by it in the long run."

"I'll be there," responded Spurge. "Out of curiosity if for nothing else. You mayn't see me at first, but let the lawyer from London call my name out, and Zachary Spurge'll step forward."

There was abundant cover for Zachary Spurge and for half a dozen like him in the village schoolhouse when the inquest was opened at ten o'clock that morning. It seemed to Copplestone that it would have been a physical impossibility to crowd more people within the walls than had assembled. The local coroner was obviously testy, irritable, self-important, and afflicted with deafness; he took his seat and looked sourly on the crowd of faces. Copplestone had already seen him in conversation with the village doctor, the village police, Chatfield, and Marston Greyle's solicitor. He began to see the force of Spurge's shrewd remarks. What was most desired was secrecy and privacy. The Scarhaven powers had no wish that the attention of all the world should be drawn to this quiet place. But outsiders were there in plenty. Stafford and several members of Bassett Oliver's company had motored over from Norcaster. There were half a dozen reporters from Norcaster and Northborough, and plainclothes police from both towns. And there, too, were all the principal folk of the neighborhood, Mrs. Greyle and her daughter, and a little distance from Audrey, alert and keenly interested, was Addie Chatfield.

It needed very little insight on the part of an intelligent specta- tor to see how things were going. The twelve good men and true, required to form a jury, were all of them either Scarhaven tradesmen or Scarhaven householders or laborers on the estate. Their counte- nances showed plainly that they regarded the whole thing as a nec- essary formality and that they were already prepared with a verdict. This impression was strengthened by the coroner's opening remarks. In his opinion the whole affair, to which he did not even refer as unfortunate, was easily and quickly explained and understood. The deceased had come to the village to look around—on a Sunday be it observed—had somehow obtained access to the Keep, where he had no right to be, the ruins being strictly private and not open to the public on any consideration on Sunday, had indulged his curiosity by climbing to the top of the ancient tower, and had paid for it by falling down from that terrible height and breaking his neck. All that was necessary was for them to hear evidence bearing out these facts, after which they would return a verdict in accordance with what they had heard. Fortunately the facts were plain, and it would not be necessary to call many witnesses.

Sir Cresswell Oliver turned to Copplestone who sat at one side of him, while Petherton sat on the other.

"I don't know if you notice that Greyle isn't here?" he whispered grimly. "In my opinion, he doesn't intend to show. We'll see."

Certainly the Squire was not in the place. And there were soon signs that those who conducted the proceedings evidently did not consider his presence necessary. The witnesses were few: Sir Cresswell Oliver, to give formal identification; Mrs. Wooler, to prove that the deceased man came to her house; one of the foremen of the estate, to prove the great care with which the Squire had searched for traces of the missing man; one of the estate laborers, to prove the actual finding of the body; and the doctor, to prove beyond all doubt that the deceased had broken his neck. Each examination was perfunctory; each was out of the makeshift witness box as soon as he was in it.

The coroner, obviously well satisfied with the trend of things, took off his spectacles and turned to the jury.

"You have heard everything there is to be heard, gentlemen," said he. "As I remarked at the opening of this inquest, the case is one of great simplicity. You will have no difficulty in deciding that the deceased came to his death by accident. As to the exact wording of your verdict, you had better put it in this way: that the deceased Bassett Oliver died as the result—"

Petherton, who had noticed the coroner's deafness, had contrived to seat himself as close to his chair as possible and quietly rose.

"Before the jury considers any verdict," he said in his loudest tones, "they must hear certain evidence which I wish to call. And first of all, is Mr. Marston Greyle present in this room?"

The coroner frowned, and the Squire's solicitor turned to Petherton.

"Mr. Greyle is not present," he said. "He is not at all well. There is no need for his presence; he has no evidence to give."

"If you don't have Mr. Greyle down here at once," said Petherton, "this inquest will have to be adjourned for his attendance. You had better send for him, or I'll get the authorities to do so. In the meantime we'll call one or two witnesses. Daniel Ewbank, to begin with."

There was a brief and evidently anxious consultation between Greyle's solicitor and the coroner; there were dark looks at Petherton and his companions. Then the foreman of the jury spoke sullenly.

"We don't want to hear no Ewbanks!" he said. "We're quite satisfied, us as sits here. Our verdict is—"

"You'll have to bear Ewbank and anybody I like to call, my good sir," retorted Petherton. "I am better acquainted with the law than you are." He turned to the coroner's officer. "I warned you this morning to produce Ewbank," he said. "Now, where is he?"

Out of a deep silence a shrill voice came from the rear of the crowd.

"Knows better than to be here, does Dan'l Ewbank, mister! He's off!"

"Very good—or bad—for somebody," remarked Petherton. "Then until Mr. Marston Greyle comes, we will call Zachary Spurge."

The assemblage, jurymen included, broke into derisive laughter as Spurge suddenly appeared from the most densely packed corner of the room. It was at once evident to Copplestone that whatever the poacher might say, no one there would attach any importance to it. The laughter continued and increased while Spurge was under examination. Petherton appealed to the coroner; the coroner affected not to hear. And once more the foreman of the jury interrupted.

"We don't want to hear no more o' this stuff!" he said. "It's an insult to us to put a fellow like that before us. We don't believe a word o' what he says. We don't believe he was within a mile o' them ruins on Sunday afternoon. It's all a put-up job!"

Petherton leaned towards the reporters.

"I hope you gentlemen of the press will make a full note of these proceedings," he observed suavely. "*You*, at any rate, are not biased or prejudiced."

The coroner heard that in spite of his deafness, and he grew purple.

"Sir!" he exclaimed. "That is a most improper observation! It's a reflection on my position, sir, and I've a great mind—"

"Mr. Coroner," observed Petherton, leaning towards him, "I shall hand in a full report concerning your conduct of these proceedings to the Home Office tomorrow. If you attempt to interfere with my duty here, all the worse for you. Now, Spurge, you can stand down. And as I see Mr. Greyle there, call Marston Greyle!"

The Squire had appeared while Spurge was giving his evidence and had heard what the poacher alleged. He entered the box very pale, angry, and disturbed, and the glances which he cast on Sir Cresswell Oliver and his party were distinctly those of displeasure.

"Swear him," commanded Petherton. "Now, Mr. Greyle—"

But Greyle's own solicitor was on his legs, insisting on his right to put a first question. In spite of Petherton, he put it.

"You heard the evidence of the last witness, Spurge? Is there a word of truth in it?"

Marston Greyle, who certainly looked very unwell, moistened his lips.

"Not one word," he answered. "It's a lie."

The solicitor glanced triumphantly at the coroner and the jury, and the crowd raised unchecked murmurs of approval. Again the foreman endeavored to stop the proceedings.

"We regard all this here as very rude conduct to Mr. Greyle," he said angrily. "We're not concerned—"

"Mr. Foreman!" said Petherton. "You are interfering with justice. I warn you, if the coroner doesn't. Mr. Greyle, I must ask you certain questions. Did you see the deceased Bassett Oliver on Sunday last?"

"No!"

"I needn't remind you that you are on your oath. Have you ever met the deceased man in your life?"

"Never!"

"You never met him in America?"

"I may have met him, but not to my recollection. If I did, it was in such a casual fashion that I have completely forgotten all about it."

"Very well. You are on your oath, mind. Where did you live in America, before you succeeded to this estate?"

The Squire's solicitor intervened.

"Don't answer that question," he said sharply. "Don't answer any more. I object altogether to your line," he went, turning to Petherton. "I claim the coroner's protection for the witness."

"I quite agree," said the coroner. "All this is absolutely irrelevant. You can stand down," he continued, turning to the Squire. "I will have no more of this, and I will take the full responsibility!"

"And the consequences, Mr. Coroner," replied Petherton calmly. "And the first consequence is that I now formally demand an indefinite adjournment of this inquest."

"On what grounds, sir?" demanded the coroner.

"To permit me to bring evidence from America," replied Petherton with a side glance at Marston Greyle. "Evidence already being prepared."

The coroner hesitated, looked at Greyle's solicitor, and then turned sharply to the jury.

"I refuse that application," he said. "You have heard all I have to say, gentlemen," he went on, "and you can return your verdict."

Petherton quietly gathered up his papers and motioned to his friends to follow him out of the schoolroom. The foreman of the jury was returning a verdict of accidental death as they passed through the door. They emerged into the street to an accompaniment of loud cheers for the Squire and groans for themselves.

"What a travesty of justice!" exclaimed Sir Cresswell. "That fellow Spurge was right, you see, Copplestone. I wish we hadn't brought him into danger."

Copplestone suddenly laughed and touched Sir Cresswell's arm. He pointed to the edge of the moorland just outside the schoolyard. Spurge was disappearing over that edge and in a moment had vanished.

Chapter 13

Mr. Dennie

A mongst the little group of actors and actresses who had come over from Norcaster to hear all that was to be told concerning their late manager sat an old gentleman. With hands folded on the head of his walking cane and chin settled on his hands, he watched the proceedings with silent and concentrated attention. He was a striking figure of an old gentleman—tall, distinguished-looking, handsome. He had a face full of character, the strong lines and features further accentuated by his silvery hair. He was a stylish old gentleman, too, scrupulously attired and groomed. His fellow members of the Oliver company seemed to pay him great attention, and at various points of the proceedings whispered questions to him as to an acknowledged authority.

This old gentleman, when the inquest came to its extraordinary end, separated himself from his companions and made his way towards Mrs. Greyle and her daughter, who were quietly setting out homewards. To Audrey's surprise the two elders shook hands in silence and inspected each other with a palpable wistfulness of look.

"It's twenty-five years since we met," said the old gentleman, almost as if he were talking to himself. "But I knew you at once. I was wondering if you remembered me?"

"Why, of course," responded Mrs. Greyle. "Besides, I've had an advantage over you. I've seen you several times at Norcaster when we go to the theater. Audrey, this is Mr. Dennie. You've seen him too."

"On the stage. On the stage," murmured the old actor, as he shook hands with the girl. "Um! I wonder if any of us are ever really off it! This affair, for instance. There's a drama for you! By the-bye, this young Squire, he's your relation, of course?"

"My nephew-in-law and Audrey's cousin," replied Mrs. Greyle.

Mr. Dennie, who had walked along with them towards their cottage, stopped in a quiet stretch of the quay and looked meditatively at Audrey.

"Then this young lady," he said, "is next heir to the Greyle estates, eh?"

"That's something that isn't worth thinking about," replied Mrs. Greyle hastily. "Don't put notions into the girl's head, Mr. Dennie. The Greyle estates are not entailed, you know. The present owner can do what he pleases with them. Besides that, he's sure to marry."

"All the same," observed Mr. Dennie imperturbably, "if this young man had not been in existence, this child would have inherited, eh?"

"Why, of course," agreed Mrs. Greyle a little impatiently. "But what's the use of talking about that, my old friend? The young man is in possession, and there you are!"

"Do you like the young man?" asked Mr. Dennie. "I take an old fellow's privilege in asking direct questions, you know."

"No, we don't," replied Mrs. Greyle. "And we don't know *why* we don't. So there's a woman's answer for you. Kinsfolk though we are, we see little of each other."

Mr. Dennie made no remark on this. He walked along at Audrey's side, apparently in deep thought, and suddenly he looked across at her mother.

"What do people here think about this extraordinary story of Bassett Oliver's having met a Marston Greyle over there in America?" he asked abruptly.

"We're not in a position to hear much of what other people think," answered Mrs. Greyle. "But what *I* think is that if this Marston Greyle ever did meet such a very notable and noticeable man as Bassett Oliver, it's a very, very strange thing that he's forgotten all about it."

Mr. Dennie laughed quietly.

"Aye, aye," he said. "But don't you think we folk of the profession are a little bit apt to magnify our own importance? You say 'Bless me, how could anybody ever forget an introduction to Bassett Oliver!' But we must remember that to some people even a famous actor is of no more importance than a respectable grocer? Marston Greyle may be one of those people. It's quite possible he may have been introduced quite casually to Oliver at some gathering over there and have quite forgotten all about it. Quite possible, I think."

"I agree with you as to the *possibility*, but certainly not as to the *probability*," said Mrs. Greyle dryly. "Bassett Oliver was the sort of man whom nobody would forget. But here we are at our cottage. You'll come in, Mr. Dennie?"

"It will only have to be for a little time, my dear lady," said the old actor, pulling out his watch. "Our people are going back very soon, and I must join them at the station."

Mr. Dennie followed Audrey into the little parlor as Mrs. Greyle disappeared to another part of the house. And the instant they were alone, he tapped the girl's arm and gave her a curiously warning look.

"Hush, my dear!" he whispered. "Not a word. Don't want your mother to know! Listen. Have you a specimen—letter, anything— of your cousin, the Squire's handwriting? Anything so long as it's his. Give it to me, but say nothing to your mother. Wait until tomorrow morning. I'll run over to see you again about noon. It's important, but silence!"

Audrey, scarcely understanding the old man's meaning, opened a desk and drew out one or two letters. She selected one and handed it to Mr. Dennie, who made haste to put it away before Mrs. Greyle returned. He gave Audrey another warning look.

"That was what I wanted," he said mysteriously. "I thought of it during the inquest. Never mind why just now. You shall know tomorrow."

He lingered a few minutes, chatting with his hostess about old times, then he went off to the station, joined Stafford and his fellow actors and actresses, and returned with them to Norcaster. And at Norcaster Mr. Dennie separated himself from the rest and repaired to his quiet lodgings. Once safely inside his room, he pulled out an old-fashioned trunk which he had owned since boyhood and lugged about wherever he went. From it, after much methodical unpacking, he disinterred a brown paper parcel, neatly tied up with green ribbon. From this parcel he drew a thin packet of typed matter and a couple of letters; the typed script he laid aside; the letters he opened out on his table. Then he took from his pocket the letter which Audrey Greyle had given him and put it side by side with those taken from the parcel. And after one brief glance at all three Mr. Dennie made typescript and letters up again into a neat packet, restored them to his trunk, locked them up, and turned to the two hours' rest he always took before going to the theater for his evening's work.

He was back at Scarhaven by eleven o'clock the next morning with his neat packet under his arm, and he held it up significantly to Audrey, who opened the door of the cottage to him.

"Something to show you," he said with a quiet smile as he walked in. "To show you and your mother." He stopped short on the threshold of the little parlor where Copplestone was just then talking to Mrs. Greyle. "Oh," he said, a little disappointedly, "I hoped to find you alone. I'll wait."

Mrs. Greyle explained who Copplestone was, and Mr. Dennie immediately brightened. "Of course, of course," he explained. "I know! Glad to meet you, Mr. Copplestone. You don't know me, but I know you—or your work—well enough. It was I who read and recommended your play to our poor dear friend. It's a little secret, you know," continued Mr. Dennie, laying his packet on the table, "but I have acted for a great many years as Bassett Oliver's literary adviser—his taster, you might say. You know, he had a great number of plays sent to him, of course, and he was a very busy man; he used to hand them over to me in the first place to take a look at, a taste of, you know, and if I liked the taste, why, then he took a mouthful himself, eh? And that brings me to the very point, my dear ladies and my dear young gentleman, that I have come 'specially to Scarhaven this morning to discuss. It's a very, very serious matter indeed," he went on as he untied his packet of papers, "and I fear that it's only the beginning of something more serious. Come round me here at this table, all of you, if you please."

The other three drew up chairs, each wondering what was coming, and the old actor picked up his eyeglasses and gave obvious signs of making a speech.

"Now I want you all to attend to me, very closely," he said. "I shall have to go into a detailed explanation, and you will very soon see what I am after. As you may be aware, I have been a personal friend of Bassett Oliver for some years and a member of his company without break for the last eight years. I accompanied Bassett Oliver on his two trips to the United States; therefore, I was with him when he was last there years ago.

"While we were at Chicago that time, Bassett came to me one day with the typescript of a one-act play and told me that it had been sent to him by a correspondent signing himself Marston Greyle, who in a cover letter said that he sprang from an old English family and that the play dealt with a historic, romantic episode in its history. The principal part, he believed, was one which would suit Bassett, therefore he begged him to consider the matter. Bassett asked me to read the play, and I took it with the writer's letter for that purpose. But we were just then very busy, and I had no opportunity of reading anything for a time. Later on we went to St. Louis, where Bassett as usual was much honored and went out a great deal, lunching with people and so on. One day he came to me, 'By-the-bye, Dennie!' he said, 'I met that Mr. Marston Greyle today who sent me that romantic one-act thing. He wanted to know if I'd read it, and I had to confess that it was in your hands. Have you looked at it?' I, too, had to confess that I hadn't. 'Well,' said he, 'read it, and let me know what you think. Will it suit me?' I made time to read the little play during the following week, and I told Bassett that I didn't think it would suit him, but I felt sure it might suit Montagu Gaines, who plays just such parts. Bassett thereupon wrote to the author and said what I, his reader, thought. Bassett kindly offered, as he knew Gaines intimately, to show the play to him on his return to England. Mr. Marston Greyle wrote back, thanking Bassett warmly and accepting his kind offer. Accordingly I brought the play with me to England, however, Montagu Gaines had just set off on a two years' tour to

Australia. Consequently, the play and the author's two letters have remained in my possession ever since. And here they are."

Mr. Dennie laid his hand dramatically on his packet, looked significantly at his audience, and went on.

"Now when I heard all that I did hear at that inquest yesterday," he said, "I naturally remembered that I had in my possession two letters which were undoubtedly written to Bassett Oliver by a young man named Marston Greyle, whom Oliver—just as undoubtedly!—had personally met in St. Louis. And so when the inquest was over, Mr. Copplestone, I reintroduced myself to Mrs. Greyle here, whom I had known many years ago. I walked back to this house with her and her charming daughter, and—don't be angry, Mrs. Greyle—while the mother's back was turned on hospitable intentions, I got the daughter to secretly lend me a letter written by the present Squire of Scarhaven. Armed with that, I went home to my lodgings in Norcaster, found the letter written by the American Marston Greyle, and compared it with them. And here is the result!"

The old actor selected the two American letters from his papers, laid them out on the table, and placed the letter which Audrey had given him beside them.

"Now," he said, as his three companions bent eagerly over these exhibits, "Look at those three letters. All bear the same signature, Marston Greyle, but the handwriting of those two is as different from that of this one as chalk is from cheese!"

Chapter 14

By Private Treaty

There was little need for the three listeners to look long at the letters. One glance was sufficient to show even a careless eye that the hand which had written one of them had certainly not written the other two. The letter which Audrey had handed to Mr. Dennie was plain, commonplace, and of the sort which one comes across every day in shops and offices and banks. But the other two letters were evidently written by a man of literary and artistic sense, possessing imagination, flourish, and a liking for effect. It needed no expert in handwriting to declare that two totally different individuals had written those letters.

"And now," observed Mr. Dennie, breaking the silence and putting into words what each of the others was vaguely feeling, "the question is, what does all this mean? To start with, Marston Greyle is a most uncommon name. Is it possible there can be two persons of that name? That is the first thing that strikes me."

"It is not the first thing that strikes me," said Mrs. Greyle. She took up the script which the old actor had brought in his packet and held its title page before him. "That is the first thing that strikes me," she exclaimed. "The Marston Greyle who sent this to Bassett Oliver said, according to your story, that he sprang from a very old family in England, and that this is a dramatization of a romantic episode in its history. Now there is no other old family in England named Greyle; this episode is, of course, the famous legend of how Prince Rupert once sought refuge in the Keep yonder and had a secret passage to a lady of the house. Am I right, Mr. Dennie?"

"Quite right, ma'am, quite correct," replied the old actor. "You have guessed correctly!"

"Very well then. The Marston Greyle who wrote this play and those letters, and who met Bassett Oliver was without doubt the son of Marcus Greyle, who went to America many years ago. He was the same Marston Greyle, who, his father being dead, succeeded his uncle, Stephen John Greyle. That seems an absolute certainty." Mrs. Greyle looked earnestly from one to the other. "And in that case, who is the man now at Scarhaven Keep?"

A dead silence fell on the little room. Audrey started at her mother's pregnant question; Mr. Dennie sat up very erect and took a pinch of snuff from his old-fashioned box. Copplestone pushed his chair away from the table and began to walk about. And Mrs. Greyle continued to look from one face to the other as if demanding a reply to her question.

"Mother," said Audrey in a low voice. "You aren't suggesting—"

"Ahem," interrupted Mr. Dennie. "A moment, my dear. There is nothing, I believe," he continued, waxing eloquent, "nothing like plain speech. We are all friends. We have a common cause—justice! It may be that justice demands our best endeavors not only as regards our deceased friend, Bassett Oliver, but in the interests of this young lady. So—"

"I wish you wouldn't, Mr. Dennie!" exclaimed Audrey. "I don't like this at all. Please don't!"

She turned, almost instinctively, to seek Copplestone's aid in repressing the old man. But Copplestone was standing by the window, staring moodily at the wind-swept quay beyond the garden, and Mr. Dennie waved his snuff-box and went on.

"An old man's privilege," he said. "In your interests, my dear. Allow me." He turned again to Mrs. Greyle. "In plain words, ma'am, you are wondering if the present holder of the estates is really what he claims to be. Plain English, eh?"

"I am," answered Mrs. Greyle with a distinct ring of challenge and defiance. "And now that it comes to the truth, I have wondered that ever since he came here. There!"

"Why, mother?" asked Audrey wonderingly.

"Because he doesn't possess a single Greyle characteristic," replied Mrs. Greyle, readily enough. "I ought to know. I married Valentine Greyle, and I knew Stephen John. I saw plenty of both and something of their father too. Even a little of Marcus before he emigrated. This man does not possess one single scrap of the Greyle temperament!"

Mr. Dennie put away his snuff-box and drumming on the table with his fingers looked out of his eye corners at Copplestone who still stood with his back to the rest, staring out of the window.

"And what," said Mr. Dennie softly, "what does our good friend Mr. Copplestone say?"

Copplestone turned swiftly and gave Audrey a quick glance.

"I say," he answered in a sharp, businesslike fashion, "that Gilling, who's staying at the inn, you know, is walking up and down outside here, evidently very anxious to see me. With your permission, Mrs. Greyle, I'd like to ask him in. Now that things have got to this pitch, I'd better tell you something I needn't conceal any longer. Gilling isn't an invalid curate at all! He's a private detective. Sir Cresswell Oliver and Petherton, the solicitor, sent him down here to watch Greyle—the Squire, you know. That's Gilling's job. They suspect Greyle. Have suspected him from the very first, but of what I don't know. Not of this, I think. But they do suspect him, and Gilling's had his eye on him ever since he came here. I'd like to fetch Gilling in here, and I'd like him to know all that Mr. Dennie's told us. Because, don't you see, Sir Cresswell and Petherton ought to know all that immediately, and Gilling's their man."

Audrey's brows had been gathering in lines of dismay and perplexity all the time Copplestone was talking, but her mother showed no signs of anything but complete composure, crowned by something very like satisfaction, and she nodded a ready acquiescence in Copplestone's proposal.

"By all means," she responded. "Bring Mr. Gilling in at once."

Copplestone hurried out into the garden and signaled to the pseudocurate, who came hurrying across from the quay. One glance at him showed Copplestone that something had happened.

"My! I thought I would never attract your attention!" said Gilling hastily. "Been trying to catch your eye for ten minutes. I say, Greyle's off!"

"Off? How do you mean *off*?"

"Left Scarhaven, anyhow, for London," replied Gilling. "An hour ago I happened to be at the station buying a paper, when he drove up, luggage and man with him, so I knew he was off for some time. And I took good care to dodge round by the booking office when the man bought the tickets. King's Cross. So that's all right for the time being."

"How do you mean *all right?*" asked Copplestone. "I thought you were to keep him in sight?"

"All right," repeated Gilling. "I have more eyes than these, my boy! I've a particularly smart partner in London, name of Swallow. So soon as the gentleman had left, I repaired to the nearest post office and wired a coded message to Swallow. Swallow will meet that train at King's Cross. It doesn't matter if Greyle hides himself in one of the spikes on top of the monument or inside the lion house at the zoo, Swallow will be there. No man ever got away from Swallow once Swallow had set eyes on him."

Copplestone looked, listened, and laughed.

"Professional pride," he said. "All right. I want you to come in here with me to Mrs. Greyle's. Something's happened here too, and of such a serious nature that I've taken the liberty of telling them who and what you really are. You'll forgive me when you hear what it is that we've learned here this morning."

Gilling had looked rather doubtful at Copplestone's announcement, but he immediately turned towards the cottage.

"Oh, well," he said good-naturedly. "I'm sure you wouldn't have told if you hadn't felt there was good reason. What is this fresh news? Something about him?"

"Very much about him," answered Copplestone. "Come in."

He himself, at Mrs. Greyle's request, gave Gilling a brief account of Mr. Dennie's revelations, the old actor supplementing it with a shrewd remark or two, and then all four turned to Gilling as to an expert in these matters.

"Odd," observed Gilling. "Decidedly odd. There may be some explanation, you know. I've known stranger things than that turn out to be perfectly straight and plain when they were gone into. But putting all the facts together, I don't think there's much doubt that there's something considerably wrong in this case. I should like to repeat it to my principals. Better let me have all those documents, Mr. Dennie. I'll give you a proper receipt for them. There's something very valuable in them anyhow."

"What?" asked Copplestone.

"The address in St. Louis from which that Marston Greyle wrote to Bassett Oliver," replied Gilling. "We can communicate with that address at once, and we may learn something there. But," he went on, turning to Mrs. Greyle, "I want to learn something here and now. I want to know where and under what circumstances the Squire came to Scarhaven. You were here then, Mrs. Greyle? You can tell me?"

"He came very quietly," replied Mrs. Greyle. "Nobody in Scarhaven, unless it was Peter Chatfield, knew of his coming. In fact nobody in all these parts knew he was in England. The family solicitors in London may have known. But nothing was ever said or written to me, even though my daughter, failing this man, is the next in succession."

"I do wish you'd leave all that out, Mother!" exclaimed Audrey. "I don't like it."

"Whether you like it or not, it is the fact," said Mrs. Greyle, "and it can't be left out. As I say, no one knew the Squire had come to England, until one day Chatfield calmly walked down the quay with him, introducing him right and left. He brought him here."

"That's interesting," said Gilling. "Did you find out if he was well up in the family history?"

"Not then, but afterwards," answered Mrs. Greyle. "He is particularly well studied in the Greyle records. Suspiciously well studied."

"Why suspiciously?" asked Cobblestone.

93

"He knows more, in a sort of antiquarian and historian fashion, than you'd suppose a young man of his age would," said Mrs. Greyle. "He gives you the impression of having read and studied it deeply. And his usual tastes don't lie in that direction."

"Bad sign, ma'am," observed Mr. Dennie. "Bad sign! Looks as if he had been, shall we say, put up to over studying his part. That's possible. I have known men who were so anxious to be what one calls letter-perfect, Mr. Copplestone, that though they knew their parts, they didn't know how to play them. Fact, sir!"

While the old actor was chuckling over this reminiscence, Gilling turned quietly to Mrs. Greyle.

"I think you suspect this man?" he said.

"Frankly, yes," replied Mrs. Greyle. "I always have, though I have said so little—"

"Mother," interrupted Audrey. "Is it really worth while saying so much now? After all, we know nothing, and if this is all mere supposition—" She broke off, rising and going away from the group. "Perhaps I had better say nothing."

Copplestone too rose and followed her into the window recess.

"I hope you don't think me interfering," he said entreatingly. "I assure you—"

"You?" she exclaimed. "Oh, no! I think you're anxious to clear things up about Mr. Oliver, but I don't want my mother dragged into it for a simple reason. We've got to live here, and Chatfield is a vindictive man."

"You're frightened of him?" said Copplestone incredulously.

"Not for myself," she answered, giving him a warning look and glancing apprehensively at Mrs. Greyle, who was talking eagerly to Mr. Dennie and Gilling. "But my mother is not as strong as she looks, and it would be a blow to her to have to leave this place. We are the Squire's tenants, and therefore at Chatfield's mercy. And you know that Chatfield does as he likes. Now do you understand?"

"It maddens me to think that you should be at Chatfield's mercy," muttered Copplestone. "But do you really mean to say that if Chatfield thought you, that is, your mother, were mixed up in anything relating to the clearing up of this affair he would—"

"Drive us out without mercy," replied Audrey. "That's dead sure."

"And that your cousin would let him?" exclaimed Copplestone. "Surely not!"

"I don't think the Squire has any control over Chatfield," she answered. "You have seen them together."

"If that's so," said Copplestone, "I shall begin to think there is something strange about the Squire in the way your mother suggests. It looks as if Chatfield had a hold on him. And in that case—"

He suddenly broke off as a smart automobile drove up to the cottage door and let out a tall, distinguished-looking man who after a glance at the little house walked quickly up the garden. Audrey's face showed surprise.

"Mother," she said, turning to Mrs. Greyle. "Lord Altmore is here!"

Mrs. Greyle left the room hastily. The others heard her welcome the visitor, lead him up the tiny hall, and then they heard a door shut. Audrey looked at Copplestone.

"You've heard of Lord Altmore, haven't you?" she said. "He's our biggest man in these parts. He owns all the country at the back—mountains, valleys, everything. The Greyle land shuts him off from the sea. In the old days, Greyles and Altmores used to fight over their boundaries, and—"

Mrs. Greyle suddenly showed herself again and looked at her daughter.

"Will you come here, Audrey?" she said. "You gentlemen will excuse both of us for a few minutes?"

Mother and daughter went away, and the two young men drew up their chairs to the table at which Mr. Dennie sat and exchanged views with him on the curious situation. Half an hour went by; then steps and voices were heard in the hall and the garden; Mrs. Greyle and Audrey were seeing their visitor out to his car. In a few minutes the car sped away, and they came back to the parlor. One glance at their faces showed Gilling that some new development had cropped up, and he nudged Copplestone.

"Here is remarkable news," said Mrs. Greyle as she went back to her chair. "Lord Altmore called to tell me of something that he thought I ought to know. It is almost unbelievable, yet it is a fact. Marston Greyle—if he *is* Marston Greyle—has offered to sell Lord Altmore the entire Scarhaven estate by private treaty. Imagine that! Sell the estate which has belonged to the Greyles for five hundred years!"

Chapter 15

The Cablegram from New York

The two younger men received this announcement with no more than looks of astonished inquiry, but the elder one coughed significantly and turned to Mrs. Greyle with a knowing glance.

"My dear lady," he said impressively. "Now this is a matter in which I believe I can be of service, real service! You may have forgotten the fact—it is all so long ago, and perhaps I never mentioned it in the old days—but the truth is that before I went on the stage, I was in the law. The fact is, I am a duly and fully qualified solicitor," he added, with a dry chuckle, "it is a good five and twenty years since I paid the six pounds for the necessary annual certificate. But I have not forgotten my law, or all of it, and no doubt I can polish up a little more if necessary. You say that Mr. Marston Greyle, the present owner of Scarhaven, has offered to sell his estate to Lord Altmore? But is not the estate entailed?"

"No," replied Mrs. Greyle. "It is not."

Mr. Dennie's face fell unmistakably. He shook his head.

"Then in that case," he said dryly, "all the lawyers in the world can't help. It's his absolutely, and he can do what he pleases with it. Five hundred years, you say? Remarkable that a man should want to sell land his forefathers have walked over for half a thousand years. Extraordinary."

"Did Lord Altmore say if any reason had been given him as to why Mr. Greyle wished to sell?" asked Gilling.

"Yes," replied Mrs. Greyle, who was obviously greatly upset by the recent news. "He did. Mr. Greyle gave as his reason that the north does not suit him, and that he wishes to buy an estate in the south of England. He approached Lord Altmore first because it is well-known that the Altmores have always been anxious to extend their own borders to the coast."

"Does Lord Altmore want to buy?" asked Gilling.

"It is very evident that he would be quite willing to buy," said Mrs. Greyle.

"What made him come to you?" continued Gilling. "He must have had some reason."

"He had a reason," Mrs. Greyle answered with a glance at Audrey. "He knows the family history and is well aware that my daughter is at present the heir apparent. He therefore thought we ought to know of this offer. But that is not quite all. Lord Altmore has read the accounts of the inquest in this morning's paper. Also his steward was present at the inquest. From what he has read, and from what his steward told him, Lord Altmore thinks there is something wrong. He thinks that Marston Greyle should explain this mystery about the meeting with Bassett Oliver in America. At any rate, he will go no further in any negotiations until that mystery is properly cleared up. Shall I tell you what Lord Altmore said on that point? He said—"

"Is it worthwhile, Mother?" interrupted Audrey. "It was only his opinion."

"It is worthwhile amongst ourselves," insisted Mrs. Greyle. "Why not? Lord Altmore said in so many words, 'I have a sort of uneasy feeling that this man calling himself Marston Greyle may not be Marston Greyle at all. I shall want good proof that he is before I even consider the proposal he has made to me.' There! So what's to be done?"

"The law, ma'am," observed Mr. Dennie solemnly, "the law must step in. You must get an injunction, ma'am, to prevent Mr. Marston Greyle from dealing with the property until his own title to it has been established. That, at any rate, is my opinion."

"May I ask a question?" said Copplestone who had been listening and thinking intently. "Did Lord Altmore say when this offer was made to him?"

"Yes," replied Mrs. Greyle. "A week ago."

"A week ago!" exclaimed Copplestone. "That is before last Sunday, before the Bassett Oliver episode. Then the offer to sell is quite independent of that affair."

"Strange and significant," muttered Gilling.

He rose from his chair and looked at his watch.

"Well," he went on, "I am going off to London. Will you give me leave, Mrs. Greyle, to report all this to Sir Cresswell Oliver and Mr. Petherton? They ought to know."

"I'm going too," declared Copplestone, also rising. "Mrs. Greyle, I'm sure will entrust the whole matter to us. And Mr. Dennie will trust us with those papers."

"Oh, certainly, certainly," asserted Mr. Dennie, pushing his packet across the table. "Take care of 'em, my boy! You don't know how important they may turn out to be."

"And Mrs. Greyle?" asked Copplestone.

"Tell whatever you think it best to tell," replied Mrs. Greyle. "My own opinion is that a lot will have to come out yet."

"We can catch a train in three-quarters of an hour, Copplestone," said Gilling. "Let's get back, settle up with Mrs. Wooler, and be off."

Copplestone contrived to draw Audrey aside.

"You'll see me back here before many days are over," he whispered. "But if anything happens here, if you want anybody's help in any way, promise you'll wire to me at this address. Promise or I won't go."

"Very well," said Audrey, "I promise."

An hour later he and Gilling were on their way to London, and from opposite corners of a compartment which they had contrived to get to themselves, they exchanged looks.

"This is a curious business, Copplestone," said Gilling. "It strikes me it's going to be a big one too. And it's coming to a point round Squire Greyle."

"Do you think your man will have tracked him?" asked Copplestone.

"It will be the first time Swallow's ever lost sight of anybody he hasn't," answered Gilling. "He's a human ferret! I wired him just before we left, telling him to meet me at King's Cross, so we'll get his report. He'll have followed him all right. I don't imagine for a moment that Greyle is trying to evade anybody at this juncture at any rate."

But four hours later, when the train drew into King's Cross, a young and sharp-looking man presented himself. It was with a long and downcast face and a lugubrious shake of the head.

"Done! For the first time in my life!" he growled in answer to Gilling's eager inquiry. "Lost him. Never failed before, as you know. Well, it had to come, I suppose. Can't go on without an occasional defeat. But I'm a bit licked as to the whole thing, unless your man is dodging somebody. Is he?"

"Tell your tale," commanded Gilling, motioning Copplestone to follow him and Swallow aside.

"I was up here in good time this afternoon to meet his train," reported Swallow. "I spotted him and his man at once; no difficulty, as your description of both was so full. They were together while the luggage was got out; then he, Greyle, gave some instructions to the man and left him. He himself got into a taxi cab; I got into another close behind and gave its driver certain orders. Greyle drove straight to the Fragonard Club."

"Ah," exclaimed Gilling. "Did he now? That's worth knowing."

"What's the Fragonard Club?" asked Copplestone. "Never heard of it."

"Club of folk connected with the stage and the music halls," answered Gilling testily. "In a side street, off Shaftesbury Avenue. Tell you more of it later. Go on, Swallow."

"He paid his driver there and went in," continued Swallow. "I paid mine and hung about. There's only one entrance and exit to that spot, as you know. He came out again within five minutes, stuffing some letters into his pocket. He walked away across Shaftesbury Avenue into Wardour Street; there he went into a tobacconist's shop. Of course, I hung about again. But this time he didn't come. So at last I walked in . . . to buy something. He wasn't there!"

"He'd slipped out, walked out, when you weren't looking?" said Gilling. "Why didn't you keep your eye on the man? You!"

"You yourself!" retorted Swallow. "Never had an eyelash off that shop door from the time he entered until I too entered."

"Then there's a side door to that shop into some alley or passage," said Gilling.

"Not that I could find," answered Swallow. "Might be at the rear of the premises perhaps, but I couldn't ascertain. He may have stopped on the premises. There's that possibility. I know the shop and the name."

"Why didn't you bring somebody else with you to follow the man and the luggage?" demanded Gilling, half-petulantly.

Swallow shook his head.

"There I made a mess of it, I confess," he admitted. "But it never struck me they'd separate. I thought, of course, they'd drive straight to some hotel, and—"

"And the long and the short of it is, Greyle's slipped you," said Gilling. "Well, there's no more to be done tonight. The only thing of value is that Greyle called at the Fragonard. What's a country squire, only recently come to England, to do with the Fragonard? That is worth something. Copplestone, we'd better meet in the morning at Petherton's. You be there at ten o'clock, and I'll get Sir Cresswell Oliver to be there too."

Copplestone took himself to his own rooms in Jermyn Street; it seemed an age, several ages, since he had last seen the familiar things in them. During the few days which had elapsed since his hurried setting-off to meet Bassett Oliver, so many things had happened that he felt as if he had lived a week in a totally different world. He had met death, and mystery, and what appeared to be sure evidence of deceit and cunning, and perhaps worse—fraud and crime blacker than fraud.

The next morning Copplestone was late for the appointment which Gilling had made at Mr. Petherton's office. By the time he arrived, Gilling had already reported all that had taken place the day before to the solicitor and to Sir Cresswell Oliver. And at that point

Copplestone produced the papers entrusted to him by Mr. Dennie, and they all compared the handwritings afresh.

"There is certainly something wrong somewhere," remarked Petherton after a time. "We are in a position to begin a systematic inquiry. Here," he went on, drawing a paper from his desk, "is a cablegram which arrived first thing this morning from New York from an agent who has been making a search for me in the shipping lists. This is what he says: 'Marston Greyle, St. Louis, Missouri, booked first-class passenger from New York to Falmouth, England, by S.S. *Araconda*, September 28th, 1912.' There. That's something definite. So the next thing," concluded the old lawyer with a shrewd glance at Sir Cresswell, "is to find out if the Marston Greyle who landed at Falmouth is the same man whom we have recently seen."

Chapter 16

In Touch with the Missing

S ir Cresswell Oliver took the cablegram from Petherton and read it over slowly, muttering the precise and plain wording to himself.

"Seems to me, Petherton, that the time's come to know exactly where we are," he said as he laid it back on the solicitor's desk. "As I understand it, the case is this: rightly or wrongly we suspect the present holder of the Scarhaven estates. We suspect that he is not the rightful owner, and that he is no more the real Marston Greyle than you are. We think that he's an impostor posing as Marston Greyle. Other people, Mrs. Valentine Greyle, for example, evidently think so too. Am I right?"

"Quite," responded Petherton. "That's our position exactly."

"Then in that case, what I want to get at is this," continued Sir Cresswell. "How does this man relate to my brother's death? What's the connection? That is the first thing of importance. Of course I have a theory: that the impostor *did* see my brother last Sunday afternoon; that he knew that my brother would at once know that he was an impostor, not the real Marston Greyle; and that the discovery would lead to detection. And therefore he put him out of the way. He might accompany him to the top of the tower and fling him down. It's possible. Do you follow me?"

"Precisely," replied Petherton. "I, too, incline to that conclusion, though I've worked it out in a different fashion. My reconstruction of what took place at Scarhaven Keep is as follows: I think that Bassett Oliver met the Squire—we'll call this man that for the sake of clarity—when he entered the ruins. He probably introduced himself and mentioned that he had met a Marston Greyle in America.

Then the Squire saw the probabilities of detection, and what subsequently took place was most likely what you suggest. It may have been that the Squire recognized Bassett Oliver and knew that he'd met Marston Greyle; it may have been that he didn't know him and didn't know anything until Bassett Oliver enlightened him. But, either way, I firmly believe that Bassett Oliver came to his death by violence. That he was murdered. So there's the case in a nutshell. Murdered to keep his tongue still."

"What's to be done then?" asked Sir Cresswell as Petherton tapped the cablegram.

"The first thing," he answered, "is to make use of this. We now know that the real Marston Greyle, who certainly did live in St. Louis where his father had settled, left New York for England to take up his inheritance on September 28th, 1912. He booked a passage to Falmouth and would land about October 5th. He no doubt stayed a night at Falmouth. Somebody must go to Falmouth and make inquiries. You'd better go, Gilling, and at once. While you're away, your partner had better resume his search for the man we know as the Squire. You've two good clues, the fact that he visited both the Fragonard Club and that tobacconist's shop. Urge Swallow to do his best; the man must be kept in sight. See to both these things immediately."

"Swallow is at work already," replied Gilling. "He's got good help too, and his failure yesterday has put him on his mettle. As for me, I'll go to Falmouth by the next express. Let me have that cablegram."

"I'll go with you," said Copplestone. "I may be of some use. But," he paused and looked questioningly at the old solicitor. "What about the other news we brought you?" he asked. "About this sale of the estate, you know? If this man is an impostor . . ."

"Leave that to me," replied Petherton with a shrewd glance at Sir Cresswell. "I know the Greyle family solicitors. Highly respectable people and only a few doors away. In fact, I'm going round to have a quiet little chat with them in a few minutes. There will be no sale! Leave me to deal with that matter."

It was late that night when Copplestone and Gilling arrived at the far-off seaport, so nothing could be done until the following morning. To Copplestone it seemed as if they were in for a difficult task. Over twelve months had elapsed since the real Marston Greyle left America for England; he might not have stayed the night in Falmouth; he might not have conversed with anybody there who would recollect him. How were they going to trace him? But Gilling, now free of his clerical attire and presenting himself as a smart young professional man, was quick to explain that system, accurate and definite system, would expedite matters.

"We know the approximate date on which the *Araconda* would touch here," he said as they breakfasted together. "As things go, it would be from October 4th to 6th, according to the quickness of her run across the Atlantic. If Marston Greyle stayed here, he'd have to stay at some hotel. Accordingly, we visit all the Falmouth hotels and examine their registers of that date, first week of October, 1912. If we find his name, good! We can then go on to make inquiries. If we don't find any trace of him, then we know he probably went straight by train after landing. We'll begin with this hotel first."

There was no record of any Marston Greyle at that hotel, nor at the next half-dozen at which they called. A visit to the shipping office of the line to which the *Araconda* belonged revealed the fact that she reached Falmouth on October 5th at half-past ten in the evening, and that the name of Marston Greyle was on the list of first-class passengers. Gilling left the office in cheery mood.

"That simplifies matters," he said. "As the *Araconda* reached here late in the evening, the passengers who landed from her would be almost certain to stay the night in Falmouth. So we've only to resume our round of these hotels in order to hit something pertinent. This is plain and easy work, Copplestone. We'll strike oil before noon."

In fact, they struck oil at the very next hotel they called at, an old-fashioned house in close proximity to the harbor. There was a communicative landlord there who evidently possessed and was proud of a retentive memory, and he no sooner heard the reason of

Gilling's call upon him than he bustled into activity and produced the register of the previous year.

"But I remember the young gentleman you're asking about," he remarked, as he took the book from a safe and laid it open on the table in his private room. "Not a common name, is it? He came here about eleven o'clock of the night you've mentioned. There you are! There's the entry. And there, higher up, is the name of the man who came to meet him. He came the day before to be here when the *Araconda* got in."

The two visitors, bending over the book, mutually nudged each other as their eyes encountered the signatures on the open page. There, in the handwriting of the letters which Mr. Dennie had so fortunately preserved, was the name Marston Greyle. But it was not the sight of that name which surprised them; they had expected to see it. What made them both thrill with the joy of an unexpected discovery was the sight of the other signature inserted some lines above it, under date October 4th. Lest they should exhibit that joy before the landlord, they mutually affected the unconcern of indifference.

But there the signature was—*Peter Chatfield.* Peter Chatfield! They both knew that they were entering on a new stage of their quest, that the fact that Chatfield had traveled to Falmouth to meet the new owner of Scarhaven meant much—possibly meant everything.

"Oh," said Gilling, as steadily as possible. "That gentleman came to meet the other, did he? Just so. Now what sort of man was he?"

"Big, fleshy man, elderly, very solemn in manner and appearance," answered the landlord. "I remember him well. Came in about five o'clock in the afternoon of the fourth just after the London train arrived and booked a room. He told me he expected to meet a gentleman from New York and was very fidgety about fixing it up to go off in the small boat to meet the *Araconda* when she came into the bay. I found out for him that she wouldn't be in until next evening, so of course he settled down to wait. Very quiet, reserved old fellow. Never said much."

"Did he go off on the boat the next night?" asked Gilling.

"He did and came back with this other gentleman and his baggage. This Mr. Greyle," answered the landlord. "Mr. Chatfield had booked a room for Mr. Greyle."

"And what sort of man was Mr. Greyle?" inquired Gilling. "That's really the important thing. You've an exceptionally good memory; I can see that. Tell us all you can recollect about him."

"I can recollect plenty," replied the landlord, shaking his head. "As for his looks: a tallish, slightly-built young fellow, between, I should say, twenty-five and twenty-eight. Stooped a good bit. Very dark hair and eyes. Eyes a good deal sunken in his face. Very pale. Good-looking. Good features. But ill. Oh, my sakes! He was ill!"

"Ill!" exclaimed Gilling with a glance at Copplestone. "Really?"

"He was so ill," said the landlord, "that me and my wife never expected to see him get up that next morning. We wanted them to have a doctor, but Mr. Greyle himself said that it was nothing, but that he had some heart trouble and that the voyage had made it worse. He said that if he took some medicine, which he had with him, and got a good night's sleep, he'd be all right. And next morning he seemed better, and he got up to breakfast. But my wife said to me that if she'd ever seen death on a man's face, it was on his! She's a bit of a persuasive tongue, has my wife; and when she heard that these two gentlemen were thinking of going a long journey—right away to the far north, it was, I believe—she got 'em to go and see the doctor first, for she felt that Mr. Greyle wasn't fit for the exertion."

"Did they go?" asked Gilling.

"They did. I talked, myself, to the old gentleman," replied the landlord. "And I showed them the way to our own doctor, Dr. Tretheway. And as a result of what he said to them, I heard them decide to break up their journey into stages, as you might term it. They left here for Bristol that afternoon to stay the night there."

"You're sure of that? Bristol?" asked Gilling.

"Ought to be," replied the landlord with curt assurance. "I went to the station with them and saw them off. They booked to Bristol first class."

Gilling looked at his companion.

"I think we'd better see this Dr. Tretheway," he remarked.

Dr. Tretheway, an elderly man of grave manners and benevolent appearance, remembered the visit of Mr. Marston Greyle well enough when he had turned up its date in his case book. He also remembered the visitor's companion, Mr. Chatfield, who seemed unusually anxious and concerned about Mr. Greyle's health.

"And as to that," continued Dr. Tretheway, "I learned from Mr. Greyle that he had been seriously indisposed for some months before setting out for England. The voyage had been rather a rough one; he had suffered much from seasickness, and, in his state of health, that was unfortunate for him. I made a careful examination of him, and I came to the conclusion that he was suffering from a form of myocarditis which was rapidly assuming a very serious complexion. I earnestly advised him to take as much rest as possible, to avoid all unnecessary fatigue and all excitement. And I strongly disparaged his traveling in one journey to the north, whither I learned he was bound. On my advice, he and Mr. Chatfield decided to break that journey at Bristol, at Birmingham, and at Leeds. By so doing, you see, they would only have a short journey each day, and Mr. Greyle would be able to rest for a long time at a stretch. But I formed my own conclusions."

"And they were . . . what?" asked Gilling.

"That he would not live long," said the doctor. "Finding that he was going to the neighborhood of Norcaster, where there is a most excellent school of medicine, I advised him to get the best specialist he could, and to put himself under his treatment. But my impression was that he had already reached a very, very serious stage."

"You think he was then likely to die suddenly?" suggested Gilling.

"It was quite possible. I should not have been surprised to hear of his death," answered Dr. Tretheway. "He was, in short, very ill indeed."

"You never heard anything?" inquired Gilling.

"Nothing at all, though I often wondered. Of course," said the doctor with a smile, "they were strangers. I often have transatlantic passengers drop in, and they forget that a physician would sometimes like to know how a case has turned out. No, I never heard any more."

"Did they give you any address, either of them?" asked Copplestone, seeing that Gilling had no more to ask.

"No," replied the doctor, "they did not. I knew from what they told me that Mr. Greyle had come off the *Araconda* the night before, and that he was passing on. But I only gathered that they were going to the neighborhood of Norcaster from the fact that Mr. Greyle asked if a journey to that place would be too much for him. He said with a laugh that over there in the United States a journey of five hundred miles would be considered a mere jaunt! He was very plucky, poor fellow, but—"

Dr. Tretheway ended with a significant shake of the head, and his two visitors left him and went out into the autumn sunlight.

"Copplestone," said Gilling as they walked away. "That chap, the real Marston Greyle, is dead. I'm as certain he's dead as I'm certain we're alive. And now the next thing is to find out where he died and when. And that's going to be a big job!"

"How are you going to set about it?" asked Copplestone. "It seems as if we are up against a blank wall now."

"Not at all, my friend," retorted Gilling, cheerfully. "One step at a time. That's the sure thing to go on in my calling. We've found out a lot here, and quickly too. And we know where our next step lies. Bristol! Like looking for needles in a bundle of hay? Not a bit of it. If those two broke their journey at Bristol, they'd have to stop at a hotel. Well, now we'll adjourn to Bristol, bearing in mind that we're on the track of Peter Chatfield!"

Chapter 17

The Old Playbill

G illing's cheerful optimism was the sort of desirable quality that is a good thing to have, but all the optimism in the world is worthless in the face of insurmountable difficulty. And the difficulty of tracing Chatfield and his sick companion in a city the size of Bristol did indeed seem impossible when Gilling and Copplestone had been attacking it for twenty-four hours. They had spent a whole day in endeavoring to get news; they had gone in and out of hotels until they were sick of the sight of one; they had made exhaustive inquiries at the railway station and of the cabmen who congregated there. Nobody remembered anything at all about a big, heavy-faced man and a man in his company who seemed to be very ill. And on the second night Copplestone intimated plainly that in his opinion they were wasting their time.

"How do we even know that they ever came to Bristol?" he asked, as he and Gilling refreshed themselves with a much needed dinner. "The Falmouth landlord saw Chatfield take tickets for Bristol. That's not much to go on. Put it to yourself in this way. Greyle may have found even that journey too much for him. In that case, they may have left the train at Plymouth, or at Exeter, or at Taunton. It would stop at each place. Seems to me we're wasting time here. Far better to get nearer more tangible things. Chatfield, for instance. Or go back to town and find out what your friend Swallow has done."

"Swallow," replied Gilling, "has done nothing so far, or I would have heard. Swallow knows exactly where I am and where I shall be until I give him further notice. Don't be discouraged, my friend. One is often on the very edge of a discovery when one seems to be miles away from it. Give me another day, and if we haven't found out something by tomorrow evening I'll consult with you as to our next step. But I've a plan for tomorrow morning which ought to yield some result."

"What?" demanded Copplestone doubtfully.

"This. There is in every center of population an official who registers births, marriages, and deaths. Now we believe the real Marston Greyle to be dead. Let us suppose, for argument's sake, that he died here in Bristol. What would happen? Notice of his death would have to be given to the Registrar by the nearest relative or by the person in attendance on the deceased. That person would in this case be Chatfield. If the death occurred suddenly and without medical attendance, an inquest would have to be held. If a doctor had been in attendance, he would give a signed certificate of the cause of death, which he would hand to the relatives or friends in attendance, who in their turn would hand over to the Registrar. Do you see the value of these points? What we must do tomorrow morning is to see the Registrar, or, as there will be more than one in a place this size, each of them in turn in the endeavor to find out if early in October, 1912, Peter Chatfield registered the death of Marston Greyle here. He may not have registered it under that name. He may, indeed, not have used his own name. He's deep enough for anything. That, however, is our next best chance, the search of the registers. Now, as we've had a stiff day, I propose we dismiss all thought of this affair for the rest of the evening and take ourselves to some place of amusement. Theater, eh?"

Copplestone made no objection; and, when dinner was over, they walked around to the principal theater in time for the first act of a play which having been highly successful in London had just started on a round of the local theaters. Between the second and third acts of this production there was a long interval, and the two companions moved to the foyer to recuperate their energies. While there, Copplestone encountered an old school friend with whom he exchanged a few words. Gilling meanwhile strolled about, inspecting the pictures, photographs, and old playbills on the walls. And suddenly, he turned back, waited until Copplestone's acquaintance had gone away, and then hurried over and smacked his cosearcher on the shoulder.

"Didn't I tell you that one's often close to a thing when one seems furthest off it!" he exclaimed triumphantly. "Come here, my son, and look at what I've just found."

He drew Copplestone away to a quiet corner and pointed out an old playbill, framed and hung on the wall. Copplestone stared at it and saw nothing but the title of a well-known comedy, the names of one or two fairly celebrated actors and actresses, and the usual particulars which appear on all similar announcements.

"Well?" he asked. "What of this?"

"That," replied Gilling, pointing the tip of his finger to a line in the bill. "That my boy!"

Copplestone looked again. He started at what he read.

Margaret Sayers . . . . MISS ADELA CHATFIELD.

"And now look at that!" continued Gilling with an accentuation of his triumphal note. "See! These people were here for a fortnight from October 3rd to 17th, 1912. Therefore, if Peter Chatfield brought Marston Greyle to Bristol on October 6th, Peter Chatfield's daughter would also be in the town!"

Copplestone looked over the bill again, rapidly realizing possibilities.

"Would Chatfield know that?" he asked reflectively.

"It's likely that he would," replied Gilling. "Even if father and daughter don't quite hit things off in their tastes, it's only reasonable to suppose that Peter would usually know his daughter's whereabouts. And if he brought Greyle here ill, and they had to stop, it's only likely that Peter would turn to his daughter for help. Anyway, Copplestone, here are two undoubted facts: Chatfield and Greyle booked from Falmouth for Bristol on October 6th, 1912, and may therefore be supposed to have come here. That's one fact. The other is: Addie Chatfield was certainly in Bristol on that date and for eleven days after it."

"Well, what next?" asked Copplestone.

"I've been thinking that over while you stared at the bill," answered Gilling. "I think the best thing will be to find out where Addie Chatfield herself stayed. You know that in most of these towns there are lodgings almost exclusively devoted to the theatrical profession. Actors and actresses go to them year after year; what's more, your theatrical landlady always remembers names and faces, and has her favorites. Now in my stage experience, I never came to Bristol, so I don't know much about it; but I know where we can get information. The stage doorkeeper. He'll tell us where the recognized lodgings are, and then we begin a round of inquiry. When? Just now, my boy, and a good time, too, as you'll see."

"Why?" asked Copplestone.

"Best hour of the evening," replied Gilling with glib assurance. "Landladies enjoying an hour of ease before beginning to cook supper for their lodgers, now busy on the stage. Always ready to talk, theatrical landladies, when they've nothing to do. Trust me for knowing the ropes! Come round to the stage door, and let's ask the keeper a question or two."

But before they departed the foyer, an interruption came in the shape of a gentleman in evening dress, who wore his hat at a rakish angle and seemed to be very much at home as he strolled about, hands in pockets, looking around him at all and sundry. He suddenly caught sight of Gilling, smiled surprisedly and expansively, and came forward with outstretched hand.

"Bless our hearts, is it really yourself, dear boy?" exclaimed this apparition. "Really, now? And what brings you here? Bless my soul and eyes, why I haven't seen you this . . . how long is it, dear boy?"

"Three years," answered Gilling, promptly clasping the outstretched hand. "But what are you doing here, boss, eh?"

"Lessee's manager, dear boy. Nice job too," whispered the other. "Been here two years." He deftly steered Gilling towards the refreshment bar and glanced out of his eye corner at Copplestone. "Friend of yours?" he suggested hospitably. "Introduce us, dear boy. My name is the same as before, you know!"

"Mr. Copplestone, Mr. Montmorency," said Gilling. "Mr. Montmorency, Mr. Copplestone."

"Your servant, sir," said Mr. Montmorency. "Pleased to meet any friend of my friend! And how are things with you, Gilling, old man? Now who on earth would have thought of seeing you here?"

Copplestone held his peace while Gilling and Mr. Montmorency conversed. He was sure that his companion would turn this unexpected meeting to account, and he therefore felt no surprise when Gilling, after giving him a private nudge, asked the manager a direct question.

"Did you see Addie Chatfield when she was here about a year ago?" he asked. "You remember? She was here in *Mrs. Swayne's Necklace* for a fortnight."

"I remember very well, dear boy," responded Mr. Montmorency. "I saw the lady several times. What's more, I accidentally witnessed a curious little scene between Miss Addie and a gentleman whom nature appeared to have specially manufactured for the part of heavy parent. You know the type. One morning when that company was here, I happened to be standing in the vestibule, when a large, solemn-faced individual, Quakerish in attire, and evidently not accustomed to the theater walked in and peered about him at our rich carpets and expensive fittings, pretty much as if he was appraising their value. At the same time I observed that he was in what one calls a state—a good deal upset about something. Wherefore I addressed myself to him in my politest manner and inquired if I could serve him. Thereupon he asked if he could see Miss Adela Chatfield on very important business. Now, I wasn't going to let him see Miss Addie, for I took him to be a man who might have a legal document about him, or something nasty of that sort. But at that very moment, Miss Addie, who had been rehearsing and had come out by the house instead of going through the stage door, came tripping into the vestibule and let off a sharp note of exclamation. After which she and old wooden-face stepped into the street together and immediately exchanged a few words. That the old man told her something very serious was abundantly evident from the expression of their respective countenances. But I never knew what it was, nor who *he* was, dear boy. Not my business, don't you know."

"They went away together, those two?" asked Gilling, favoring Copplestone with another nudge.

"Up the street together certainly, talking most earnestly," replied Mr. Montmorency.

"Ever see that old chap again?" asked Gilling.

"I never did, dear boy. Once was sufficient," said Mr. Montmorency lightly. "But," he continued, dropping his bantering tone, "are these questions pertinent? Has this to do with this new profession of yours, dear boy? If so, mum's the word, you know."

"I'll tell you what, Monty," answered Gilling. "I wish you'd find out for me where Addie Chatfield lodged when she was here that time. Can it be done? Between you and me, I do want to know about that old chap. Never mind why now. I will tell you later. But it's serious."

Mr. Montmorency tapped the side of his handsome nose.

"All right, my boy," he said. "I understand. Wicked, wicked world! Done, dear boy, it shall be done! Come down to the stage door. Our man knows every landlady in the town!"

By various winding ways and devious passages he led the two young men down to the stage door. Its keeper was reading the evening newspaper in his glass-walled box and glanced inquiringly at the strangers as Mr. Montmorency pulled them up before him.

"Prickett," said Mr. Montmorency, leaning into the chamber over its half-door and speaking confidentially. "You keep a sort of register of lodgings don't you? Now I wonder if you could tell me where Miss Adela Chatfield of the *Mrs. Swayne's Necklace* Company stopped when she was last here? That's a year ago or about it. Prickett," he went on, turning to Gilling, "puts all this sort of thing down methodically, so that he can send callers on or send up urgent letters or parcels during the day. Isn't that it, Prickett?"

"That's about it, sir," answered the doorkeeper. He had taken down a sort of ledger as the manager spoke and was now turning over its leaves. He suddenly ran his finger down a page and stopped its course at a particular line.

"Mrs. Salmon, 5 Montargis Crescent, second to the right outside," he announced briefly. "Very good lodgings, too, are those."

Gilling promised Mr. Montmorency that he would look him up later on and went away with Copplestone to Montargis Crescent. Within five minutes they were standing in a comfortably furnished sitting room, liberally ornamented with the photographs of actors and actresses. They confronted a stout, sharp-eyed little woman who listened intently to all that Gilling said and sniffed loudly when he had finished.

"Remember Miss Chatfield being here!" she exclaimed. "I should think I do! I ought to! Bringing mortal sickness into my house . . . and then death . . . and then a funeral . . . and her and her father going away never giving me an extra penny for the trouble!"

Chapter 18

The Lie on the Tombstone

G illing's glance at his companion was quiet enough, but it spoke volumes. Here was such a revelation as they had never dreamed of hearing! Here was the probable explanation of at least half the mystery. He turned composedly to the landlady.

"I've already told you who and what I am," he said, pointing to the card which he had handed to her. "There are certain mysterious circumstances about this affair which I want to get at, and what you've said just now is abundant evidence that you can help. If you do help, you'll be well paid for your trouble. Now, you speak of sickness, death, a funeral. Will you tell us all about it?"

"I never knew there was any mystery about it," answered the landlady, as she motioned her visitors to seat themselves. "It was all aboveboard as far as I knew. Of course, I've always been sore about it; I had a great deal of trouble, and as I say, I never got anything for it, that is, anything extra. And me doing it really just to oblige her and her father!"

"They brought a sick man here?" suggested Gilling.

"I'll tell you how it was," said Mrs. Salmon, seating herself and showing signs of a disposition to confidence. "Miss Chatfield, she'd been here, I think, three days that time. One morning—I'm sure it was about the third day that the *Swayne Necklace* Company was here—she came in from rehearsal in a regular fit. She said that her father had just called on her at the theater. She said he'd been to Falmouth to meet a relation of theirs who'd come from America and had found him to be very ill on landing, so ill that a Falmouth doctor had given strict orders that he mustn't travel any further than Bristol on his way wherever he wanted to go. They'd got to Bristol

117

and the young man was so done in that Mr. Chatfield had had to drive him to another doctor, one close by here, Dr. Valdey, as soon as they arrived. Dr. Valdey said he must go to bed at once and have at least two days' complete rest in bed. He advised Mr. Chatfield to get quiet rooms instead of going to a hotel. So Mr. Chatfield, knowing that his daughter was here, do you see, sought her out and told her all about it. She came to me and asked me if I knew where they could get rooms. Well now, I had my drawing room floor empty that week; and as it was only for two or three days that they wanted rooms, I offered to take Mr. Chatfield and the young man in. Of course, if I'd known how ill he was, I wouldn't have. What I understood—and mind you, I don't say they willfully deceived me, for I don't think they did—what I understood was that the young man simply wanted a real good rest. But he was evidently a deal worse than what even Dr. Valdey thought. Much worse. And the doctor had to be fetched to him more than once during the afternoon. Still Dr. Valdey himself never said to me that there was any immediate danger. But that's neither here nor there. The young fellow died that night."

"That night!" exclaimed Gilling, "the night he came here?"

"Very same night," assented Mrs. Salmon. "Brought in here about two in the afternoon and died suddenly. It was just before midnight and soon after Miss Chatfield came in from the theater."

"Were you present?" asked Copplestone.

"I wasn't. Nobody was with him but Mr. Chatfield. Miss Chatfield was getting her supper down here," replied Mrs. Salmon. "And I was busy elsewhere."

"Was there an inquest then," inquired Gilling?"

"Oh, no," said Mrs. Salmon, shaking her head. "No, there was no need for that as the doctor had been seeing him all day. Oh, no. The cause of death was evident enough. Heart."

"Did they bury him here then?" asked Gilling.

"Two days after," replied Mrs. Salmon. "Kept everything very quiet, they did. I don't believe Miss Chatfield told any of the theater people. She went to her work just the same, of course. The old gentleman saw to everything, funeral and all. I'll say this for them, they gave me no unnecessary trouble; but still, there's trouble that is necessary when you've death in a house and a funeral at the door, and they ought to have given me something for what I did. Mr. Chatfield stayed two days after the funeral, and when he left he just said that his daughter would settle up with me. But when she came to pay, she added nothing to my bill; and she walked out remarking that if her father hadn't given me anything extra, she was sure she shouldn't. I considered it very mean. Shabby, in fact."

"Very shabby," agreed Gilling. "Well, you won't find my clients quite so mean, ma'am. But please, don't mention this matter to anybody until you hear from me. And as I like to give some earnest of payment, here's a bank note in advance which you can slip into your purse."

The landlady spirits rose visibly on receipt of the bank note.

"Now, just a question or two," Gilling continued. "Did you hear the young man's name?"

She appeared to reflect on this question and finally shook her head as if surprised at her own inability to answer it satisfactorily.

"Well, now," she said, "it may seem surprising, but I don't recollect that I ever heard his name! You see, I didn't see much of him after he once got here. I was never in his room with them, and they didn't mention his name that I can remember when they spoke about him. I understood he was a relative, a cousin or something of that sort."

"Didn't you see any name on the coffin?" asked Gilling.

"I didn't," replied Mrs. Salmon. "You see, the undertaker fetched him away when him and his men brought the coffin the next day. He took charge of the coffin for the second night, and the funeral took place from there. But I'll tell you what, the undertaker'll know the name, and of course the doctor does. They're both close by."

Gilling took names and addresses and, once more pledging the landlady to secrecy, led Copplestone away.

"That's the end of another chapter," he said when they were clear of that place. "We know now that Marston Greyle died there in that very house, Copplestone, and that Peter Chatfield was with him. That's fact!"

"And it's fact, too, that the daughter knows," observed Copplestone in a low voice.

"Fact, too, that Addie Chatfield was in it," agreed Gilling. "But what happened next? Before we go on to that, there are three things to do. We must see this Dr. Valdey, and the undertaker, and Marston Greyle's grave."

"And then?" asked Copplestone.

"Big question," sighed Gilling. "Go back to town and report, I think, and find out if Swallow has discovered anything. My, there's a lot to discover! For you see we're certain now that a conspiracy began, a conspiracy between Chatfield, his daughter, and the man who's been passing himself off as Marston Greyle. So who is the man? Where did they get hold of him? Is he some relation of theirs? All that's got to be found out. Of course, their object is very clear. The real Marston Greyle was dead on their hands, and his legal successor was Miss Audrey, his cousin. Chatfield knew that when Miss Audrey came into power, his own reign as steward of Scarhaven would be brief. And so . . . but the thing is so plain that one needn't waste breath on it. And I tell you what's plain too, Copplestone, Miss Audrey Greyle is the lady of Scarhaven! Good luck to her. You'll no doubt be glad to communicate the glad tidings."

Copplestone made no answer. He was utterly confounded by all these revelations and was wondering what the mother and daughter in the little cottage would say when all was told to them.

"Let's make dead certain of everything," he said after a long pause. "Don't let's leave any loophole."

"Oh, we'll leave nothing, here at any rate," replied Gilling confidently. "But you'll find in the morning that we already know almost everything."

And he was right. The doctor's story was a plain one. The young man was very ill indeed when brought to him, and though he did not anticipate so early or sudden an end, he was not surprised when death came and had no difficulty giving the necessary certificate.

Just as plain was the undertaker's account of his connection with the affair; it was a very ordinary transaction in his eyes. And having heard both stories, there was nothing left to do but to visit one of the adjacent cemeteries and find a certain grave, the number of which they had learned from the undertaker's books. It was easily found, and Copplestone and Gilling found themselves standing at a new tombstone, whereon the stone mason had carved four lines:

Mark Grey
Born April 12th, 1884
Died October 6th, 1912
Aged 28 Years

"Short, simple, and suited to the purpose," murmured Gilling as the two turned away. "Somebody thought things out quickly and well, Copplestone, when this poor fellow died. Do you know I've been thinking as we walked up here that if Bassett Oliver had never taken it into his head to visit Scarhaven that Sunday, this fraud would never have been found out! Consider this. A young man who is an absolute stranger in England comes to take up an inheritance, having on him, no doubt, the necessary proofs of identification. He's met by one person only—his agent. He dies the next day. The agent buries him under a false name, takes his effects and papers, gets some accomplice to impersonate him, introduces that accomplice to everybody as the real man, and there you are! Oh, Chatfield knew what he was doing. Who on earth wandering in this cemetery would ever connect Mark Grey with Marston Greyle?"

"Just so, but there was one danger spot which must have given Chatfield and his accomplices a good many uneasy hours," answered Copplestone. "You know that Marston Greyle actually registered in his own name at Falmouth and was known to both the landlord and the doctor there."

"Yes, but Falmouth is three hundred miles from London and five hundred from Scarhaven," replied Gilling dryly. "Do you suppose that whoever saw Marston Greyle at Falmouth cared two pins about what became of him after he left there? No, Chatfield was almost safe from detection as soon as he'd got that unfortunate young fellow laid in the grave. However, we know now. The next thing, now that we know Marston Greyle lies behind us there, is to get back to town and catch the chap who took his place. We'll wire to Swallow and to Petherton and get the next express."

Sir Cresswell Oliver and Petherton were in conference with Swallow at the solicitor's office when Gilling and Copplestone arrived there in the early afternoon, and Gilling interrupted their conversation to tell the result of his investigations. Copplestone, watching the effect, saw that neither Sir Cresswell nor Petherton showed surprise. In fact Petherton smiled as if he had anticipated all that Gilling had to say.

"I told you that I knew the Greyle family solicitors," he observed. "I find that they have only once seen the man whom we will call the Squire. Chatfield brought him there. He produced proofs of identification—papers which Chatfield no doubt took from the dead man. Of course, the solicitors never doubted for a moment that he was the real Marston Greyle, never dreamed of fraud. Now to the next step. We must concentrate on finding this man. And Swallow has nothing to tell yet; he has seen nothing more of him. You'd better turn all your attention to that, Gilling, you and Swallow. As for Chatfield and his daughter, I suppose we shall have to approach the police."

Copplestone presently went home to his rooms in Jermyn Street, puzzled and wondering. And there, lying on top of a pile of letters, he found a telegram from Audrey Greyle. It had been dispatched from Scarhaven at an early hour of the previous day, and it contained but three words: *Can you come?*

Chapter 19

The Steam Yacht

C opplestone had learned enough of Audrey Greyle during his brief stay at Scarhaven to know that she would not have sent for him except for very serious reasons, especially since it had been with great reluctance that she had promised to do so in the first place. He had never expected that she would send for him. Here, however, was her summons, as definite as it was brief. He was wanted. He snatched up the whole pile of letters, thrust it into his pocket, hurriedly made preparation for his journey, and raced off to King's Cross.

He fumed and fretted with impatience during the six hours' journey to Norcaster. It was ten o'clock when he arrived there, and since the last train to Scarhaven had left at half-past-nine, he hurried to find a motor car to take him the last twenty miles of his journey. He had wired Audrey from Peterborough, telling her that he was on his way and would come straight to Mrs. Greyle's cottage close by Scarhaven church. Just then he heard a voice calling his name, and turning saw a young man running out of the station, much wrapped and cloaked, who waved a hand at him.

"Mr. Copplestone?" panted the new arrival, coming up hurriedly. "I almost missed you. I got on the wrong platform to meet your train. You don't know me, though you may have seen me at the inquest on Mr. Bassett Oliver the other day. My name's Vickers. Guy Vickers."

"And?" said Copplestone.

"I'm a solicitor, here in Norcaster," answered Vickers. "I—at least, my firm, you know—we sometimes act for Mrs. Greyle at Scarhaven. I got a wire from Miss Greyle late this evening, asking me to meet you here when the London train got in and to bring you on to Scarhaven at once. She added the words *urgent business*."

"Then let's be off!" exclaimed Copplestone. "It'll take us a good hour and a quarter as it is." As they moved away through the Norcaster streets, he asked, "Have you any notion what this urgent business is?"

"None whatever," replied Vickers. "But I'm quite sure that it is urgent, or Miss Greyle wouldn't have said so. I don't know what her exact meaning was; but I know there's something wrong about the whole thing at Scarhaven, seriously wrong!"

"You do, eh?" exclaimed Copplestone. "What now?"

"Ah, that I don't know," replied Vickers with a dry laugh. "I wish I did. But you know how people talk in these provincial places? Ever since that inquest there have been all sorts of rumors. Every public place in Norcaster has been full of gossip, surmise, and speculation."

"But about what?" asked Copplestone.

"Squire Greyle, of course," said the young solicitor. "That inquest was enough to set the whole country talking. Everybody thinks— they couldn't think otherwise—that something is being hushed up. Everybody's agog to know if Sir Cresswell Oliver and Mr. Petherton are applying for a re-opening of the inquest. You've just come from town, I believe. Did you hear anything?"

Copplestone was wondering whether he ought to tell his companion of his own recent discoveries. Like all laymen, he had an idea that you can tell anything to a lawyer, and he was half-minded to pour out the whole story to Vickers, especially as he was Mrs. Greyle's solicitor. But on second thought, he decided to wait until he had ascertained the state of affairs at Scarhaven.

"I didn't hear anything about that," he replied. "Of course, that inquest was a travesty of what such an inquiry should have been."

"Oh, an utter farce," agreed Vickers. "However, it produced the opposite effect to what those manipulators wanted. Of course, Chatfield had squared that jury! But he forgot the press, and the local reporters were so glad to get hold of what was really spicy news. The Norcaster and Northborough papers have been full of it, and everybody's talking of it, as I said. People are asking what this evidence from America is; why there is such mystery about the whole thing; and so on. And everybody knows that Squire Greyle has since left Scarhaven."

"Have you seen Mrs. or Miss Greyle since the inquest?" asked Copplestone, who was anxious to keep off subjects on which he might possess information. "Have you been over there?"

"No, not since that day," replied Vickers. "And I'm a bit anxious about this telegram. Something must have happened."

Copplestone looked out of the window on his side of the car. Already they were clear of the Norcaster streets and on the road which led to Scarhaven. That road ran along the coast, often at the very edge of the high cliffs with no more between it and the rocks far beneath than a low wall. It was a dangerous road with curves and corners that needed care even in broad daylight, and this was a black, moonless night. But Copplestone and his companion were both so full of their purpose that they paid little heed to the danger they ran as the car tore around turns and down deep cuts at a speed which at other times would have been considered suicidal. At just under the hour they ran onto the level stretch by the Admiral's Arms. Looking down at the harbor they saw the lighted portholes of some ship which lay against the south quay and on the quay itself men moving about in the glare of lamps.

"What's going on there?" said Vickers. "Late for a vessel to be loading at a place like this where time's of no great importance."

Copplestone offered no suggestion. He was impatient to reach the cottage, and as soon as the car stopped at its gate, he burst out, bade the driver wait, and ran eagerly up to the path to Audrey, who opened the door as he advanced. In another second he had both her hands in his own.

"You're all right?" he demanded in tones which made clear to the girl how anxious he had been. "There's nothing wrong with you or your mother . . . personally, I mean? You see, I didn't get your wire until this afternoon, and then I raced off as quick—"

"I understand," she said. "You may be sure I wouldn't have wired if I hadn't felt it absolutely necessary. Somebody was wanted, and you'd made me promise, and so. Yes," she continued, drawing back as Vickers came up, "we are all right . . . personally, . . . but there's something very wrong indeed."

Mrs. Greyle, looking worn and ill, appeared just then in the hall and called to them to come in. She preceded them into the parlor and turned to the young men as soon as Audrey closed the door.

"I'm more thankful to see you gentlemen than I've ever been in my life for anything!" she said. "Something is happening here which needs your attention. Yesterday morning very early, the Squire's ship, the *Pike*, was brought into the inner harbor and moored against the quay just opposite the park gates. We, of course, could see it; and as we knew he had gone away, we wondered why it was brought in there. After it had been moored, we saw that preparations of some sort were being made. Then men—estate laborers—began coming down from the house, carrying packing cases, which were taken on board. And while this was going on, Mrs. Peller, the housekeeper, came hurrying here in a state of great consternation. She said that a number of sailors and estate men were packing up and removing all the most valuable things in the house: the finest pictures, the old silver, the famous collection of china which Stephen John Greyle had made, the rarest and most valuable books out of the library, and all sorts of things of real and great value. Everything was being taken down to the *Pike*. The estate carpenter, who was in charge of all this, said it was by the Squire's orders and produced to Mrs. Peller his written authority. Of course, Mrs. Peller could do nothing against that, but she came hurrying to tell us, because she, like everybody else, is much exercised by these recent events. And so Audrey and I pocketed our pride and went to see Peter Chatfield. But he, like his master, had gone! He had left home the previous evening, and his house was locked up tight."

Copplestone and Vickers exchanged glances, and the young solicitor signaled Mrs. Greyle to proceed.

"Then," she added, "to add to that, as we came away from Chatfield's house, we met Mr. Elkin, the bank manager from Norcaster. He had come to see me privately. He wanted to tell me that within the last few days, the Squire and Peter Chatfield had withdrawn from the bank the very large balances of two separate accounts. One was the Squire's own account in his name; the other was an estate account on which Chatfield could draw. As Mr. Elkin pointed out, it was all in order, and no objection could be raised. But it was unusual since a large balance had always existed in both these accounts. And so many strange rumors are going about Norcaster and the district, that Mr. Elkin felt seriously uneasy and thought it his duty to see me at once. What is to be done? The house is being stripped of the best part of its valuables. In my opinion, when that yacht sails it will be for some foreign port. What other purpose can there be in taking these things away? Of course, as nothing is entailed, and there are no heirlooms, everything is absolutely the Squire's property.

Copplestone, who had been realizing the serious significance of these statements, saw that it was time to speak, if action was to be taken at once.

"I'd better tell you the truth," he said interrupting Mrs. Greyle. "I might have told you, Vickers, as we came along, but I decided to wait until we got here and found out how things were. Mrs. Greyle, the man you speak of as the Squire, is no more the owner of Scarhaven than I am! In fact, he is not Marston Greyle at all. The real Marston Greyle, who came over from America, died the day after he landed in lodgings at Bristol to which Peter Chatfield and his daughter had taken him. He is buried in a Bristol cemetery under the name of Mark Grey. Gilling and I found that out during these last few days. It's an absolute fact. So the man who has been posing here as the rightful owner is an impostor!"

A dead silence followed this declaration. The mother and daughter after one long look at Copplestone turned and looked at each other. But Vickers, quick to comprehend the situation, started from his seat with evident intention of doing something.

"That's the truth?" he exclaimed, turning to Copplestone. "No possible flaw in it?"

"None," replied Copplestone. "It's sheer fact."

"Then in that case," said Vickers, "Miss Greyle is the owner of Scarhaven, of everything in the house, of every stick, stone and pebble about the place! And we must act at once. Miss Greyle, you will have to assert yourself. You must do what I tell you to do. You must get ready at once—this minute!—and come with me and Mrs. Greyle to that yacht and stop all these proceedings. In our presence you must lay claim to everything that's been taken from the house, yes, and to the yacht itself. Come, let's hurry!"

Audrey hesitated and looked at Mrs. Greyle.

"Very well," she said quietly. "But not my mother."

"Very well," said Vickers. "You will have us with you."

Audrey hurried from the room, and Mrs. Greyle turned anxiously to Vickers.

"What shall you do?" she asked.

"Warn all concerned," answered Vickers with a snap of the jaw which showed Copplestone that he was a man of determination. "Warn them, if necessary, that the man they have known as Marston Greyle is an impostor, and that everything they are handling belongs to Miss Greyle. The Scarhaven people know me, of course. There ought not to be any great difficulty with them, and as regards the yacht people—"

"You know," interrupted Mrs. Greyle, "that this man, the impostor, has made himself very popular with the people here? You saw how they cheered him after the inquest? You don't think there is danger in Audrey going down there?"

"Wouldn't it be enough if you and I went?" suggested Copplestone. "It's very late to drag Miss Greyle out."

"I'm sorry, but it's absolutely necessary," said Vickers. "If your story is true . . . I mean, of course, *since* it is true, Miss Greyle is owner and mistress, and she must be on the spot. It's all we can do anyway," he continued, as Audrey, wrapped in a big overcoat, came back to the parlor. "Even now we may be too late. And if that yacht once sails away from here—"

There were signs that the yacht's departure was imminent when they went down to the south quay and came abreast of her. The lights on the shore were being extinguished; the estate laborers were gone; only two or three sailors were busy with ropes and gear. And Vickers hurried his little party up a gangway and on to the deck. A hard-faced, keen-eyed, man, evidently in authority, came forward.

"Are you the captain of this vessel?" demanded Vickers in tones of authority. "I am Mr. Vickers, solicitor, of Norcaster. I give you formal warning that the man you have known as Marston Greyle is not Marston Greyle at all, but an impostor. All the property which you have removed from the house and now have on this vessel belongs to this lady, Miss Audrey Greyle, Lady of the Manor of Scarhaven. It is at your peril that you move it or that you cause this vessel to leave this harbor. I claim the vessel and all that is on it on behalf of Miss Greyle."

The man addressed listened in silent attention and showed no sign of any surprise. As soon as Vickers had finished he turned, hurried down a stairway, remained below for a few minutes, and came up again.

"Will you kindly step this way, Miss Greyle and gentlemen?" he said politely. "You must remember that I am only a servant. If you will, come down."

He led them down the stairs along a thickly-carpeted passage and opened the door of a lighted cabin. All unthinking, the three stepped in . . . to hear the door closed and locked behind them.

Chapter 20

The Courteous Captain

Vickers sprang back at that door as the sharp click of the turning key caught his ear, and both Copplestone and Audrey, who had advanced fearlessly into the cabin, stopped short with a sudden, sickening sense of treachery. The two young men looked at each other, and a dead silence fell on them and the girl. Then Vickers laid his hand on the door and shook it.

"Locked in," he muttered with a quick glance at his companions. "What does that mean?"

"Nothing good," growled Copplestone who was secretly cursing his own folly in allowing Audrey to leave the quay. "We're trapped! That's what it means. *Why* we're trapped isn't a question that matters very much under the circumstances. The serious thing is that we certainly are trapped."

Vickers turned to Audrey.

"My fault," he said contritely. "All my fault! I meant the best; it was the right thing to do—to act swiftly. But who on earth could have foreseen this? Look here, we've got to think quickly. Copplestone, that captain? Has he done this on his own, or is there somebody on board who's at the top of things?"

"I don't see any good in thinking quickly, or asking one's self questions," replied Copplestone. "We're locked in here. We've got Miss Greyle into this mess, and her mother will be anxious and alarmed. I wish we'd let this confounded yacht go where it liked before ever we'd—"

"Don't!" broke in Audrey. "That's no good. Mr. Vickers certainly did what he felt to be best, and who could foresee this? I'm not afraid, and as for my mother, if we don't return very soon, why, she knows where we are, and there are police in Scarhaven."

"How long are we going to be where we are?" asked Copplestone grimly. "The thing's moving!"

There was no doubt of that very pertinent fact. Somewhere beneath them, machinery began to work; above them there was hurry and scurry as ropes and stays were thrown off. But so beautifully built was that yacht, and so almost soundproof the luxurious cabin in which they were prisoners, that little of the noise of departure came to them. However, there was no mistaking the increasing throb of the engines or the fact that the vessel was moving. Vickers suddenly sprang on a lounge seat and moved away a silken screen which curtained a porthole window.

"We're going through the outer harbor; we've passed the light at the end of the quay. What do these people mean by carrying us out to sea? Copplestone, with all due respect, whether it's relevant or not, I wish we knew more of that captain chap!"

"I know him," remarked Audrey. "I have been on this yacht before. His name is Andrius. He's an American or American-Norwegian, or something like that."

"And the crew?" asked Vickers. "Are they Scarhaven men?"

"No," replied Audrey. "There isn't a Scarhaven man amongst them. My cousin, I mean . . . you know whom I mean, bought this yacht just as it stood from an American millionaire early this spring. He took over the captain, crew, and everything."

"So we're in the hands of strangers," exclaimed Vickers, while Copplestone dug his hands into his pockets and began to stamp about. "I wish I'd known all that before we came on board."

"But what harm can they do us?" said Audrey, incredulous of danger. "You don't suppose they'll want to murder us, surely! My own belief is that we never would have been locked up here if you hadn't let them know how much we know, Mr. Vickers."

"I don't understand," said Vickers.

"Why," replied Audrey, with a laugh which convinced both men of her fearlessness, "you let the captain see that we know a great deal.

He ran downstairs, presumably to tell somebody of what you said. And here's the result."

"You think, then," suggested Vickers, "you think that . . ."

"I think the somebody, whoever he is, wants to know exactly how much we do know," answered Audrey with another laugh. "And so we're being carried off to be cross-examined at somebody's leisure. Let's hope they won't use thumbscrews and that sort of thing. Anyway," she continued, looking from one to the other, "hadn't we better make the best of it? We're going out to sea. That's certain. We're crossing the bar!"

A sudden lifting of the thickly-carpeted floor, a dip to the left, another to the right, a plunge forward, a drop back, then a settling down to a steady persistent roll, showed her companions that Audrey was right. The yacht had crossed the bar which lay at the mouth of Scarhaven Bay. Outside that lay the North Sea, and Copplestone suddenly wondered which course the vessel was going to take, north, east, or south. But before he could put his thoughts into words, the door was suddenly unlocked, and Captain Andrius, suave, polite, and deprecating, walked into the cabin.

"A thousands pardons and two words of explanation!" he exclaimed, as he executed a deep bow to his lady prisoner. "First, Miss Greyle, I have sent a message to your mother that you are quite safe and will join her in due course. Second, this is merely a temporary detention. You shall all be landed, all in good time."

Vickers as a legal man, assumed his most professional air.

"Do you know what you are rendering yourself liable to, sir, by detaining us at all?" he demanded.

Captain Andrius bowed again and again assumed his deprecating smile. He waved the two men to seats and himself took a chair with his back to the door by which he entered.

"My dear sir," he said courteously, "you forget that I am but a servant. I am under orders. However, I give my word that no harm shall come to you, that you shall be treated with every polite attention, and that you shall be landed."

"When? And where?" asked Vickers.

"Tomorrow, certainly," replied Andrius. "As to where, I cannot say. But you will be in touch with, shall we say, civilization?"

He showed a set of fine white teeth in such a curious fashion as he spoke the last word that Copplestone and Vickers instinctively glanced at each other with a mutual instinct of distrust.

"Won't do!" said Vickers. "I insist that you put about and go into Scarhaven again."

Andrius spread out his open palms and shook his head. "Impossible," he answered. "We are already underway. Time presses. Be patient. Tomorrow you shall be released."

Vickers was about to answer this appeal with an angry refusal to be patient, but he suddenly stopped the words which rose to his tongue. There was something in all this, some mystery, some strange game, and it might be worthwhile to find it out.

"Where are you taking this yacht?" he demanded brusquely. "Come, now!"

"I am under orders," said Andrius with another smile.

"Whose orders?" persisted Vickers. "Look here, it's no use trying to avoid facts. Who's on board this vessel? You know what I mean. Is the man who calls himself Squire of Scarhaven here?"

Andrius shook his head quietly and gave his questioner a shrewd glance.

"Mr. Vickers," he said meaningfully, "I know you. You are a lawyer, though a young one. Lawyers are guarded in their speech. We are alone, we four. No one can hear anything we say. Tell me, is that right what you said to me on deck, that the man who has called himself Marston Greyle is not so at all?"

"Absolutely right," replied Vickers.

"An impostor?" demanded Andrius.

"He is."

"And never had any right to . . . anything?"

"No right whatever!"

"Then," said Andrius, with a polite inclination of his head and shoulders to Audrey, "the truth is that everything of the Scarhaven property belongs to this lady?"

"Everything!" exclaimed Vickers. "Land, houses, furniture, valuables—everything. All the property which you have on this yacht—pictures, china, silver, books, objects of art, as I am instructed, removed from the house—are Miss Greyle's sole property. Once more I warn you of what you are doing, and I demand that you immediately return to Scarhaven. This very yacht belongs to Miss Greyle!"

Andrius nodded, looked fixedly at the young solicitor for a moment, and then rose.

"I am obliged to you," he said. "That, of course, is your claim. But the other one, eh? It seems to me there might be something to be said for that, you know? So, all I can do is to renew my assurance of polite attention, offer you our best accommodation, and promise to land you somewhere tomorrow. Miss Greyle, we have two women servants on board; I shall send them to you at once, and they will attend to you. Please consider them your own. You, gentlemen, will perhaps join me in my quarters? I have two spare cabins close to my own which are at your service."

Copplestone and Vickers, undecided and suspicious, looked at each other and at Audrey. But Audrey was evidently neither alarmed nor uneasy; she nodded a ready assent to the Captain's proposal.

"Thank you, Captain Andrius," she said coolly. "I know the two women. You may send one of them. Do what he suggests," she murmured, turning to Copplestone, who had moved close to her, "I'm not one scrap afraid of anything, and it's only until tomorrow. He'll land us; I'm sure of it."

There was nothing to do then, but to follow Andrius to his own comfortable quarters. There, utterly ignoring the strange circumstances under which they met, he played the part of host with genuine desire to make his guests feel at ease. And when he showed them to their berths a little later, he emphasized his assurance of their absolute safety and liberty.

"You see, gentlemen, your movements are untrammeled," he said. "You can go in and out of your quarters as you like. You can go where you like on the yacht tomorrow morning. There is no restriction on you. Sleep well, and tomorrow you are all free again, eh?"

Copplestone had a word or two with Vickers . . . alone.

"What do you think?" he muttered. "Shall you sleep?"

"My impression, for I know what you're thinking about," said Vickers, "is that Miss Greyle's as safe as if she were in her mother's house. She has no fear herself, anyway. There's some mystery somewhere, and I can't make this Andrius man out at all, but I believe all's right as regards personal safety. There's Miss Greyle's cabin, anyhow, right opposite ours, and I can keep an eye and an ear open even when I'm asleep!"

But in spite of these assurances, Copplestone slept little. He was up, dressed, and on deck by sunrise, staring around him in a fresh autumn morning to get some notion of the yacht's whereabouts. He had just managed to make out a mere filmy line of land far to the west when Audrey appeared at his elbow. There was no one of any importance near them, and Copplestone impulsively seized her hands.

"I've scarcely slept!" he blurted out, gazing intently at her. "Couldn't! Blaming myself for letting you get into this confounded mess. You're all right?"

Audrey responded a little to the pressure of his hands before she disengaged her own.

"It wasn't your fault," she said. "It's nobody's fault. Don't blame Mr. Vickers; he couldn't foresee this. Yes, I'm all right, and I slept like a top. What's the use of worrying? Do you know," she went on, lowering her voice and drawing nearer to him, "I believe something's going to come of all this, something that'll clear matters up once and for all."

"Why?" asked Copplestone. "What makes you think that?"

"Don't know—instinct, intuition, perhaps," she answered. "Besides, I'm dead certain we're not the only people—I don't mean crew and Captain—aboard the *Pike*. I believe there's somebody else. There's some mystery anyway. Keep that to yourself," she said as Andrius and Vickers appeared from below. "Don't show any sign. Wait to see how things turn out."

She turned away from him to greet the other two as unconcernedly as if there were nothing unusual in the situation, and Copplestone marveled at her coolness. He himself, not so well equipped with patience, was feverishly anxious to know how things would turn out, and when. But the day went by and nothing happened, except that Captain Andrius was very polite to his guests and that the yacht, a particularly fast sailor, continued to make headway through the gray seas, sometimes in bare sight of land and sometimes out of it. To inquiries as to the fulfillment of his promise Andrius made no more answer than a reassuring nod, and when pressed, he replied curtly that the day was not yet over.

Vickers drew Copplestone aside.

"Look here," he said. "I can make out that we've been running due north, or north-east ever since we left Scarhaven last night. I reckon, too, that this vessel makes nearly twenty-two or three knots an hour. We must be off the extreme north-east coast of Scotland. And night's coming on!"

"There are ports there that he can put into," said Copplestone. "The thing is, will he keep his promise? He must know that if we land anywhere within reach of a telegraph office, we can wire particulars about him to every port in the world if we like. And he's got to land somewhere eventually, you know."

Vickers shook his head. It was beyond him, he said, to even guess at what Andrius was after, or what was going to happen. And nothing did happen until, as the three prisoners sat at dinner with their polite jailer, the *Pike* came to a sudden stop and hung gently on a quiet sea. Andrius looked up and smiled.

"A pleasant night for your landing," he remarked. "Don't hurry, but there will be a boat ready for you as soon as dinner is over."

"And where are we?" asked Vickers.

"That, my dear sir, you will see when you land." replied Andrius. "You will be quite comfortable for the night; in the morning, I think, you will be able to journey wherever you wish to go to."

There was something in the smile which accompanied the last words which made Copplestone uneasy. But the prospect of regaining their liberty was too good; he kept his own counsel. Thirty minutes later, he, Audrey, and Vickers stood on deck, looking down on a boat alongside, in which were three of the crew and a man holding a lantern. In front was the dark sea, and ahead a darker mass which they took to be land.

"You won't tell us what this place is?" said Vickers as he was about to follow the others into the boat. "Is it on the mainland?"

"The morning light, my good sir, will show you everything," replied Andrius. "Be content that I have kept my promise; you have come off safely," he added with a significant look.

Vickers felt a strange sense of alarm as the boat left the yacht. He noticed two or three suspicious circumstances. As soon as they got away, he saw that all the yacht's lights had been darkened or entirely obscured; at a dozen boat lengths, they could see her no more. Then a boat, swiftly pulled, passed them in the darkness, evidently coming from the shore to which they were being taken; it, too, carried no light. Nor were there any lights on the shore itself; all was in utter blackness. They arrived at the stony beach within a quarter of an hour; another minute or two more, and the yachtsmen had helped all three onto the beach, had carried up certain boxes and packages which had been placed in the boat, had set down the lighted lantern, jumped into the boat again, and vanished in the darkness. The silence was broken only by the drip of water from the retreating oars and by the scarcely-noticed ripple of the waves. Audrey voiced exactly what her two companions felt.

"Andrius has both kept his word *and* cheated us! We're stranded!"

From somewhere out of the darkness came a groan, deep and heartfelt, as if in entire agreement with Audrey's declaration. That it proceeded from a human being was evident enough, and Vickers hastily snatched up the lantern and strode in the direction from which it came. And there, seated on the stones, his whole attitude one of utter dejection and misery, the three castaways found a sharer of their sorrows—Peter Chatfield!

Chapter 21

Marooned

To each of these three, this was the most surprising moment which life had yet afforded. It was astonishing to find a fellow mortal there at all, but to find that mortal was the Scarhaven estate agent was nothing short of marvelous. What was also astounding was to see Chatfield's only too evident distress. Swathed in a heavy, old-fashioned overcoat with a plaid shawl around his shoulders, he wore a deerstalker hat tied over his head and ears with a bandanna. He sat on the beach nursing his knees, slightly rocking his fleshy figure to and fro, and moaning softly with the regularity of a tolling bell. His eyes were fixed on the dark expanse of waters at his feet; his lips—when he was not moaning—worked incessantly; as he rocked his body, he beat his toes on the beach. Clearly, Chatfield was in a bad way mentally. That he was not so badly off materially was made evident by the presence of a half-open knapsack, which obviously contained food and a bottle of spirits.

He took no notice of them. Audrey, Vickers, and Copplestone might have been no more than the pebbles on which they stood, in spite of the fact that Vickers shone the light on Chatfield's fat face. He continued to stare moodily out to sea and took no notice of his newly arrived company. So utterly extraordinary was his behavior and attitude that Audrey suddenly and almost involuntarily stepped forward and laid a hand on his shoulder.

"Mr. Chatfield!" she exclaimed. "What's the matter? Are you ill?"

The emphasis which she gave to the last word roused some quality of Chatfield's subtle intellect. He flashed a swift look at his questioner, a look of mingled contempt and derision, spiced with a dash of sneering humor. And he found his tongue.

"Ill!" he snorted. "Ill! She asks if I'm ill. Me, a respectable man what's maltreated and robbed before his own eyes by them as ought to fall in humble gratitude at his feet. Ill. Aye, ill with something that's worse than any bodily aches and pains. Let me tell you that! But not done for neither!"

"He's all right," said Copplestone. "That's a flash of his old spirit. You're all right, Chatfield, aren't you? Who's robbed and maltreated you? And how and when—especially when—did you come here?"

Chatfield looked up at his old assailant with a glare of dislike.

"You keep your tongue to yourself, young feller," he growled. "I shouldn't never ha' been here at all if it hadn't been for the likes of you a pokin' your nose where it isn't wanted. It's 'cause o' you three comin' aboard o' that there yacht last night as I am here a castaway!"

"Well, we're castaways too, Mr. Chatfield," said Audrey. "And we can't help believing that it's all your naughty conduct that's made us so. Why don't you tell the truth?"

Chatfield uttered a few grumpy and inarticulate sounds.

"It'll be a bad day for more than one when I do that," he muttered presently. "Oh, aye, I'll tell the truth. When it suits me! But I'll be out o' this first."

"You'll never get out of this first or last, until you tell us how you got in," said Vickers, assuming a threatening tone. "You'd better tell us all about it. Come now, you know me and my firm."

Chatfield laughed grimly and shook his much-swathed head.

"I ought to," he said. "I've given 'em more than one nice job and said naught about their bills o' costs neither, my lad. You keep a civil tongue in your mouth. I ain't done for yet, no ways! You let me get off this here place, wherever it is, and within touch of a telegraph office, and I'll make somebody suffer!"

"Andrius, of course," said Copplestone. "Come now, he put you ashore before he sent us off, didn't he? Why don't you own up?"

"Never you mind, young feller," retorted Chatfield. "I was feeling very cast down, but I'm better. I've something that'll keep me going. Revenge! I'll show 'em, once I'm off this place. I will so!"

"Look here, Chatfield," said Vickers. "Do you know where this place is? Is it on the mainland, or is it an island, or where are we? It's all very well talking about getting off, but when and how are we to get off? Why don't you be sensible and tell us what you know?"

The estate agent arose slowly and ponderously, drawing his shawl about him. He looked out seawards. In that black waste the steady beat of the yacht's propellers could be clearly heard, but not a gleam of light came from her, and it was impossible to decide in which direction she was going. And Chatfield suddenly shook his fist at the throbbing sound which came in regular pulsations through the night.

"Never mind," he said sneeringly. "We aren't at the North Pole. I ain't a seafaring man, but I've a good idea of where we are. And perhaps there won't be naught to take me off when it's daylight. And perhaps there won't be no telegraphs near at hand nor within a hundred miles. Oh, no! Just you wait, my fine fellers. That's all!"

"He's not addressing us, Vickers," said Copplestone. "You're decidedly better, Chatfield; you're quite better. The notion of revenge and of circumvention has come to you like balm. But you'd a lot better tell us who you're referring to and why you were put ashore. Listen, Chatfield, there's property of your own on that yacht, eh? That it?"

Chatfield gave his questioner a look of indignant scorn. He stooped for the knapsack, picked it up, and turned away.

"I don't want to have naught to do with you," he remarked over his shoulder. "You keep yourselves to yourselves, and I'll keep myself to myself. If it hadn't been for what you blabbed out last night, them ungrateful devils 'ud never have had such ideas put into their heads."

As if he knew his way, Chatfield plodded heavily up the beach and was lost in the darkness. The three left behind stood helplessly staring at each other. For a long time there was silence, broken only by the agent's heavy tread on the rocky beach. At last Vickers spoke.

"I think I can see through all this," he said. "Chatfield's cryptic utterances were somewhat suggestive. 'Robbed,' 'maltreated,' 'them as ought to have fallen in humble gratitude at his feet,' 'revenge,' 'ungrateful devils.' Ah, I see it! Chatfield had associates on the *Pike*, probably the impostor himself and Andrius. Probably, too, he had property of his own, as you suggested to him, Copplestone. The whole gang was doubtless off with their loot to far quarters of the globe. And now the other members have shelved Chatfield. They're done with him. But not if he can help it! That man will hunt the *Pike* and her people, whoever they are, relentlessly when he gets off this."

"I wish we knew what it is that we're on," said Copplestone.

"Impossible till daybreak," replied Vickers. "But I've an idea. This is probably one of the seventy-odd islands of the Orkneys. I've sailed round here before. If I'm right, it's most likely one of the out-lying and uninhabited ones. Andrius, or his controlling power, has dropped us and Chatfield here, knowing that we may have to spend a few days on this island before we succeed in getting off. Those few days will mean a great deal to the *Pike*. She can be run into some safe harbor, given a new coat of paint and a new name, and be off before we can do anything to stop her. I allow Chatfield to be right in this: that my perhaps too hasty declaration to Andrius revealed to that gentleman how he could make off with other people's property."

"Nothing will make me believe that Andrius is the solely responsible person for this last development," said Copplestone. "There had to be other people on board, cleverly concealed. What are we going to do?"

Audrey had stepped away from the circle of light made by the lantern and was gazing steadily in the direction which Chatfield had taken.

"Those are surely cliffs," she said presently. "Hadn't we better go up the beach and see if we can't find some shelter until morning? Fortunately we're all warmly clad, and Andrius was considerate enough to throw rugs and things into the boat, as well as provisions. We're not so badly off after all, and we have the satisfaction of knowing that we can keep Chatfield under observation. Remember that!"

But in the morning, when the first gleam of light came across the sea, Vickers set out to make a first examination of their surroundings, leaving his companions to prepare some breakfast from the provisions which had been sent ashore with them. The agent was nowhere to be seen. What *was* to be seen was a span of rock, sand, beach, not a mile in length, lying at the foot of high cliffs; and on the gray sea in front not a sign of a sail, nor a wisp of smoke from a passing steamer. The apparent solitude and isolation of the place was as profound as the silence which hung over everything.

Vickers made his way up the cliffs to their highest point and from its summit took a leisurely view of his surroundings. He saw at once that they were on an island, and that it was but one of many which lay spread out over the sea towards the north and the west. It was a wedge-shaped island, and the cliffs on which he stood and the beach beneath formed the widest side of it; from there its lines drew away to a point in the distance which he judged to be two miles off. Between him and that point lay a sloping expanse of rough land, whereon there were vast masses of rock and boulder but nary a sign of human life. No curling column of smoke went up from hut or cottage; no bleating of sheep nor the cry of shepherd. All was still as only such places can be still. Nor could he perceive any signs of life on the adjacent islands, which, to be sure, were not very near. From the sea mists which wrapped one of them, he saw projecting the cap of a mountainous hill that he recognized as being on one of the principal islands of the group. And then he knew that he and his companions had been set down on one of the outlying islands, one not in the immediate way of passing vessels nor likely to be visited by fishermen.

He was turning away from the top of the cliff after a long and careful inspection when he caught sight of a man's figure crossing the rocky slope low. That, he said to himself, was Chatfield. Did Chatfield know of a place visited by fishing craft from the other islands? Had Chatfield ever been in the Orkneys before? Was there any method in his wanderings? Or was he, too, merely examining his surroundings and considering which was the likeliest part of the island from which to attract attention?

In the midst of these speculations a sudden resolution came to Vickers: one or other of the three must keep an eye on Chatfield. Night or day, Chatfield must be watched. And having already seen that Copplestone and Audrey had an unmistakable liking for each other's society and would certainly not object to being left together, he determined to watch Chatfield himself. Hurrying down the cliffs, he hastily explained the situation to his companions, took some food in his hands, and set out to follow the agent wherever he went.

Chapter 22

The Old Hand

Half an hour later, when Vickers regained the top of the cliff and once more looked across the island, the figure which he had previously seen was now plodding steadily across the coarse grass- and rock-strewn moorland in his own direction. Chatfield had evidently taken a bird's eye view of the situation from the vantage point of the slope and had come to the conclusion that the higher part of the island was the most likely point from which to attract attention. He came steadily forward, a big, lumbering figure in the light mist. Vickers went to meet him and eyed him with a lively curiosity, wondering what secrets lay carefully locked up in the man's heart and what happened on the *Pike* that made its captain bundle Chatfield out of it like a box of bad goods for which there was no more use. And as he speculated, they met, and Vickers saw at once that the old fellow's mood had changed during the night. An atmosphere of smug oiliness sat upon Chatfield in the freshness of the morning, and he greeted the young solicitor in tones which were suggestive of a chastened spirit.

"Morning, Mr. Vickers," he said. "A pretty spot it is that we find ourselves in, sir. Nevertheless, one's affairs sometimes makes us long to quit the side of beauty, however much we would tarry by it. In plain words, Mr. Vickers, I want to get out o' this. And I've been looking round, and my opinion is that the best thing we can do is to start as big a fire as we can on yon bluff and keep a-feeding it. In the meantime, while you're considering that, I'll burn something of my own. I'm weary."

He dropped down on a convenient boulder of limestone, settled his big frame comfortably, and, producing a pipe and a tobacco pouch, proceeded to smoke. Vickers himself took another boulder and looked inquisitively at his strange companion. He felt sure that Chatfield was up to something.

"You say 'we' now," he remarked suddenly. "Last night you said you didn't want to have anything to do with us. We were to keep to ourselves, and—"

"Well, well, Mr. Vickers," broke in Chatfield. "One says things at one time that one wouldn't say at another, you know. Facts is facts, sir, and we are companions in distress. I've naught against you nor against the girl; as for t'other young man, he's of a interfering nature, but I forgive him. He's young. I don't bear no ill will, things being as they are. I've had time to reflect since last night, and I don't see no reason why Miss Greyle and me shouldn't come to terms . . . through you."

Vickers took some time over this.

"What are you after, Chatfield?" he asked at length. "You say you want to come to terms with Miss Greyle. That, of course, is because you know very well that Miss Greyle is the legal owner of Scarhaven, and that—"

Chatfield waved his pipe.

"I don't!" he answered with what seemed genuine eagerness. "I don't know nothing of the sort. I tell you, Mr. Vickers, I do *not* know that the man what we've known as the Squire of Scarhaven for a year gone by is *not* the rightful Squire. I do not! Fact, sir! But," he lowered his voice, and his sly eyes became slyer and craftier, "but I won't deny that during this last week or two I may have had my suspicions aroused that there was something wrong. I don't deny that, Mr. Vickers."

Vickers heard this with amazement. Young as he was, he had had various dealings with Peter Chatfield, and subtle old fellow that he was, he believed that Chatfield was now speaking the truth. But, in that case, what of Copplestone's revelation about the Falmouth and Bristol affair and the dead man? He thought rapidly and then determined to take a strong line.

"Chatfield," he said. "You're trying to bluff me. It won't do. Things are known. I know 'em, so I'll be candid with you and tell you what I know. It'll all have to come out. You know very well that the real Marston Greyle's dead. You were with him when he died. What's more, you buried him at Bristol under the name of Mark Grey. What's the use of lying about it? You know that's all true!"

He was watching Chatfield's big face keenly, and he was astonished to see that his dramatic impeachment produced no more effect than a slightly superior smile. Instead of being floored, Chatfield was distinctly unimpressed.

"Aye," he said, reflectively. "Aye, I expected to hear somewhat like that. That's Copplestone's work, of course. I knew he was some sort of detective as soon as I got speech with him. His work and that there Sir Cresswell Oliver, him as is making a mountain out of a molehill about his brother who broke his neck quite accidental, poor man, and of that London lawyer Petherton. Aye, aye. But all the same, Mr. Vickers, it don't alter matters!"

"What do you mean, man?" exclaimed Vickers, who was becoming more and more mystified. "Do you mean to tell me—? Come, come, Chatfield, I'm not a fool! Why, Copplestone has found it all out. There's no need to keep it secret now. You were with Marston Greyle when he died; you registered his death as Marston Greyle."

Chatfield laughed softly and gave his companion a swift glance out of one corner of his right eye.

"And put another name on a bit of a tombstone six months afterwards?" he said quietly. "Mr. Vickers, when you're as old as I am, you'll know that this here world is as full o' puzzles as yon sea's full o' fish!"

Vickers could only stare at his companion in speechless silence after that. There was some mystery about which Chatfield evidently knew a great deal, while he knew nothing. The old fellow's coolness, his ready acceptance of the Bristol facts and almost contemptuous brushing aside of them, reduced Vickers to a feeling of helplessness. He continued to stare at Chatfield, and in the end he could only think of one word. "Well?" he asked lamely. "Well?"

"As to what now?" inquired Chatfield with a sly smile.

"About what you said," replied Vickers. "Miss Greyle, you know. I'm thoroughly tied up with all this. You evidently know a lot, but of course you won't tell. You're devilish deep, Chatfield. But between you and me, what do you mean when you say that you don't see why you and Miss Greyle shouldn't come to terms?"

"Didn't I say that during this last week or two I'd had my suspicions about the Squire?" answered Chatfield. "I did. I have had them suspicions, got 'em stronger than ever since last night. So what I say is this. If things should turn out that Miss Greyle's the rightful owner of Scarhaven, and if I help her to establish her claim, and if I help, too, to recover them valuables that are on the *Pike*—there's a good sixty to eighty thousand pounds worth of stuff, silver, china, paintings, books, tapestry, on that there craft, Mr. Vickers—if, I say, I do all that, what will Miss Greyle do for me? That's it in a plain way of speaking."

"Indeed it is," said Vickers dryly. "Very well. You'd better come now and talk to Miss Greyle."

Copplestone and Audrey, having made a breakfast from the box of provisions which Andrius had been good enough to send ashore with them, had climbed to the head of the cliff after Vickers, and they were presently astonished beyond measure to see him returning with Chatfield under outward signs which suggested amity if not friendship. They paused by a convenient nook in the rocks and silently awaited the approach of these two strangely assorted companions. Vickers, coming near, gave them a knowing look.

"Mr. Chatfield," he said gravely, "has had the night in which to reflect. Mr. Chatfield desires peaceable relations. Mr. Chatfield doesn't see, now having reflected, why he and Miss Greyle should not be on good terms. Mr. Chatfield desires to discuss these terms. Is that right, Chatfield?"

"Quite right, sir," assented the agent. He had been regarding the couple who faced him benevolently and indulgently, and he now raised his hat to them. "Servant, ma'am," he said with a bow to Audrey. "Servant, sir," he continued with another bow to

Copplestone. "Ah, it's far better to be at peace one with another than to let misunderstandings exist forever. Mr. Copplestone, sir, you and me's had words in times past; I brush 'em away, sir, like that there. The memory's departed! I desire naught but better feelings. Mr. Vickers'll repeat what's passed between him and me."

Copplestone stood rooted to the spot with amazement while Vickers hastily summarized the recent conversation; his mouth opened but his speech failed him. Audrey laughed and looked at Vickers as if Chatfield were a new sort of entertainment.

"What do you say to this, Mr. Vickers?" she asked.

"Well, if you want to know," replied Vickers, "I believe Chatfield when he says that he does *not* know that the Squire is *not* the Squire. May seem strange, but I do. As a solicitor, I do."

"You believe that?" exclaimed Copplestone, finding his tongue.

"I've said so," retorted Vickers.

"Thank you, sir," said Chatfield. "I'm obliged to you. Mr. Copplestone, sir, doesn't yet understand that there's a deal of conundrum in life. He'll know better someday. He'll know, too, that the poet spoke truthful when he said that things isn't what they seem."

Copplestone turned angrily on Vickers.

"Is this a farce?" he demanded. "You know what I told you!"

"Mr. Chatfield has a version," answered Vickers. "Why not hear it?"

"Terms, Mr. Vickers," remarked Chatfield. "Speak on my terms, sir."

"What terms?" asked Audrey. "To Mr. Chatfield's personal advantage, I'm sure."

Chatfield, who was still the most unconcerned of the group, seated himself on the rocks and looked at his audience.

"I've said to Mr. Vickers here that if I help Miss Greyle to gain the estate, I ought to be rewarded . . . handsome," he said. "Mind you, I don't know that I can. As I say, I do not know as a matter of strict fact that this man as we've called the Squire isn't the Squire. But recent events—very recent events—has made me suspicious that he isn't; and it happens I can do a good bit to turning him out. Now, if I help in that there work, will Miss Greyle continue me in my post of estate agent at Scarhaven?"

"Not for any longer than it will take to turn you out of it, Mr. Chatfield," replied Audrey, with an energy and promptness which surprised her companions. "So we need not discuss that. You will never be my agent."

"Very good, ma'am. That's quite according to my expectations," said Chatfield meekly. "I was always a misunderstood man. Perhaps this here proposition will be more welcome. It's always been understood that I was to have a retiring pension of five hundred pounds per year. The family has always promised it; I've letters to prove it. Will Miss Greyle stand to that if she comes in? I've been a faithful servant for nigh on to fifty years, Mr. Vickers, as all the neighborhood is aware."

"If I *come in*, as you call it, you shall have your pension," said Audrey.

Chatfield slowly felt in a capacious inner pocket and produced a large notebook and a fountain pen. He passed them to Vickers.

"We'll have that there in writing, signed and witnessed," he said. "Put, if you please, Mr. Vickers, 'I agree that if I come into the Scarhaven estate, Peter Chatfield shall at once be pensioned off with five hundred pounds a year to be paid quarterly. Same to be properly assured to him for his life.' And then if Miss Greyle'll sign that document and you gentlemen'll witness it, I shall consider that henceforth I'm in Miss Greyle's service. And," he added, with a significant glance all around, "I shall be a deal more use as a friend than I should be as what you might term an enemy. Mr. Vickers knows that."

Vickers held a short consultation with Audrey, the result of which was that the paper was duly signed, witnessed, and deposited in Chatfield's pocket. And Chatfield nodded his satisfaction.

"All right," he said. "Now then, ma'am and gentlemen, the next thing is to get away out o' this and get on the track of them as put us here. We'd better start a big fire out o' this dry stuff."

"But what about these revelations you were going to make?" said Vickers. "I understood you were to tell us—"

"Sir," replied Chatfield, "I'll tell and I'll reveal in due course and in good order. Events, sir, is the thing! Let me get to the nearest telegraph office, and we'll have some events, right smart. Let me attract attention. I've sailed in these seas before. There's steamers goes out of Kirkwall yonder frequent; we must get hold of one. A telegraph office! That's what I want. I'm a-going to set up a blaze here, and I'll set up a blaze elsewhere as soon as I can lay hands on a bundle o' telegraph forms!"

He leisurely took off his shawl and overcoat, laid them on a shelf of rock, and moved away to collect the dry stuff which lay about. The three young people exchanged glances.

"What's this new mystery?" asked Audrey.

"All bluff! Some deep game of his own," growled Copplestone. "He's the most consummate old liar I ever—"

"You're wrong this time, old chap," interrupted Vickers. "He's a bad 'un, but he's on our side now, I'm convinced. It is a game he's playing and a deep one, and I don't know what it is, but it's for our benefit. Chatfield's simply transferred his interest and influence to us. That's all. For his own purposes, of course. And," he suddenly paused, gazed seaward, and then jumped to his feet. "Chatfield," he called. "You needn't light any fire. Here's a steamer!"

Chapter 23

The Yacht Comes Back

C hatfield, his arms filled with masses of dried bracken and coarse grass, turned sharply on hearing Vickers's call and stared hard and long in the direction the young solicitor pointed. His eyes took on a look of cunning satisfaction, and throwing away his burdens he drew out a big handkerchief and mopped his high forehead as if the perspiration was the result of intense mental relief.

"Didn't I know we should be rescued from this here imprisonment," he cried with smug joy. "Thought they'd pinned me here for best part of a week, no doubt, while they could get theirselves quietly away far away!"

"Enough of that," said Vickers, curtly. "What we'd better think about is the chance of that steamer sighting us. We'll light that fire anyway."

"She's coming straight on for the island," remarked Copplestone, who had been narrowly watching the approaching vessel. "So straight that you'd think she was actually making for it."

"She'll be some craft bound for Kirkwall," said Vickers, pointing northward to the main group of islands. "And in that case she'll probably take this channel on our west. Come on all of you, and let's make as big a smoke as we can get out of this stuff."

The weather being calm and the grass and bracken which they heaped together as dry as tinder, there was little difficulty raising a thick column of smoke, which presently rose high in the sky. But Audrey, turning away from the successful result of their labors, suddenly glanced at Copplestone with a look that challenged an answer to her own thoughts. They were standing a little apart from the others, and she lowered her voice.

"I say," she murmured. "I don't think we need have bothered ourselves to light that fire. That vessel, whatever it is, is coming to us. Look!"

Copplestone shaded his eyes and stared out across the sea. The steamer was by that time no more than two or three miles away. But she was coming towards them in a dead straight line, and as she was accordingly bow on, and as her top deck and lamps were obscured by clouds of black smoke pouring furiously from her funnels, they could make little out of her appearance. Copplestone's first notion was that she was a naval patrol boat or a torpedo destroyer. Whatever she was, it seemed certain that she was heading directly for the island at that very point on which the fugitives had been landed the previous night. And it was very evident that she was in a great hurry.

"I think you're right," he said, turning to Audrey. "But it's strange that any vessel should be making for an uninhabited island like this. But you've got some notion in your mind?" he broke off suddenly, seeing her glance at him again. "What is it?"

Audrey shook her head with a cautious look at Chatfield.

"I was wondering if that's the *Pike* come back," she whispered. "And if it is, why?"

Copplestone took a longer and keener look at the vessel. Before he could speak again, Vickers called out cheerily across the rocks.

"Come on, you two!" he cried. "She's seen us; she's coming in. They'll have to send off a boat. Let's get down to the beach, so that they'll know where there's a safe landing."

He sprang over the edge of the cliff and hurried down the rough path; Chatfield, picking up his coat and shawl, prepared to follow him; Audrey and Copplestone lingered until he had begun to lumber downward.

"If that is the *Pike*," said Audrey, "there is something wrong. Whoever it is that is on the *Pike* wouldn't come back to take us."

"You think there is somebody on the *Pike*, somebody other than Andrius?" suggested Copplestone.

"I believe the man who calls himself Marston Greyle was on the *Pike*," announced Audrey. "I've thought so from the start. My belief is that Chatfield knew this too. I think that Chatfield was in with them, as the saying is, and they were all running away with as much of the Scarhaven property as they could lay hands on. And having got it, they bundled Chatfield out here and dumped him down, having no further use for him. And, if that's the *Pike*, and they're returning here, it's because they want Chatfield!"

Copplestone suddenly recognized that she had solved a puzzle which his own reason had so far left unsolved.

"Then, if that is so," he exclaimed softly, "this is merely another of Chatfield's games. You don't believe him?"

"I would think myself within approachable distance of lunacy if I believed a word that Peter Chatfield said," she answered calmly. "Of course he is playing a game of all his own. He shall have his pension, if I have the power to give it; but believe him, oh, no!"

"Let's follow them," said Copplestone. "Something's going to happen, if that is the *Pike*."

"Look there," said Audrey as they began to descend the cliff. "Chatfield's already uneasy."

She pointed to the beach below where Chatfield, now fully overcoated and shawled again, had mounted a ridge of rock, and while gazing intently at the vessel, was exchanging remarks with Vickers, who had evidently said something which had alarmed him. They caught Chatfield's excited ejaculations as they hurried over the sand.

"Don't say that, Mr. Vickers!" he was saying imploringly. "Mr. Vickers, don't suggest them there sort of thoughts. It's worse than a bad dream, Mr. Vickers, to say such. No, sir, no, surely you're mistaken!"

"Bet you a fiver to a halfpenny it's the *Pike*," retorted Vickers. "I know her lines. Besides, she's heading straight here. Copplestone," he cried, turning to the advancing couple. "Do you know, I believe that's the *Pike*!"

Copplestone gave Audrey's elbow a gentle squeeze.

"Look at old Chatfield," he whispered. "Just look at him. Yes," he called out loudly, "We know it's the *Pike*; we saw that from the top of the cliffs. She's coming straight in."

"Yes, it is the *Pike*," exclaimed Audrey. "Aren't you delighted, Mr. Chatfield?"

The agent suddenly turned his big fat face towards the three young people with such an expression of craven fear on it that the jest which Copplestone was about to voice died away on his lips. Chatfield's creased cheeks and heavy jowl had become white as chalk; great beads of sweat rolled down them; his mouth opened and shut silently, and suddenly, as he raised his hands and wrung them, his knees began to quiver. And as they watched him in amazed wonder, his eyes began to search the shore and the cliffs as if he were some hunted animal seeking any hole or cranny in which to hide. A sudden swelling of the light wind brought the steady throb of the oncoming engines to his ears, and he turned on Vickers with a look that made the onlookers start.

"For goodness sake, Mr. Vickers," he said in a strained voice. "Let's get ourselves away! Mr. Vickers, it ain't safe for none of us. We'd best to run, sir. Let's get to the other side of the island. There's caves there—places. Let's hide till something comes from the other islands or till these folks goes away. I tell you it's dangerous for us to stop here!"

"I'm not afraid, Chatfield," replied Vickers. "What ails you? Why man, you couldn't be more afraid if you'd murdered somebody! What do you suppose these people want? You, of course. And you can't escape if they want you; they'll search the island till they get you. You've been deceiving us, Chatfield. There's something you've kept back. Now, what is it? What have they come back for?"

"Yes, Mr. Chatfield, what has the *Pike* come back for?" repeated Audrey, coming nearer. "Come now, hadn't you better tell?"

"It is the *Pike*," remarked Copplestone. "Look there! And they're going to send in a boat. Better be quick, Chatfield."

The agent turned an ashen face towards the yacht. She had swung around and come to a halt, and the rattle of a boat being let down came menacingly to the frightened man's ears. He exhaled a deep groan, and his eyes again sought the cliffs.

"It's not a bit of good, Chatfield," said Vickers. "You can't get away. What are you so frightened for?"

Chatfield moaned and drew haltingly nearer to the other three, as if he found some comfort in their mere presence.

"It's the money," he whispered. "The money as was in the Norcaster Bank—two lots of it. The Squire gave me authority to get out his lot what was standing in his name and the other, the estate lot, that was standing in mine, some fifty thousand pounds in all, Mr. Vickers. I had it all in gold, packed in sealed chests, and those on board there thought I took them chests aboard the *Pike* with me. I did take chests, d'ye see, but they'd lead in 'em. The real stuff is hidden, buried. Never mind where. And I know what they've come back for! They've opened the chests I took on board, and they've found there's naught but lead. And they want me, me, me! They'll torture me to make me tell where the real chests, the money is. Torture me! Oh, keep 'em away from me. Help me to hide. Help me to get away, and I'll tell Miss Greyle then where the money's hid. Oh, they're coming! Mr. Vickers! Mr. Vickers!"

He cast himself bodily at Vickers, but Vickers stepped agilely aside, and Chatfield fell on the sand, where he lay groaning while the others looked from him to each other.

"So that's it, is it, Chatfield?" said Vickers at last. "Trying to cheat everybody all round, eh? I suppose you'd have told Miss Greyle later that these people had collared all that gold, and then you'd have helped yourself to it? And now I know what you were doing on that yacht when we boarded it; you were one of the gang, and you meant to pilfer it with them."

"I didn't!" screamed Chatfield, beating the sand with his hands and feet. "I meant to slip away from 'em at a Scotch port we was to call at, and then—"

"Then you'd have gone back to the hidden chests and helped yourself," said Vickers. "Chatfield, you're a wicked old scoundrel and an unmitigated liar! Give me that paper that Miss Greyle signed, this instant!"

"No," interjected Audrey. "Let him keep it. He'll have trouble enough presently. It's very evident they mean to have him."

Chatfield heard the last few words and looked around at the edge of the surf. The boat had grounded on the beach, and half a dozen men had leapt from it and were coming rapidly up the beach.

"Armed!" exclaimed Copplestone. "There's no chance for you, Chatfield!"

The agent suddenly sprang to his feet with a howl of terror. He gave one more glance at the men, and then he ran, clumsily, but with a speed made desperate by terror. He made straight for the rocks; and at that, two of the men at a word from their leader raised their rifles and fired. And with a shriek that set all the echoes ringing, the sea birds screaming, and made Audrey clap her hands to her ears, Chatfield threw up his arms and dropped heavily on the sands.

"That's sheer murder!" exclaimed Vickers, as the yachtsmen came running up. "You'll answer for that, you know, unless you mean to murder all of us."

The leader touched his cap respectfully and grinned from ear to ear.

"Bless you, sir, we shot twenty feet over his head," he said. "He's too precious to shoot; they want him badly on board there. Now then, men, pick him up and get him into the boat. He'll come round quick enough when he finds he hasn't even a pellet in him. Handy, now! Captain's compliments, sir," he went on, turning again to Vickers and pointing to certain things which were being unloaded from the boat, "and as he understands that no vessel will pass here for two more days, sir, he's sent you further provisions, some more wraps, and some books and papers."

Chapter 24

The Torpedo-Boat Destroyer

Before Vickers and his companions had recovered from the surprise which this extraordinarily cool message had given them, the men had bundled Chatfield across the beach and into the boat and were rowing quickly back to the *Pike*.

Audrey broke the silence with a ringing laugh.

"Captain Andrius is certainly the perfection of polite pirates," she exclaimed. "More food, more wraps, and books and papers! Was any marooned mariner ever half so well treated?"

"What's the fellow mean about no vessel passing here for two more days?" growled Copplestone, who was glaring angrily at the yacht. "What's he so meticulously correct for?"

"I should say that he's referring to some weekly or biweekly steamer which runs between Kirkwall and the mainland," replied Vickers. "Well, it's good to know that, anyhow. We'll wait until the *Pike's* vamoosed again, and we'll make up such a column of smoke that it'll be seen for many a mile. In fact, I'll go and gather a lot of dried stuff now; you two can drag those boxes and things up the beach and see what our jailers have been good enough to send us."

He went away up the cliffs, and Audrey and Copplestone, once more left alone, looked at each other and laughed.

"That's right," said Copplestone. "What I like about you is that you take things that way."

"Is it any use taking them any other way?" she asked. "Besides I've never been at all frightened nor particularly concerned. I've always felt that we were only put here so that we should be out of the way while our captors got safely away with their booty; and as regards my mother, I know her well enough to feel sure that she quickly sized things up, and that she'll have taken measures of her own. Don't be surprised if we're rescued through her means or if she has set somebody to work to catch the predatory *Pike*."

"Good!" said Copplestone. "But as regards the *Pike*, I wonder if you observed something during the few minutes she was here. I'm sure Vickers didn't; he was too busy watching Chatfield."

"So was I," replied Audrey. "What was it?"

"I believe I'm unusually observant," answered Copplestone. "I seem to see things, all at once, don't you know. I saw that since we made her acquaintance and were unceremoniously bundled off her, the *Pike* has got a new and quite different coat of paint. And I daresay she's changed her name too. From all of which I argue that when they got rid of us here, the people who are working all this slipped quietly back to some cove or creek on the Scotch coast, did the repainting, and meant to sail off to the other side of the world under new colors. And while this painting was going on, Andrius, or his co-villain, found time to examine those chests that Chatfield told us of; and when they found that Chatfield had duped them, they came back here quick. Now they're off to make him reveal the whereabouts of the real chests."

"Won't they be rather running their necks into a noose?" suggested Audrey. "I'm dead certain that my mother will have raised a hue and cry after them."

"They're smart enough," said Copplestone. "But they'll run a good many risks for the sake of fifty thousand pounds. Perhaps they will sail into some very quiet inlet—there are hundreds on these northern coasts—and take Chatfield to his hiding place. Chatfield's like all scoundrels of his type, a horrible coward if a pistol's held to his head. Now that they've got him, they'll force him to disgorge. This compulsory inactivity will do me in! My nerves are all a-tingle to get going at things!"

"Let's occupy ourselves with the things our generous jailers have been kind enough to send us then," suggested Audrey. "We'd better carry them up to our shelter."

The boat's crew had deposited on the beach a couple of small packing cases, a bundle of wraps and cushions, and some books, magazines, and newspapers. Copplestone picked up a paper with a cry which suggested a discovery of importance.

"Look at that!" he exclaimed. "Do you see? A *Scotsman*. Today's date. And here, *Aberdeen Free Press*. Same date."

"Well?" asked Audrey. "So what then?"

"What then?" demanded Copplestone. "Where are your powers of deduction? Why, that shows that the *Pike* was somewhere this morning where she could get the morning papers from Aberdeen and Edinburgh; therefore, she's been, as I suggested, somewhere on the Scotch coast all night. It's now noon; she's a fast sailer. I guess she's been within sixty miles of us ever since she left us."

"Isn't it more pertinent to speculate on where she'll be when we want to find her?" asked Audrey.

"More pertinent still to wonder when somebody will come to find us," answered Copplestone as he shouldered one of the cases. "However, there's a certain joy in uncertainty, so they say."

The joys of uncertainty, however, were not to endure. They had scarcely completed the task of carrying up the newly-arrived stores to their shelter in an angle of the rocks when Vickers hailed them from the cliffs and waved his arms excitedly.

"I say, you two!" he shouted. "There's a craft coming from the south-west. Come up! There!" he added, a few minutes later, when they arrived, breathless, at his side. "Out yonder. A mere black blot, but unmistakable. Do you know what that is, either of you? I do. I ought to, because I'm a Royal Navy Volunteer Reserve man myself. That's a torpedo-boat destroyer, my friends. A torpedo-boat destroyer. What's more, far off as she is, my experienced eye and sure knowledge tell me exactly what she is. She's a class H boat built last year. Oil fuel. Turbines. Runs up to thirty knots, and she's doing 'em, too, just now! Come on, Copplestone, more stuff on this fire!"

"I don't think we need be uneasy," said Copplestone. "Miss Greyle thinks that her mother will have raised a hue and cry after the *Pike*. This torpedo thing is probably looking round for us. She—what's that?"

The sudden sharp crack of a gun came across the calm surface of the sea, and the watchers turning from their fire towards the black object in the distance saw a cloud of white smoke drifting away from it.

"Hooray!" shouted Vickers. "She's seen our smoke pillar! Shove more on, just to let her know we understand. Saved! This time anyway."

Half an hour later, a spick-and-span and youthful-looking naval lieutenant raised his cap to the three folk who stood eagerly awaiting his approach at the edge of the surf.

"Miss Greyle? Mr. Vickers? Mr. Copplestone?" he asked as he sprang from his boat and came up. "Right! We're searching for you. Had wireless messages this morning. Where's the pirate, or whatever he is?"

"Somewhere away to the southward," answered Vickers, pointing into the haze. "He was here two hours ago, but he's about as fast as they make 'em, and he's good reason to show a clean pair of heels. However, we've ample grounds for believing him to have gone due south again. Where are you from?"

"Got the message off Dunnett Head, and we'll run you to Thurso," replied the rescuer, motioning them to enter the boat. "Come on. Our commander's got some word or other for you. What's all this been?" he went on, gazing at Audrey as they moved away from the shore. "You don't mean to say you've actually been kidnapped?"

"Kidnapped and marooned," replied Vickers. "And I hope you'll catch our kidnapper. He's got a tremendous amount of property on him which belongs to this lady, and he'll make tracks for the other side of the Atlantic as soon as he gets hold of some more, which he's gone to collect."

The lieutenant regarded Audrey with still more interest. "All right," he said confidently. "He'll not get away. I guess they've sent messages all over the place. Ours came from the Admiralty!"

"That's Sir Cresswell's doing," said Copplestone, turning to Audrey. "Your mother must have wired to him. I wonder what the message is?" he asked, facing the lieutenant. "Do you know?"

"Something about if you're found to tell you to get south as fast as possible," he answered. "And we've worked that out for you. You can get on by train from Thurso to Inverness, and from Inverness, of course, you'll get the southern express. We'll put you off at Thurso by two o'clock, just time to give you such lunch as our table affords. A bit rough, you know. So you've really been all night on that island?" he went on with unaffected curiosity. "What a lark!"

"You'd have had an opportunity of studying character if you'd been with us," replied Vickers. "We lost a fine specimen of humanity two hours ago."

"Tell about it aboard," said the lieutenant. "We'll be thankful; we've been round this endless coast for a month, and we're tired. It's quite a boon to have a little adventure."

Copplestone had been right in surmising that Sir Cresswell Oliver had bestirred himself to find him and his companions. They were presently shown his message. They were to get to Norcaster as quickly as possible and to wire their whereabouts as soon as they were found. If, as seemed likely, they were picked up on the north coast of Scotland, they were to ask at Inverness railway station for telegrams. And, after being landed at Thurso, to Inverness they took themselves, while the torpedo-boat destroyer set off to nose around for the *Pike*, in case she came that way back from wherever she had gone to.

Copplestone came out of the station master's office at Inverness with a couple of telegrams and read their contents to his companions in the dining room to which they adjourned.

"This is from Mrs. Greyle," he said. " 'All right and much relieved by wire from Thurso. Bring Audrey home as quick as possible.' That's good! And this from Gilling. Listen. 'Just heard from Petherton of your rescue. Come straight and sharp to Norcaster. Meet me at the Angel. Big things afoot. Spurge most anxious see you. Important news. Gilling.' So things have been going on," he concluded, turning the second telegram over to Vickers. "I suppose we'll have to travel all night?"

"Night express in an hour," replied Vickers. "We shall make Norcaster about five-thirty tomorrow morning."

"Then let us wire the time of our arrival to Gilling. I'm anxious to know what has brought him up there," said Copplestone. "And we'll wire your mother too," he added, turning to Audrey. "She'll know then that you're absolutely on the way."

"I wonder what we're on the way to?" remarked Vickers with a grim smile. "It strikes me that our recent alarms and excursions will have been almost nothing compared to what awaits us at Norcaster."

What did await them on a cold, dismal morning at Norcaster was Gilling, stamping up and down a windswept platform. And Gilling seized on Copplestone almost before he could alight from the train.

"Come to the Angel straight off!" he said. "Mrs. Greyle's there awaiting her daughter. That chap Spurge is somewhere about the Angel too; been hanging round there since yesterday, heavy with news that he'll give to nobody but you."

Chapter 25

The Squire

A night porter, a waiter, and a chambermaid were up and about at the Angel hotel that gray morning, and each wondered why the two old gentlemen who had arrived from London the day before should rise from their beds to hold a secret and mysterious conference with the three young ones who, with a charming if tired-looking young lady, drove up before the city clocks had struck six. But Sir Cresswell Oliver and Mr. Petherton knew that there was no time to be lost, and as soon as Audrey had been restored her mother's room, they summoned Vickers and Copplestone to a private parlor and demanded their latest news. Sir Cresswell listened eagerly and in silence, until Copplestone described the return of the *Pike*; at that he broke his silence.

"That's precisely what I feared!" he exclaimed. "If she's been hurriedly repainted and renamed, she stands a fair chance of getting away. Our instructions to the patrol boats up there are to look for a certain vessel, the *Pike*. Naturally they won't look for anything else. We must get the wireless to work at once."

"But there's this," said Copplestone. "They certainly captured old Chatfield to make him hand over the gold, and they won't go away without that. He said that he'd hidden the gold somewhere near Scarhaven. Therefore, they'll have to come down this coast to get it."

"Not necessarily," replied Sir Cresswell with a knowing shake of the head. "You may be sure they're alive to all the possibilities of the situation. They could do several things once they'd got Chatfield on board again. Some of them could land with him at some convenient port and make him take them to where he's hidden the money; they could recapture that and go off to some other port to which the yacht had meanwhile been brought round. If we only knew where Chatfield had planted that money."

"He said near Scarhaven, unmistakably," remarked Vickers.

"Near Scarhaven," repeated Sir Cresswell, laughing dismally. "That's a wide term, a very wide one. Behind Scarhaven, as you all know, are hills and moors and valleys and ravines in which one could hide a battleship! Well, all I can think of is getting into communication with patrol boats and coast guard stations all along the coast between here and Wick. And that mayn't be the least good. Somebody may have escorted Chatfield ashore after they left you yesterday, brought him hereabouts by rail or motor car, and the yacht may have already made a wide detour round the Shetlands and now be well on her way to the North Atlantic."

"But in that case, the money?" asked Copplestone.

"They would get hold of the money, take it clean away, and ship it from Liverpool, or Glasgow, or anywhere," replied Sir Cresswell. "You may be sure they've plenty of resources at their command, and that they'll work secretly. Of course, we must keep a lookout round about here for any sign or reappearance of Chatfield; but, as I say, this country is so wild that he and his companions can easily elude observation, especially as they're sure to come by night. We must do what we can and at once. But first, there are one or two things I want to ask you young men. You said, Mr. Vickers, that Chatfield solemnly insisted to you that he did not know that the man who had posed as Marston Greyle was not Marston Greyle?"

"He did," replied Vickers, "and though Chatfield is an unmitigated old scoundrel, I believe him."

"You do?" exclaimed Gilling, who was listening eagerly. "Oh, come!"

"I do . . . as a professional man," answered Vickers, stoutly, and with an appealing glance at his fellow solicitor. "Mr. Petherton will tell you that we lawyers have a curious gift of intuition. With all Chatfield's badness, I do really believe that the old fellow does not know whether the man we'll call the Squire is Marston Greyle or not! He's doubtful; he's puzzled, but he doesn't know."

"Odd," murmured Sir Cresswell, after a minute's silence. "Odd. Very, very odd. That shows that there's still some extraordinary mystery about this which we haven't even guessed at. Well, now, another question. You got the idea that someone else was aboard the yacht?"

"Someone other than Andrius in authority, yes," answered Vickers. "We certainly thought that."

"Did you think it was the Squire?" asked Sir Cresswell.

"We had a notion that he might be there," replied Vickers, with a glance at Copplestone. "Especially after what happened to Chatfield. Of course, we never saw him, or heard his voice, or saw a sign of him. Still, we fancied."

Sir Cresswell rose from his chair and motioned to Petherton.

"I think you and I, Petherton," he said, "had better complete our grooming for this day, and then give a look in at the authorities here and find out if anything has been learned about the yacht. In the meantime," he added, turning to Vickers and Copplestone, "Gilling can tell you what's been going on in your absence. You'll learn from it that our impression is that the Squire was on the *Pike* with you."

The two elder men went away, and Copplestone turned to Gilling.

"What have you got?" he asked eagerly. "Live news!"

"Might have been livelier and more satisfactory," answered Gilling. "We tracked the Squire."

"You did?" exclaimed Copplestone. "Where?"

"When I said we, I should have said Swallow," continued Gilling. "You remember that afternoon of our return from Bristol, Copplestone? It seems ages away now, though as a matter of time it's only four days ago. Well, that afternoon Swallow, who had two or three more keeping a sharp lookout for the Squire, got a telephone message from one of 'em saying that he'd tracked his man to the Fragonard Club. I'd gone home to my chambers to rest a bit after our adventures at Bristol and Falmouth, so Swallow had to act on his own. He set off for the Fragonard Club, and outside it met his contact. This particular man had been keeping a watch for days on that tobacconist's shop in Wardour Street. That afternoon he suddenly saw the Squire leave it by a side door. He followed him to the

Fragonard Club, watched him enter; then he himself turned into a neighboring bar and telephoned to Swallow. The Squire was still in the Fragonard when Swallow got there. From that time he kept a watch. The Squire remained in the Club for an hour—"

"Which proves," interrupted Copplestone, "that he's a member, and that I ought to have followed up my attempt to get in there."

"Well, anyway," continued Gilling, "there he was, and thence he eventually emerged with a knapsack. He got into a taxi, and Swallow heard him order its driver to go to King's Cross. Now Swallow was there alone, and he had just before that sent his man scooting round to see if there was a rear exit from the Fragonard, and he hadn't returned. Swallow, of course, couldn't wait; every minute was precious. He followed the Squire to King's Cross and heard him book for Northborough."

"Northborough!" exclaimed Copplestone in surprise. "Not Norcaster? Ah, well, Northborough's a port, too, isn't it?"

"Northborough is as near to Scarhaven as Norcaster is, you know," said Gilling. "To Northborough he booked anyhow. So did Swallow, who, now that he'd got him, was going to follow him to the North Pole, if need be. The train was just starting; Swallow had no time to communicate with me. The train didn't stop until it reached Grantham. There he sent me a wire, saying he was on the track of his man. Well, they went on to Northborough, where they arrived late in the evening. There—what is it, Copplestone?" he broke off, seeing signs of a desire to speak on Copplestone's part.

"You're talking of the very same afternoon and evening that I came down, four evenings ago," said Copplestone. "My train was the four o'clock. I got to Norcaster at ten. Surely they didn't come on the same train?"

"I feel sure they did, but these trains to the north are usually very long ones, and you were probably in a different part," replied Gilling. "Anyway, they got to Northborough soon after nine. Swallow followed his man on to the platform out to some taxi cabs, and heard him commission one of the chauffeurs to take him to Scarhaven. When they'd gone, Swallow got hold of another taxi and told its driver to take him to Scarhaven too. Off they went in a pitch-black night, I'm told."

"We know that," said Vickers with a glance at Copplestone. "We motored from Norcaster just about the same time."

"Well," continued Gilling, "it was at any rate so dark that Swallow's driver, who appears to have been a very nervous chap, made very poor progress. He also took one or two wrong turns. Finally he ran his car into a guide post which stood where two roads forked, and there Swallow was stuck, scarcely halfway to Scarhaven. They couldn't get the car to move, and it was some time before Swallow could persuade the landlord at the nearest inn to hire out a horse and carriage to him. Altogether, it was near or just past midnight when he reached Scarhaven; and when he did get there, it was to see the lights of a steamer going out of the bay."

"The *Pike*, of course," muttered Copplestone.

"Of course, and some men on the quay told him," continued Gilling. "Well, that put Swallow in a fix. He was dead certain, of course, that his man was on that yacht. However, he didn't want to rouse suspicion, so he didn't ask any of those quayside men if they'd seen the Squire. Instead, remembering what I'd told him about Mrs. Greyle, he asked for her house and was directed to it. He found Mrs. Greyle in a state of great anxiety. Her daughter had gone with you two to the yacht and had never returned; Mrs. Greyle, watching from her windows, had seen the yacht go out to sea and was seriously alarmed. Of course, he told her what he had come down for and they consulted. Next morning—"

"Stop a bit," interrupted Vickers. "Didn't Mrs. Greyle get any message from the yacht about her daughter? Andrius said he'd sent one."

"A lie," replied Gilling. "She got no message. The only consolation she had was that you and Copplestone were with Miss Greyle. Well, first thing next morning Swallow and Mrs. Greyle set every possible means to work. They went to the police; they wired to places up the coast and down the coast to keep a lookout; Swallow also wired full particulars to Sir Cresswell Oliver, with the result that Sir Cresswell went to the naval authorities and got them to set their craft up north to work. Having done all this and finding that he could be of no more service at Scarhaven, Swallow returned to town to see me and to consult. Now we were in a position to approach that Fragonard Club."

"Ah!" exclaimed Copplestone. "Just so!"

"The man, whoever he is, had been there an hour on the day Swallow and his man tracked him," continued Gilling. "Therefore, something must be known of him. Swallow and I went there, but we could find out next to nothing. The hall porter there said he dimly remembered such a gentleman coming in and going upstairs, but he himself was new to his job and didn't know all the members as there are hundreds of 'em. He took this man for a regular guest. A waiter also had some sort of recollection of the man, seeing him in conversation with another man whom he, the waiter, knew better, though he didn't know his name. Swallow is now moving everything to find anybody who knows our man. Something will come of it in the end. It must. In the meantime I came down here with Sir Cresswell and Mr. Petherton to be on the spot. And from your information, things will happen here! That hidden gold is the thing; they'll not leave that without an effort to get it. If we could only find out where that is and watch it, then our present object would be achieved."

"What is the present object?" asked Copplestone.

"Why," replied Gilling, "we've got warrants out against both Chatfield and the Squire for the murder of Bassett Oliver! The police here have them in hand. Petherton's seen to that. And if they can only be laid hands on—What is it?" he asked, turning to a sleepy-eyed waiter who, after a gentle tap at the door, put a shaggy head into the room. "Somebody want me?"

"That there man, sir, you know," said the waiter. "Here again, sir. Stable yard, sir."

Gilling jumped up and gave Copplestone a look.

"Spurge," he muttered. "He said he'd be back at daybreak. Wait here. I'll fetch him."

Chapter 26

The Reaver's Glen

G illing ushered in Zachary Spurge, who carefully closed the door behind them both looking as if his recent lodging had been of an even rougher nature than that in which Copplestone had found him at their first meeting. The rough horseman's cloak buttoned to the edge of a red neckerchief beneath a stubbly chin was liberally ornamented with bits of straw, scraps of furze, and other odds and ends picked up in woods and hedgerows. Spurge bore unmistakable evidence of having slept out in wild places for some nights, and his general appearance was little more respectable than that of a scarecrow. But he grinned cheerfully at Copplestone, and then frowned at Vickers.

"I didn't count on meeting no lawyers, gentlemen," he said, pausing on the outer boundaries of the parlor, "I ain't a-goin' to talk before 'em neither!"

"He's got a grudge against me. I've had to appear against him once or twice," whispered Vickers to Copplestone. "Soothe him down. I want to know what he's got to tell."

"It's all right, Spurge," said Copplestone. "Come. Mr. Vickers is on our side this time; he's one of us. You can say anything you like before either him or Mr. Gilling. We're all in it. Pull your chair up here alongside of me, and tell us what you've been doing."

"Well, of course, if you puts it that way, Mr. Copplestone," replied Spurge, coming to the table a little doubtfully. "Though I hadn't meant to tell nobody but you what I've got to tell. However, I can see that this here ain't no one-man job; it's a job as'll want a lot o' men! No offense to you, Mr. Vickers, only you see I've had experience o' your sort before. But if you are taking a hand in this here, well, all right. But now, gentlemen," he continued, dropping into a chair at the table and laying his fur cap on its polished surface, "afore ever I says a word, d'ye think that I could be provided with a cup o' hot coffee or tea? I'm cold and starved. If you'd been where I been this last twelve hours or so, you'd be perished."

The sleepy waiter was summoned to attend to Spurge's wants, and until they were satisfied, the poacher sat staring fixedly at his cap and occasionally shaking his head. But after a first hearty gulp of strong coffee, the color came back into his face; he sighed with relief and signaled to the three watchful young men to draw their chairs close to his.

"Ah!" he said, setting down his cup. "And nobody never wanted aught more badly than I wanted that! And now then, the door being shut on us quite safe, ain't it, gentlemen? No eavesdroppers? Well, this here it is. I don't know what you've been a-doing of these last few days, nor what may have happened to each and all, but *I've* news. Serious news as I reckons it to be. Of Chatfield!"

Copplestone kicked Vickers under the table and gave him a look.

"Chatfield again," he murmured. "Go on, Spurge."

"There's a lot to go on with, guv'nor," said Spurge, after taking another evidently welcome drink. "I'll try to put it all in order, as it were, same as if I was in a witness box," he added with a sly glance at Vickers. "You remember that day of the inquest on the actor gentleman, guv'nor? Well, of course, when I went to give evidence at Scarhaven at that there inquest, I never expected but what the police 'ud collar me at the end of it. However, I didn't mean that they should if I could help it, so I watched things pretty close, intending to slip off when I saw a chance. You'll recollect that there was a bit of a dustup when the thing was over; some of 'em cheering the Squire and some of 'em grousing about the verdict, and between one and t'other I popped out and off, and you yourself saw me making for the moors. Me knowing them moors back o' Scarhaven as I do, it was easy work to make myself scarce on 'em in ten minutes. Not all the police north o' the Tees could ha' found me a quarter of an hour after I'd hooked it out o' that schoolroom! But the thing then was . . . where to go next? 'Twasn't no good going to Hobkin's Hole again. Now that them chaps knew I was in the neighborhood, they'd soon ha' smoked me out o' there. I thought of making for Norcaster here and going into hiding down by the docks. I've one or two harbors o' refuge there. But I had reasons for wishing to stop in my own country, for a bit at any rate. And so, after reckoning things up, I made for a spot as Mr. Vickers there'll know by name of the Reaver's Glen."

"Good place for hiding," remarked Vickers with a nod.

"Best place on this coast, seashore and inland," said Spurge. "And as you two London gentlemen doesn't know it, I'll tell you about it. If you was to go out o' Scarhaven harbor and turn north, you'd sail along our coast line up here to the mouth of Norcaster Bay, and you'd think there was never an inlet between 'em. But there is. About half-way between Scarhaven and Norcaster there's a very narrow opening in the cliffs, and inside that opening there's a cove that's big enough to take a thousand-ton vessel. It was a favorite place for smugglers in the old days, and they call it Darkman's Dene to this day in memory of a famous old smuggler that used it a good deal. Well, now, at the land end of that cove there's a narrow valley that runs up to the moorland and the hills, full o' rocks and crags and precipices and such like, something o' the same sort as Hobkin's Hole but a deal wilder. That's known as the Reaver's Glen, because in other days the cattle lifters used to bring their stolen cattle down there where they could pen 'em in, as it were. There's piles o' places in that glen where a man can hide. I picked out one right at the top at the edge of the moors, where there's the ruins of an old peel tower. I could get shelter in that old tower, and at the same time slip out of it if need be into one of fifty likely hiding places amongst the rocks. I got into touch with my cousin Jim Spurge that night, and I got in a supply of meat and drink, and there I was. And as things turned out, Chatfield had got his eye on the very same spot!"

Spurge paused for a minute, and picking out a match from a stand which stood on the table, began to trace imaginary lines on the mahogany.

"This is how things is there," he said, inviting his companions' attention. "Here, like, is where this peel tower stands. That's a thick wood as comes close up to its walls; that there is a road as crosses the moors and the wood about, maybe a hundred yards or so behind the tower on the land side. Now, there, one afternoon as I was in that there tower, a-reading of a newspaper that Jim had brought me the night before, I hears wheels on that moorland road. And I looked out through a convenient peephole, and who should I see but Peter Chatfield in that old pony trap of his. He was coming along from the direction of Scarhaven, and when he got abreast of the tower he pulled up, got out, left his pony to crop the grass, and came strolling over in my direction. Of course, I wasn't afraid of him. There's as many ways in and out of that old peel as there is out of a rabbit warren. Besides, I felt certain he was there on some job of his own. Well, he comes up to the edge of the glen, and he looks into it and round it, and up and down at the tower, and he wanders about the heaps of fallen masonry that there is there, and finally he went slowly back to his trap. 'But you'll be coming back, my old swindler!' says I to myself. 'You'll be back again, I doubt not at all!' And back he did come. That very night. Oh, yes!"

"Alone?" asked Copplestone.

"A-lone!" replied Spurge. "It had got to be dark, and I was thinking of going to sleep, having nought else to do and not expecting cousin Jim that night, when I heard the sound of horses' feet and of wheels. So I cleared out of my hole to where I could see better. Of course, it was Chatfield, same old trap and pony, but this time he came from Norcaster way. Well, he gets out, just where he'd got out before, and he leads the pony and trap across the moor to close by the tower. I could tell by the way that trap went over the grass that there was some sort of a load in it, and it wouldn't have surprised me, gentlemen, if the old reptile had pulled a dead body out of it. After a bit I hear him taking something out which he bumped down on the ground with a thump. I counted nine o' them thumps. And then after a bit I heard him begin a moving some of the loose masonry what lies in such heaps at the foot o' the peel tower. Dark though it was, there was light enough in the sky for him to see to do that. But after he'd been at it sometime, puffing and groaning and grunting, he evidently wanted to see better, and he suddenly flashed a light on things from one o' them electric torches. And then I see—me being not so many yards away from him—nine small white wood boxes, all clamped with metal bands, lying in a row on the grass. And I see, too, that Chatfield had been making a place for 'em amongst the stones. That was it, nine small white wood boxes; so small, considering, that I wondered what made 'em so heavy."

Copplestone favored Vickers with another quiet kick. They were, without doubt, hearing the story of the hidden gold.

"Well," continued Spurge. "Into the place he'd cleared out, them boxes went; and once they were all in, he heaped the stones over 'em as natural as they were before, and he kicked a lot o' small loose stones round about and over the place where he'd been standing. And then the old sinner let out a great groan as if something troubled him, gentlemen, and he wiped his forehead with his handkerchief and groaned again. He'd had his light on all that time, but he doused it then; and after that he led the old pony away across the bit of moor to the road, and presently in he gets and drives slowly away towards Scarhaven. And so there was I, d'ye see, Mr. Copplestone, left, as it were, sole guardian of . . . what?"

The three young men exchanged glances with each other while Spurge refreshed himself with his coffee, and their eyes asked similar questions.

"You don't know what, Spurge?" observed Copplestone at last. "You haven't examined one of those boxes?"

Spurge set his cup down and gave his questioner a knowing look.

"I'll tell you my line o' conduct, guv'nor," he said. "So certain sure have I been that something 'ud come o' this business of hiding them boxes and that something valuable is in 'em that I've taken partiklar care ever since Chatfield planted 'em there that night never to set foot within a dozen yards of 'em. Why? Cause I know he'll ha' left footprints of his own there, and them footprints may be useful.

No, sir! Them boxes has been guarded careful ever since Chatfield placed 'em where he did. For Chatfield's never been back!"

"Never back, eh?" said Copplestone, winking at the other two.

"Never been back, self nor spirit, substance nor shadow, since that night," replied Spurge. "Unless he's been back since four o'clock this morning when I left there. However, if he's been 'twixt then and now, my cousin Jim Spurge, he was there. Jim's been helping me to watch. When I first came in here to see if I could hear anything about you, Jim having told me that some London gentlemen was up here again, I left him in charge. And there he is now. And now you know all I can tell you, gentlemen, and as I understand there's some mystery about Chatfield and that he's disappeared, happen you'll know how to put two and two together. And if I'm of any use—"

"Spurge," said Gilling. "How far is it to this Reaver's Glen or rather to that peel tower?"

"Matter of eight or nine miles, guv'nor, over the moors," replied Spurge.

"How did you come in then?" asked Gilling.

"Cousin Jim Spurge's bike, down in the stable yard now," answered Spurge. "Did it comfortable in under the hour."

"I think we ought to go out there, some of us," said Gilling. "We ought—"

At that moment the door opened and Sir Cresswell Oliver came in, holding a bit of flimsy paper in his hand. He glanced at Spurge and then beckoned the three young men to join him.

"I've had a message from the North Sea. It puzzles me," he said. "One of our ships up there has had news from a fishing vessel of what is surely the *Pike*. She was seen late yesterday afternoon going due east. Due east, mind you! If that was she—and I'm sure of it— our quarry's escaping us."

Chapter 27

The Peel Tower

G illing took the message from Sir Cresswell and read it over.
Then he handed it back and motioned the old seaman to look
at Spurge.

"I think you ought to know what this man has just told us, sir,"
he said. "We've got a story from him that fits exactly with what
Chatfield told Mr. Vickers when the *Pike* returned to carry him off
yesterday. Chatfield, you'll remember, said that the gold he'd withdrawn from the bank is hidden somewhere. There's no doubt that
this man Zachary Spurge knows where it is hidden. It's there now,
and the presumption is that these people on the *Pike* will certainly
come into this coast, somehow, to get it. Eh?"

"That's valuable!" said Sir Cresswell, glancing again at Spurge
and with awakened interest. "Let me hear this story."

Copplestone summarized Spurge's account, while the poacher
listened admiringly, checking off the main points and adding a word
or two where he considered the summary lacking.

"Very smart of you, my man," remarked Sir Cresswell, nodding
benevolently at Spurge when the story was over. "You're in a fair way
to find yourself well rewarded. Now gentlemen," he continued, sitting down at the table, and engaging the attention of the others, "I
think we had better have a council of war. Petherton has just gone
to speak to the police authorities about those warrants which have
been taken out against Chatfield and the impostor, but we can go
on in his absence. Now there seems to be no doubt that those chests
which Spurge tells us of contain the gold which Chatfield procured
from the bank and concerning which he seems to have played his
associates more tricks than one. However, his associates, whoever

they are, have now got a tight grip on Chatfield, and they'll force him to show them where that gold is. They'll certainly not give up fifty thousand pounds without a stiff try to get it. So considering all the possibilities and probabilities, we may conclude that sooner or later, somebody will visit this old peel tower that Spurge talks of. But who? And we're faced with this wireless message. I've no doubt the vessel referred to here is the *Pike*; no doubt at all. She was seen making due east near late last night so that it would look as if these men were making for Denmark, or Germany, rather than for this coast. But since receiving this message, I have thought that point out. The *Pike* is a very fast vessel?"

"Very," answered Vickers. "She can do twenty-seven or eight knots an hour."

"Exactly," said Sir Cresswell. "Then in that case they may have put in at some northern port, landed Chatfield and two or three men to keep an eye on him and to accompany him to this old tower, while the *Pike* herself has gone off till a more fitting opportunity arises of dodging in somewhere to pick up the chests which Chatfield and his party will in the meantime have recovered. From what I have seen of it, this is such a wild part of the coast that Chatfield and such a small gang as I am imagining could easily come back here, keep themselves hidden, and recover the chests without observation. So our plain duty is to now devise some plan for going to the Reaver's Glen and keeping a watch there until somebody comes. Eh?"

"There's another thing that's possible, sir," said Vickers, who had listened carefully to all that Sir Cresswell had said. "The *Pike* is fitted for wireless telegraphy."

"And?" said Sir Cresswell expectantly.

"You suggested that there may be more people than Chatfield and the Squire in at this business," continued Vickers. "Just so! We, Copplestone and myself, know very well that the skipper of the *Pike*, Andrius, is in it. That's undeniable. But there may be others, one or two, on shore here. Since the *Pike* can communicate by wireless, those on board her may have sent a message to their shore confederates to remove those chests."

"Capital suggestion," said Sir Cresswell, who saw his point at once. "So we'd better lose no time in arranging our expedition out there. Spurge, you're the man who knows the spot best. What ought we to do about getting there in force?"

Spurge, obviously flattered at being called upon to advise the great man, entered into the discussion with enthusiasm.

"Your honor mustn't go in force at all," he said. "What's wanted, gentlemen, is strategy! Now if you'll let me put it to you, me knowing the lie of the land, this is what had ought to be done. A small party ought to go with me to lead. We'll follow the road that cuts across the moorland to a certain point; then we'll take a by-track that gets you to High Nick; there we'll take to a thick bit o' wood that runs right up to the peel tower. Nobody'll track us nor see us from any point going that way. Three or four of us, these here young gentlemen, now, and me'll be enough for the job if armed. A revolver apiece, your honor. That'll be plenty. And as for the rest, what you might call a reserve force, your honor said something just now about some warrants. Is the police to be in at it then?"

"The police hold warrants for the two men we've been chiefly talking about," replied Sir Cresswell.

"Well, let your honor come on a bit later with not more than three police plainclothes fellows as far as High Nick," said Spurge. "The police'll know where that is. Let 'em wait there. Don't let 'em come further until I send back a message by my cousin Jim. You see, guv'nor," he added, turning to Copplestone, whom he seemed to regard as his own special associate, "we don't know how things may be. We might have to wait hours. As I view it, me having listened careful to what his honor the admiral there says—best respects to your honor—them chaps'll never come a-nigh that place till it's night again, or at any rate, dusk, which'll be about seven o'clock this evening. But they may watch during the day, and it 'ud be a foolish thing to have a lot of men about. A small force such as I can hide in that wood and another in reserve at High Nick, that's the ticket!"

"Spurge is right," said Sir Cresswell. "You youngsters go with him. Get a motor car, and I'll see about following you over to High Nick with the detectives. Now what about being armed?"

"I've a supply of service revolvers at my office down this very street," replied Vickers. "I'll go and get them. Let's apportion our duties. I'll see to the weapons. Gilling, you see about the car. Copplestone, you order some breakfast for us sharp."

"And I'll go round to the police," said Sir Cresswell. "Now be careful to take care of yourselves. You don't know what you've got to deal with, remember."

The group separated, and Copplestone went off to find the hotel people and order an immediate breakfast. Passing along a corridor on his way downstairs he encountered Mrs. Greyle, who came out of a room nearby and started at sight of him.

"Audrey is asleep," she whispered, pointing to the door she had just left. "Thank you for taking care of her. Of course I was afraid, but that's all over now. How are things now?"

"Coming to a head in my opinion," answered Copplestone. "But how or in what way, I don't know. Anyway, we know where that gold is, and they'll make an attempt on it. That's sure! So we shall be there."

"But what fools Peter Chatfield and his associates must be, from their own villainous standpoint, to have encumbered themselves with all that weight of gold!" exclaimed Mrs. Greyle. "The folly of it seems incredible when they could have taken it in some more easily portable form."

"Ah," laughed Copplestone. "But that just shows Chatfield's extraordinary craft. He no doubt persuaded his associates that it was better to have actual bullion where they were going and tricked them into believing that he'd actually put it aboard the *Pike*. If it hadn't been that they examined those boxes and found they contained lead or bricks, the old scoundrel would have collared the real stuff for himself."

"Take care that he doesn't collar it yet," said Mrs. Greyle with a laugh as she went into her own room. "Chatfield is resourceful enough for anything. And take care of yourselves!"

That was the second admonition to be careful, and Copplestone thought of both an hour later, as he, Gilling, Vickers, and Spurge sped along the desolate, wind-swept moorland on their way to the Reaver's Glen. It was a typical North Country autumnal morning, cold, raw, and rainy. The tops of the neighboring hills were capped with dark clouds; sea birds called dismally across the heather; and the sea looked angry and threatening.

"A fit morning for a duty of this sort!" exclaimed Gilling suddenly. "Is it pretty bare and bleak at this tower of yours, Spurge?"

"You'll be warm enough where I shall put you, guv'nor," answered Spurge. "One as has knocked about these woods and moors as much as I've had to knows as many places to hide his nose in as a fox does. I'll put you by that tower where you'll be snug enough, and where nobody'll see you neither. Well, here's High Nick, so out we get."

Exiting the car deep in the hills and instructing the driver to await the return of one or other of them at a wayside farmstead a mile back, the three adventurers followed Spurge into the wood which led to the top of the Reaver's Glen. The poacher guided them onward by narrow and winding tracks through the undergrowth for a good half-mile; then he led them through thickets where there were no paths at all; finally, after a gradual and cautious advance, he halted them at a corner of the wood and motioned them to look out through a loosely laced network of branches.

"Here we are," he whispered. "Tower. Reaver's Glen. Sea in the distance. Lone spot, ain't it, gentlemen?"

Copplestone and Gilling, who had never seen this part of the coast before, looked out on the scene with lively interest. It was a wild, almost savage beauty on which they gazed. Immediately in front of them at a distance of twenty to thirty yards stood the old peel tower; it was a solid square mass of gray stone, intact from its base to its middle stories, and crumbling from there up to what was left of its battlements. The turret tower stood at one side with fallen stone in irregular heaps on the ground at its foot; all around it were clumps of furze and bramble. From there the glen fell away in horse-shoe formation, gradually narrowing and descending, until it termi-nated in a thicket of pine that ran down to the land end of the cove of which Spurge had told them. The wide expanse of sea stretched beyond the cove with here and there a red-sailed fishing boat tossing on the white-capped waves. Over the sea and the land was a chill silence, broken only by the occasional cry of the sea birds and the bleating of the mountain sheep.

"A lone spot indeed," said Gilling in a whisper. "Spurge, where is that stuff hidden?"

"Other side of the tower . . . in the old courtyard," replied Spurge, "Can't see the spot from here."

"And where's that road you told us about?" asked Copplestone. "The moor road?"

"Top o' the bank yonder. Beyond the tower," said Spurge. "Runs round yonder corner o' this wood and goes right round it to High Nick, where we've cut across from. Hush now, all of you, gentlemen. I'm going to signal Jim."

Screwing up his face into a strange contortion, Spurge emitted from his puckered lips an outlandish cry, a cry as of some trapped animal, shrill and realistic.

"What on earth is that?" asked Gilling. "It's bloodcurdling!"

"Hare with a stoat's teeth in its neck," answered Spurge. "H'sh. I'll call him again."

No answer came to the first nor to the second summons. After a third, equally unproductive signal cry, Spurge looked at his compan-ions with a scared face.

"That's a curious thing, guv'nors," he muttered. "Can't believe as how our Jim 'ud ever desert a post. He promised me faithfully as how he'd stick here like grim death until I came back. I hope he ain't had a fit nor aught o' that sort. He ain't a strong chap at the best o' times."

"You'd better take a careful look round, Spurge," said Vickers. "Here, shall I come with you?"

But Spurge waved a hand to them to stay where they were. He himself crept along the back of a hedge until he came to a point opposite the nearest angle of the tower. And suddenly he gave a great cry, human enough this time! The three young men rushing forward found him standing by the body of a roughly clad man; Copplestone recognized the one-eyed odd-job man of the Admiral's Arms.

Chapter 28

The Footprints

The man was lying face down in the weeds which clustered thickly at the foot of the hedgerow. On the rough, weather-beaten neck which showed between his fur cap and his turned-up collar, there was a patch of dried blood. Very still and apparently lifeless he looked, but Vickers suddenly bent down, laid strong hands on him, and turned him over.

"He's not dead!" he exclaimed. "Only unconscious from a crack on his skull. Gilling! Where's that brandy you brought? Hand me the flask."

Zachary Spurge watched in silence as Vickers and Gilling busied themselves in reviving the stricken man. Then he quickly pulled Copplestone's sleeve and motioned him away from the group.

"Guv'nor," he muttered, "there's been foul play here and likely to all of them nine boxes, that I'll warrant. Look you here, guv'nor, Jim's been dragged to where we found him, dragged through this here gap in the hedge and flung where he's lying. See? There's plain marks all through the grass and stuff. Let's see where they lead."

The marks of something heavy having been dragged through the wet grass were evident, and Copplestone and Spurge followed them to a corner of the old tower where they ended. Spurge glanced around that corner and uttered a sharp exclamation.

"Just what I expected!" he said. "Leastways, what I expected as soon as I see Jim a-lying there. Guv'nor, the stuff's gone!"

He drew Copplestone after him and pointed to a corner of the weed-grown courtyard where a cavity had been made in the fallen masonry. The stones taken from it lay about, pulled loose and thrown aside.

"That's where the nine boxes were," he continued. "But there ain't one of 'em there now; naught but the hole where they was. This must ha' been during the early morning after I left Jim to go into Norcaster. And of course him as put the stuff there must be him as fetched it away. Chatfield. Let's see if there's footmarks about, guv'nor."

"Wait a bit," said Copplestone. "We'd better do it systematically. Be careful and move warily. There'd have to be some sort of a trap or vehicle to carry away those chests. Where's the nearest point of that road you spoke of?"

"Up there," replied Spurge, pointing to a flanking bank of heather. "But they, or him, wasn't forced to come that way, guv'nor. He could come up from that cove down yonder. It wouldn't surprise me if that there yacht—the *Pike*, you know—had turned on her tracks and come in here during the night. It's not more than a mile from this tower down to the shore."

At that moment Vickers called to them, and they went back to find Jim Spurge slowly opening his eyes and looking around him with consciousness of his company. His one eye lightened a little as he caught sight of Zachary, and the poacher bent down to him.

"Jim, old man," he said soothingly. "How are yer, Jim? Yer been hit by somebody. Who was it, Jim?"

"Give him a drop more to drink, and lift him up a bit," counseled Gilling. "He's improving."

But it needed more than a mere drop of water, more than cousinly pleas to bring the wounded man back to a state of speech. And when at last he managed to make a feeble response, it was only to mutter some incoherent and disjointed sentences about being struck down from behind, after which he again relapsed into semi-unconsciousness.

"That's it guv'nor," muttered Spurge, nudging Copplestone. "That's the ticket! Struck down from behind. That's what happened to him. Unawares, so to speak. I can reckon of it easy. They comes in the darkness after I'd left him here. He hears 'em, as he says, a-moving about. Then he no doubt starts watching 'em as far as he can see. Then one of 'em gives him this crack on the skull, and down he goes! An' then they drag him in here and leaves him. Don't care whether he's a goner or not, not they. An' what does it prove? That there's been more than one of 'em, guv'nor. In my opinion, where they've come from is down there."

He pointed down the glen in the direction of the sea, and the three young men, who were considerably exercised by this sudden turn of events, looked after his outstretched hand and then at each other.

"Well, we can't stand here doing nothing," said Gilling at last. "We'd better divide forces. This chap'll have to be got to some hospital. Vickers, I guess you're the quickest-footed of the lot. Will you run back to High Nick and tell that chauffeur to bring his car round here? If Cresswell and the police are there, tell them what's happened. Spurge, you go down the glen there and see if you can see any suspicious-looking craft in that bay you told us of. Copplestone, we can't do any more for this man just now; let's look round."

When everyone else had departed, they walked on towards the tower. "This is a strange business," said Gilling. "The gold's gone, of course?"

"No sign of it here anyway," answered Copplestone, leading him into the decayed courtyard and pointing to the cavity in the fallen masonry. "That's where it was placed by Chatfield, according to Zachary Spurge."

"And, of course, Chatfield's removed it during the night," remarked Gilling. "That message which Sir Cresswell read us must have been all wrong. The *Pike's* come south, and she may have been in that cove at the end of the glen, though she'll have cleared out of it hours ago." he concluded disappointedly. "We're too late."

"That theory's not necessarily correct," replied Copplestone. "Sir Cresswell's message may have been quite right. For all we know, the folks on the Pike had confederates on shore. Go carefully, Gilling. Let's see if we can make out anything in the way of footprints."

The ground in the courtyard was grassless, a flooring of grit and loose stone on which no impression could well be made by human foot. But Copplestone, carefully prospecting around and going a little way up the bank which lay between the tower and the road, suddenly saw something in the black, peat-like earth which attracted his attention.

"I say!" he called to his companion. "Look at this! There, that's unmistakable enough. And fresh too!"

Gilling bent down, looked, and stared at Copplestone with a question in his eyes.

"A woman?" he said.

"And one who wears fine footwear too," remarked Copplestone. "That's what you'd call a slender and elegant foot. Here it is again, going up the bank. Come on!"

There were more traces of this feminine footgear on the soft earth of the bank which ran between the moorland and the stone-strewn courtyard; more again on the edges of the road itself. There, too, were plain signs that a motor car of some sort had recently been pulled up opposite the tower. Gilling pointed to the indentations made by the wheels as well as traces of oil on the gravelly soil.

"That's evident enough," he said. "Those chests have been fetched away during the night by motor, and a woman's been in at it! Confederates for sure. Now then, the next thing is, which way did that motor go with its contents?"

They followed the tracks for a short distance along the road, until, coming to a place where it widened at a gateway leading into the wood, they saw that the car had been backed and turned. Gilling carefully examined the marks.

"That car came from Norcaster, and it's gone back to Norcaster," he affirmed presently. "Look here! They came up the hill at the side of the wood. Here they backed the car towards that gate, and then ran it backwards till they were abreast of the tower; then, when they'd loaded up with those chests, they went straight off by the way they'd come. Read the tracks. Plain enough."

"Then we'd better get down towards Norcaster ourselves," said Copplestone. "Call Spurge back; he'll find nothing in that cove.

This job has been done from land, and we ought to be on the track of these people. They've had several hours head start already."

By the time Zachary Spurge had been recalled, Vickers had brought the car around from High Nick, and the injured man was carefully lifted into it and driven away. But at High Nick itself they met another car, hurrying up from Norcaster and bringing Sir Cresswell Oliver and three other men who bore the unmistakable stamp of the police force. In one of them Copplestone recognized the inspector from Scarhaven.

The two cars met and stopped alongside each other, and Sir Cresswell, with one sharp glance at the rough bandage around Jim Spurge's head, rapped out a question.

"Gone," replied Gilling with equal brusqueness. "Came in a motor during the night soon after Zachary Spurge left Jim. They hit him pretty hard over his head and left him unconscious. They've carried off the boxes. Car appears to have gone to Norcaster. Hadn't you better turn?"

Sir Cresswell pointed to the Scarhaven police inspector.

"Here's news from Scarhaven," he said, bending forward to the other car, "The inspector's just brought it. The Squire, whoever he was, is dead. They found his body this morning at the foot of a cliff near the Keep. Foul play? That's what you don't know, eh, inspector?"

"Can't say at all, sir," answered the inspector. "Marston Greyle might have been thrown down, he might have fallen down; it's a bad place. Anyway, what the doctor said, just before I hurried in here to tell Mrs. Greyle as the next relative that we know of, is that he'd been dead some days. The body, you see, was lying in a thicket at the foot of the cliff."

"Some days?" exclaimed Copplestone. "Days?"

"Four or five days at least, sir," replied the inspector. "So the doctor thinks. The place is a cliff between the high road from Northborough and the house itself. There's a short cut across the park to the house from that road. It looks as if—"

"It's clear how that happened then," interrupted Gilling. "He took that short cut when he came from Northborough that night. But if he's dead too, who's engineering all this? There's the fact those chests of gold have been removed from that old tower since Zachary Spurge left his cousin in charge there early this morning. Everything looks as if they'd been carried to Norcaster."

"Turn this car round," commanded Sir Cresswell. "We must get back to Norcaster."

The two cars went scurrying back to the old shipping town. When at last they had deposited the injured man at a neighboring hospital and came to a stop near the Angel, Zachary Spurge pulled Copplestone's sleeve, and with a look full of significance, motioned him aside to a quiet place.

Chapter 29

Scarvell's Cut

The quiet place was a narrow alley, which twisted away into a labyrinth of buildings that lay between the center of the town and the river. Not until Spurge had conducted Copplestone quite away from their late companions did he turn and speak; when he spoke, his words were accompanied by a glance which suggested mystery as well as confidence.

"Guv'nor," he said. "What's going to be done?"

"Have you pulled me down here to ask that?" exclaimed Copplestone, a little impatiently. "Good heavens, man, with all these complications arising—the gold gone, the Squire dead—there'll have to be a pretty deep consultation, and we'd better get back to it."

But Spurge shook his head.

"Not me, guv'nor," he said resolutely. "I ain't giving' no opinion o' consultations with lawyers and policemen—plain clothes or otherwise. They ain't no mortal good whatever, guv'nor, when it comes to horse sense. 'Tain't their fault; it's the system. They can't do nothing, start nothing, suggest nothing! They can only do things in the official, cut-and-dried, red-tape sort 'o way, guv'nor. You and me can do better."

"Well?" asked Copplestone.

"Listen," continued Spurge. "There ain't no doubt that that gold was carried off early this morning; must ha' been between the time I left Jim and sunup, 'cause they'd want to do the job in darkness. Ain't no reasonable doubt neither that the motor car what they used came here into Norcaster. Now, guv'nor, I ask you, where is it possible they'd make for? Not a railway station, 'cause them boxes 'ud be conspicuous and easy traced when inquiry was made. And yet they'd want to get 'em away as soon as possible. Very well, what's the other way o' getting any stuff out o' Norcaster? What? Why that!"

He jerked his thumb in the direction of a patch of gray water which shone dully at the end of the alley, and while his thumb jerked his eye winked.

"The river," he went on. "The river, guv'nor! Don't this here river, running into the free and bounding ocean six miles away, offer the best chance? What we want to do is to take a look round these here docks and quays and wharves, keeping our eyes open and our ears as well. Come on with me, guv'nor; I know places all along this riverside where you could hide the Bank of England till it was wanted, so to speak."

"But the others?" suggested Copplestone. "Hadn't we better fetch them?"

"No!" retorted Spurge assertively. "Two of us is enough. You trust me, guv'nor. I'll find out something. I know these docks. I'd do the job by myself, but it'll be better to have somebody along with me in case we need to send for help or anything of that nature. Come on, and if I don't find out before noon if there's any odd craft gone out o' this since morning, then I ain't what I believe myself to be."

Copplestone, who had considerable faith in the poacher's shrewdness, allowed himself to be led into the lowest part of the town, low in more than one sense of the word. Norcaster itself, as regards its ancient and time-hallowed portions, its church, its castle, its official buildings and highly-respectable houses, stood on the top of a low hill; its docks and wharves and the mean streets which intersected them had been made on a stretch of marshland that lay between the foot of that hill and the river. And down there was the smell of tar, merchandise, and narrow alleys full of sea-going men and raucous-voiced women. There were curious nooks, and corners, there were both ships being laden and ships being stripped of their cargo, there was such noise and confusion and inextricable mingling and elbowing that Copplestone thought it was as likely to find a needle in a haystack as to succeed in their quest.

But Zachary Spurge, leading him in and out of the throngs on the wharves, now inspecting a quay, now stopping to exchange a word or two with taciturn gentlemen at the corners of narrow streets, now going into shady-looking public houses by one door and coming out at another, seemed to be remarkably well satisfied and kept remarking to his companion that they would hear something yet. Nevertheless, by noon they had heard nothing, and Copplestone, who considered a search of this sort utterly purposeless, announced that he was going to more savory neighborhoods.

"Give it another turn, guv'nor," urged Spurge. "Have a bit o' faith in me now. You see, guv'nor, I've an idea, a theory, as you might term it, of my very own; only time's too short to go into details. Trust me a bit longer, guv'nor; there's a spot or two down here that I'm keen on taking a look at. This is Scarvell's Cut."

He drew his unwilling companion around a corner of the wharf and showed him a narrow creek, hemmed in by ancient buildings and sheds full of odds and ends of merchandise. It cut into the land at an irregular angle and was affording harbor to a mass of small vessels just then lying high and dry on the banks from which the tide had retreated. Along the side of this creek there was just as much crowding and confusion as on the wider quays; men were going in and out of the sheds and lofts; men were busy about the sides of the small craft. And again the feeling of uselessness came over Copplestone.

"What's the good of all this, Spurge?" he asked testily. "You'll never—"

Spurge suddenly laid a grip on his companion's elbow and twisted him aside into a narrow entry between the sheds.

"That's the good," he answered in an exulting voice. "Look there, guv'nor! Look at that tug boat. That one lying out there! Whose face is now a-peeping out o' that hatch? Come now?"

Copplestone looked in the direction which Spurge indicated. There, lying moored to the wharf at a point exactly opposite a tumbledown sail loft, was one of those strongly-built tugs which ply between the fishing fleets and the ports. It was a businesslike craft, rakish for its class, and it bore marks of recent sea usage. But Copplestone gave no more than a passing glance at it. What attracted his eyes was the face of a man who had come up out of a hatch, looking expectantly at the sail loft. There was grime and oil on that face, and the neck which supported the unkempt head rose out of a rough jersey, but Copplestone recognized his man clear enough. In spite of the attempt to look like a deckhand, there was no mistaking the skipper of the *Pike*.

"Good heavens," he muttered, as he stared across the crowded quay. "Andrius!"

"Right you are, guv'nor," whispered Spurge. "That very same, and no mistake! And now you'll perhaps see how I put things together. No doubt those folk as sent Sir Cresswell that message did see the *Pike* going east last evening, just so. But there wasn't no reason, considering what that chap and his lot had at stake why they shouldn't put him and one or two more on one of the many tugs. What I conclude they did, guv'nor, was to charter one o' them tugs and run her in here. I expect they've got the gold on board now; and when the tide comes up, out they'll go off into the free and open sea again to pick the *Pike* up somewhere. Ah! Smart 'uns they are, no doubt. But we've got 'em!"

"Not yet," said Copplestone. "What are we to do? Better go back and get help, eh?"

He was keenly watching Andrius, and as the skipper of the *Pike* suddenly moved, he drew Spurge further into the alley.

"He's coming out of that hatchway!" whispered Copplestone. "If he comes ashore he'll see us, and then—"

"No matter, guv'nor," said Spurge reassuringly. "They can't get out o' Scarvell's Cut into the river till the tide comes in. Yes, that's Cap'n Andrius right enough."

Andrius had drawn himself out of the hatch. He was dressed in the jersey, the thick leg wear, and short sea boots of an ocean-going man. Copplestone's recollection of him on board the *Pike* was of a very smartly attired, rather dandified person. Only some deep scheme would have caused him to assume this disguise, and he watched him with interest as Andrius rolled ashore and disappeared within the lower story of the sail loft. Spurge, too, watched with all his eyes, and he turned to Copplestone with a gleam of excitement.

"Guv'nor!" he said. "We've trapped 'em beautiful! I know that place. I've worked in there in my time. I know a way into it from the back. We'll get in that way and see what's being done. 'Tain't worked no longer, that sail loft. It's all falling to pieces. But first, some help."

"How are we to get help?" asked Copplestone eagerly.

"I know a man just aback of here that'll run up to the town with a message; a chap what can be trusted, sure and faithful. I'll get him," replied Spurge. "'Bide here five minutes, sir. I'll send a message to Mr. Vickers. This chap'll know him and'll find him. He can come down with the rest and the police, if he likes. Keep your eyes skinned, guv'nor."

He twisted away like an eel into the crowd of workers and idlers and left Copplestone at the entrance to the alley watching. He had not been so left more than a couple of minutes when a woman slipped past the mouth of the alley, swiftly, quietly, looking neither to right nor left. Of her veiled head and face he caught one glance, and in that glance he recognized her—Addie Chatfield!

And in the moment of that glance Copplestone recognized something vastly more important. Here was the explanation of the footprints at the old tower. The woman who wore fashionable and elegant boots? Addie Chatfield, of course! Was she not old Peter's daughter, a chip off the old block, even though a feminine chip? And did not he and Gilling know that she had been mixed up with Peter at the Bristol affair? Why, of course! Addie was an accomplice in all these things!

If Copplestone had a shadow of doubt remaining as to this conclusion, it was utterly dissipated when he saw Addie disappear into the same old sail loft into which Andrius had taken himself. She had gone to join her fellow conspirators. He began to fume and fret over Spurge leaving him down there alone. If only they had had Gilling and Vickers with them, armed as they were.

192

"All right, guv'nor," Spurge suddenly whispered at his shoulder. "They'll be here in a quarter of an hour. I telephoned to 'em."

"Do you know what?" exclaimed Copplestone. "Old Chatfield's daughter's gone in there, where Andrius went. Just now!"

"The play actress?" said Spurge. "You don't say, guv'nor? Ha! That explains everything. That's the missing link! We'll soon know what they're after, Mr. Copplestone. Follow me, quiet as a mouse."

Once more submitting to be led, Copplestone followed his unusual guide along the alley.

Chapter 30

The Greengrocer's Cart

Spurge led Copplestone a little way up the narrow alley from which they had observed the recent proceedings, suddenly turned off into a still narrower passage, and emerged at the rear of an ancient building of wood and stones which looked as if a stout shove or a strong wind would bring it down in dust and ruin.

"Back o' that old sail loft," he whispered, glancing over his shoulder at Copplestone. "Now, guv'nor, we're going in here. I worked a spell here when I was once lying low for a month or two. I know every inch of it, and if that lot are under this roof, I know where they'll be."

"They'll show fight, you know," remarked Copplestone.

"But ain't we got something to show fight with too?" answered Spurge with a knowing wink. "I've got my revolver handy, what Mr. Vickers give me, and I reckon you can handle yours. However, it ain't come to no revolver yet. What I want is to see and hear, guv'nor. Follow me."

He had opened a ramshackle door in the rear of the premises as he spoke, and he now beckoned his companion to follow him down a passage which evidently led to the front. There was no more than a dim light within, but Copplestone could see that the whole place was falling to pieces. And it was all wrapped in a dead silence. Out on the quay was the rattle of chains, the creaking of a windlass, the voices of men and shrill laughter of women. But in there no sound existed. Spurge suddenly stopped his stealthy creeping forward and looked at Copplestone suspiciously.

"Queer, ain't it?" he whispered. "I don't hear the ghost of a voice! You'd think that if they was in here, they'd be talking."

Clambering up a pile of fallen timber which lay in the passage and beckoning Copplestone to follow his example, Spurge looked through a broken slat in the wooden partition into an open shed which lay on Scarvell's Cut. The shed was empty. Folk were passing to and fro in front of it; the North Sea tug still lay at the wharf beyond, and a man who was evidently its skipper sat on a tub on its deck placidly smoking his short pipe. But of Addie Chatfield or of Andrius there was no sign. And the silence in that crumbling, rat-haunted house was deeper than ever.

"Guv'nor," muttered Spurge, "How long is it since you see her?"

"Almost as soon as you'd gone," answered Copplestone.

"Ten minutes ago," sighed Spurge. "Guv'nor, they've fooled us! She must ha' caught sight o' me nosing round, and she came here and gave the others the word, and they bucked out at the back. And bless you, at the back o' this shanty there's a perfect rabbit warren o' places; in fact, they call it the Warren. If they've got in there, all the police in Norcaster'll never find 'em; leastways, to speak truthful, not without a deal o' trouble."

"What about upstairs?" asked Copplestone.

"Upstairs?" said Spurge with a doubtful glance at the ramshackle stairway. "Mister, I don't believe nobody could get up them stairs! No, they've hooked it through the back here into the Warren. And once in there——"

He ended with an eloquent gesture, and dismounting from his perch made his way along the passage to a door which opened into the shed. Thence he looked out on the quay and along the crowded maze of Scarvell's Cut.

"Here's some of 'em, anyway, guv'nor," he announced. "I see Mr. Vickers and t'other London gentleman, and the old Admiral getting out of a motor car. Go to meet 'em, Mr. Copplestone, while I keep my eye on this here tug and its skipper."

Copplestone elbowed his way through the crowd until he met Sir Cresswell and his two companions. Copplestone could only respond to their inquiries with a gloomy shake of the head.

"We seem to have the devil's own luck," he growled dismally. "Spurge and I spotted Andrius by sheer accident. He was on a North Sea tug along the quay here. Then Spurge ran off to summon you. While he was away Miss Chatfield appeared."

"Addie Chatfield!" exclaimed Vickers.

"Exactly. And that," continued Copplestone, glancing at Gilling, "in my opinion, anyway, explains those elegant footprints up at the tower. Addie Chatfield, I tell you. She passed me as I was hiding at the entrance to an alley, and she went into an old sail loft outside which the tug I spoke of is moored and into which Andrius had strolled a minute or two previously. But neither she nor Andrius are there now. They've gone! Spurge says that at the back of this quay there's a perfect rabbit warren of courts and alleys, and if, or *rather*, as they've escaped into that . . . then?"

The detectives, who had accompanied Sir Cresswell on the interrupted expedition to the old tower, now followed him and his companions in a second car and arrived in time to hear Copplestone's story. They looked at each other.

"That's right enough comparatively speaking," said one. "But if they're in the Warren we shall get 'em out. The first thing to do, gentlemen, is to take a look at that tug."

"Just what I was thinking!" exclaimed Sir Cresswell. "Let us find out what its people have to say."

The man who smoked his pipe in placid contentment on the deck of the tug looked up in astonishment as the posse of eight crossed the plank which connected him with the quay. Nevertheless he preserved an undaunted front, kept his pipe in his tightly closed lips, and cocked a defiant eye at everybody.

"Skipper o' this craft?" asked the principal detective curtly. "Where are you from, and when did you come in here?"

The skipper removed his pipe and spat over the rail. He put the pipe back, folded his arms, and glared.

"What may that be to you?" he inquired. "And who may you be to walk aboard my vessel without leave?"

"None of that now," said the detective. "Come now; we're police officers. We've got warrants for two men that we believe to have been on your tug; one of 'em was seen here not so many minutes ago. You'd far better tell us what you know. If you don't tell now, you'll have to tell later. And I expect you've been paid already. Come on, out with it!"

The skipper, whose gnarled countenance had undergone several changes during this address, smote one red fist on top of the other.

"How was I to know as there was something on the crook in this here affair?" he said, almost cheerily. "Well, well. Warrants, you say? And what might be the partiklar' natur' o' them warrants?"

"Murder," answered the detective. "That's one charge anyhow for one of 'em. There's others."

"Murder's enough," responded the skipper. "Of course, nobody can tell a man to be a murderer by merely looking at his mug. Not at all. Nobody. However, this here is how it is. Last night it were. Evening, to be c'rect. Dark. I was on the edge o' the fleet, out there off the Dogger Bank. A yacht comes up, very fast sailer, and hails me. Was I going into Norcaster or anywheres about? Being a Northborough tug this, I wasn't. Would I go for a fee right then and there? Whereupon I asked what payment? Then we bargains. Eventual, we struck it at thirty pounds, cash down, which was paid prompt. I was to take two men straight into Norcaster to this here very slip, Scarvell's Cut, to wait while they put a bit of a cargo on board, and then to run 'em back to the same spot where I took 'em up. Done. They come aboard; the yacht goes off east; I come west. That's all. That part of it anyway."

"And the men?" suggested the detective. "What sort were they, and where are they?"

"The men now," said the skipper. "Two of 'em, both done up in deep sea style. But hadn't never done no deep sea nor yet any other sort o' sea work in their mortal days. Hands as white and soft as a lady's. One, an old chap with a face like a full moon on him, sly old chap him! T'other a younger man, looked as if he'd be a danger-ous chap to cross. Where are they? Should I know? What I knows certain is this, we gets in here about eight o'clock this morning and makes fast here; and ever since then them two's been as it were restless, allers lookin' out, so to speak, for summun as ain't come yet. The old chap went across into that there sail maker's loft an hour ago; and t'other, he followed him, recent. I ain't seen 'em since. Try there. And I say?"

"Well?" asked the detective.

"Shall I be wanted?" asked the skipper. "Cause if not, I'm off and away as soon as the tide serves. Ain't no good me waitin' here for them chaps, if you're goin' to take and hang 'em!"

"Got to catch 'em first," said the detective, with a glance at his two professional companions. "And while we're not doubting your word at all, we'll just take a look 'round your vessel. They might have slipped on board again, you see, while your back was turned."

But there was no sign of Peter Chatfield nor of his daughter nor of the captain of the *Pike* on that tug, nor anywhere in the sail maker's loft and its environs. Presently the detectives looked at one another, and their leader turned to Sir Cresswell.

"If these people have escaped into this quarter of the town," he said, "there'll have to be a regular hunt for them. I've known a man, who was badly wanted, stow himself away here for weeks. If Chatfield has accomplices down here in the Warren, he can hide himself and whoever's with him for a long time successfully. We'll have to get a lot of men to work."

"But I say," exclaimed Gilling. "You don't mean to tell me that three people, one a woman, could get away through these courts and alleys, packed as they are, without being seen? Come now!"

The detectives smiled indulgently.

"You don't know these folks," said one of them, inclining his head towards a squalid street at the end of which they had all gathered. "But they know *us*. It's a point of honor with them never to tell the truth to a policeman. If they saw those three, they'd never admit it to us until it's made worth their while."

"*Make* it worth their while then!" exclaimed Gilling, impatiently.

"All in due course, sir," said the official voice.

Copplestone recognized the futility of their own endeavors in that moment and led his men away to discuss matters amongst themselves, while the detectives proceeded leisurely into the Warren as if they were out for a quiet stroll in its byways. Sir Cresswell Oliver remarked on the difficulty of knowing exactly what to do once you had red tape on one side and unusual craftiness on the other.

"You think there's no doubt that gold was removed this morning by Chatfield's daughter?" he said to Copplestone as they went back to the center of the town together. Gilling and Vickers had turned aside elsewhere, and Spurge had gone to the hospital to ask for news of his cousin. "You think she was the woman whose footprints you saw up there at the Reaver's Glen?"

"Seeing that she's here in Norcaster and in touch with those two, what else can I think?" replied Copplestone. "It seems to me that they got in touch with her by wireless and that she removed the gold in readiness for her father and Andrius coming in here by that North Sea tug. If we could only find where she put those boxes or where she got the car from in which she brought it down from the tower."

"Vickers has already started some inquiries about cars," said Sir Cresswell. "She must have hired a car somewhere in the town. Certainly if we could hear of that gold, we would be on their track."

But they heard nothing of gold or of fugitives or of what the police and detectives were doing until the middle of the afternoon. It was then that Mr. Elkin, the manager of the bank from which Chatfield had withdrawn the estate and the private balance, came hurrying to the Angel and to Mrs. Greyle. His usually ruddy face was now pale with emotion, and he waved a scrap of crumpled paper. Mrs. Greyle and Audrey were in consultation with Sir Cresswell Oliver and Copplestone when the bank manager burst in on them without ceremony.

"I say, I say!" he exclaimed excitedly. "Can you believe it? The gold's come back! It's all safe—every penny. I scarcely know whether I'm dreaming or not, but we've got it!"

"What's all this?" demanded Sir Cresswell. "You've got back that gold?"

"Less than an hour ago," replied the bank manager, dropping into a chair and slapping his hand on his knees in his excitement, "a man, who turned out to be a greengrocer, came with his cart to the bank and said he'd been sent with nine boxes for delivery to us. Asked who had sent him, he replied that early this morning a lady, whom he didn't know, had asked him to put the boxes in his shed until she called for them; she brought them in a motor car. This afternoon she called again at two o'clock, paid him for the storage and for what he was yet going to do, and instructed him to put the boxes on his cart and bring them to us. Which," continued Mr. Elkin, gleefully rubbing his hands together, "he did! With this! And that, my dear ladies and good gentlemen, is the most extraordinary document which in all my forty years' experience of banking matters I have ever seen!"

He laid a dirty, crumpled half-sheet of cheap note paper on the table at which they were all sitting, and Copplestone, bending over it, read aloud what was there written.

"Mr. Elkin, please place the contents of the nine cases sent herewith to the credit of the Greyle Estate. Peter Chatfield, Agent."

Amidst a chorus of exclamations Sir Cresswell asked a sharp question.

"Is that really Chatfield's signature?"

"Oh, undoubtedly!" replied Mr. Elkin. "Not a doubt. As soon as I saw it, I closely questioned the greengrocer, but he knew nothing. He said the lady was wrapped up about her face, veiled, on both her visits. Said that as soon as she'd seen him set off with his load of boxes, she disappeared. He lives, this greengrocer, on the edge of the town. I've got his address. But I'm sure he knows no more."

"And the cases have been examined?" asked Copplestone.

"Every one, my dear sir," answered the bank manager with a satisfied smirk. "Every penny is there! Glorious!"

"This is most extraordinary," said Sir Cresswell. "But what on earth does it all mean? If we could only trace that woman from the greengrocer's place."

But nothing came of the attempt to carry out this proposal, and no news arrived from the police. The evening had grown far advanced when Mrs. Greyle and Audrey with Sir Cresswell, Mr. Petherton, Vickers, Copplestone, and Gilling were all in a private parlor together. It was at this late hour when the door suddenly opened and a woman entered. She threw back a heavy veil and revealed herself as Addie Chatfield.

Chapter 31

Ambassadress Extraordinaire

I f Copplestone had never seen Addie Chatfield before, if he had not known that she was an actress of renown, her entrance into that suddenly silent room would have convinced him that here was a woman gifted with the dramatic instinct. Addie's presentation of herself to the small and select audience was intensely dramatic without being theatrical. She filled the stage. It was as if the lights had suddenly gone down in the auditorium and up on the stage, as if a hush fell and every ear opened wide to catch the first word. Addie's voice was soft and liquid and accompanied by a smile which was calculated to soften the seven hearts which had begun to beat a little quicker at her coming.

"I have come to ask . . . mercy."

Her cheeks blushed modestly as she moved towards the center table and bowed to the startled and inquisitive eyes.

There was a faint sigh of surprise from somebody. Sir Cresswell Oliver, only now realizing that a pretty woman had entered the room, made haste to place a chair for her. But before Addie could respond to his old-fashioned bow, Mr. Petherton was on his legs.

"I take it that this is the young wom—the Miss Chatfield of whom we have had occasion to speak a good deal today," he said very stiffly. "I think, Sir Cresswell, eh?"

"Yes," said Sir Cresswell, glancing from the visitor to the old lawyer. "What do you think, Petherton?"

"The situation is decidedly unpleasant," said Mr. Petherton, more icily than ever. "The fact is that the police are now searching for this . . . cr . . . this *young lady*."

"But I am here," exclaimed Addie. "I am not afraid of the police. I came of my own free will to explain. And to ask you all for mercy."

"For whom?" demanded Mr. Petherton.

"Well, for my father, if you want to know," replied Addie with another softening glance. "Come now, all of you, what's the good of being so down on an old man who hasn't got so very long to live? Two of you here are getting on in years yourself, and it doesn't become old men to be so hard. Does it, Sir Cresswell?"

Sir Cresswell turned away, obviously disconcerted; when he looked around again, he avoided the eyes of the young men and glanced a little sheepishly at Mr. Petherton.

"It seems to me, Petherton," he said, "that I should like to hear what Miss Chatfield has to say. Evidently she comes to tell us something of her own free will. I should like to know what that something is. I think Mrs. Greyle would like to know too."

"Indeed," exclaimed Mrs. Greyle, who was watching the central figure with great curiosity. "I should indeed like to know, especially if Miss Chatfield proposes to tell us something about her father."

Mr. Petherton, who frowned very much and appeared to be greatly disturbed by these irregularities, twisted sharply around on the visitor.

"Where is your father?" he demanded.

"Where you can't find him," retorted Addie with a flash of the eye that lit up her whole face. "So's Andrius. They're off, my good sir! Both of them. Neither you nor the police can lay hands on them now. And you'll do no good by laying hands on me. Come now," she went on, "I said I'd come to ask for mercy, but I came for more. This game's all over. The curtain's down. At least it's going down. Why don't you let me tell you all about it, and then we can be friends?"

Mr. Petherton gazed at Addie for a moment as if she were some extraordinary specimen of a new race. Then he took off his glasses, waved them at Sir Cresswell and dropped into a chair with a snort.

"I wash my hands of the whole thing," he said. "Do what you like, all of you. Irregular. Most irregular!"

Vickers gave Addie a sly look.

"Don't incriminate yourself, Miss Chatfield," he said. "There's no need for you to tell anything against yourself, you know."

"Me?" exclaimed Addie. "Why, I've been playing good angel all day long. Me incriminate myself, indeed! If Miss Greyle there only knew what I'd done for her. Look here," she continued, suddenly turning to Sir Cresswell, "I've come to tell all about it. And first of all, know this: every penny of that money that my father drew from the bank has been restored this afternoon."

"We know that," said Sir Cresswell.

"Well, that was me! I engineered that," continued Addie. "And second, the *Pike* will be back at Scarhaven during the night to unload everything that was being carried away. My doing again. I'm no fool, and I know when a game's up."

"So there was a game?" suggested Vickers.

Addie leaned forward from the chair which Sir Cresswell had given her at the end of the table and, planting her elbows on the table edge, began to check off her points on the tips of her slender fingers. She was well aware that she had the stage to herself, and she showed her consciousness of it.

"You have it," she answered. "There was a game, and I know more of it than anybody. I'll tell all now. It began at Bristol. I was playing there. One morning my father fetched me out from rehearsal to tell me that he'd been down to Falmouth to meet the new Squire of Scarhaven, Marston Greyle; he found him so ill that they'd had to go to a doctor, who forbade Greyle to travel far at a time. He knew that I was in Bristol, so he came to me. I got Greyle a quiet room at my lodgings. A doctor said he was very bad, but he didn't say that he was in immediate danger. However, Greyle died that very night."

Addie paused for a moment. Copplestone and Gilling exchanged glances. So far, this was all known to them, but what was coming?

"I was alone with Greyle for a while that evening," continued Addie. "It was while my father was getting some food downstairs. Greyle said to me that he knew he was dying, and he gave me a pocketbook in which were all his papers. He said I could give it to my father. He became unconscious soon after that, so he never mentioned that pocketbook to my father. Neither did I. But after Greyle was dead, I examined its contents carefully. And when I was in London at the end of the week, I showed his documents to . . . my husband."

Addie again paused, and at least two of the men glanced at each other with a look of surmise. Her husband?

"The fact is," she went on suddenly, "Captain Andrius is my husband. But nobody knew that, not even my own father. We've been married three years; I met him when I was crossing over to America once. We got married, and we kept the marriage secret . . . for reasons of our own. Well, he met me in London the Sunday after Greyle's death, and I showed him the papers which were in Greyle's pocketbook. And this was where it was very wicked of me and him, though we've tried to make up for it today. We fixed up what you two gentlemen would call a conspiracy. My husband had a brother, an actor, not up to much, nor of much experience. He had been brought up in the states and was just then in town doing nothing. We took him into confidence, coached him in everything, furnished him with all the papers in the pocketbook, and resolved to pass him off as the real Marston Greyle."

Mr. Petherton stirred angrily in his chair and turned a protesting face on Sir Cresswell.

"Apart from being irregular," he said, "this is altogether outrageous! This woman is openly boasting of conspiracy and—"

"You're wrong," said Addie. "I'm not boasting; I'm explaining. You ought to be obliged to me."

"If Mrs. Andrius—to give the lady her *real* name—cares to unburden her secrets to us, I really don't see why we shouldn't listen to her, Mr. Petherton," observed Vickers. "It simplifies matters greatly."

"That's what I say," agreed Addie. "I'm done with all this, and I want to clear things up, whatever comes of it. So as I say, we fixed that up with my brother-in-law."

"His name, his *real* name, if you please?" inquired Vickers.

"Well, his real name was Martin Andrius," replied Addie. "We gave him the papers and arranged for him to go down to Scarhaven to my father. Now I want to assure you all right here that my father never did really know that Martin was an imposter. He began to suspect something at the end, but he didn't know for a fact. Martin went down to him at Scarhaven just a week after the real Marston Greyle had died. He claimed to be Marston Greyle; he produced his papers. My father told about the Marston Greyle he'd buried. Martin pooh-poohed that; he said that that man must be a secretary of his, Mark Grey, who, after stealing some documents had come here. He no doubt meant to pass himself off as the real man until he could get something substantial out of the estate, when he would have vanished. And my father accepted that story. Why? Because he knew that if Miss Greyle came into the estate, she and her mother would have bundled one Peter Chatfield out of his stewardship quick."

"Proceed if you please," said Sir Cresswell. "There are other details about which I am anxious to hear."

"Meaning about your own brother," remarked Addie. "I'm coming to that. Well, on Martin's story and on his production of those papers—birth certificates, Greyle papers of their life in America, and so on—everybody accepted him as the real man, and things seemed to go quite smoothly till that Sunday when Bassett Oliver chose to go to Scarhaven. And now, Sir Cresswell, I'll tell you the plain and absolute truth about your brother's death. On that Sunday I was at Scarhaven, for I wanted to speak privately with Martin. I arranged to meet him in the grounds of the Keep during the afternoon, and I *did* meet him there. We hadn't been talking many minutes when Bassett Oliver came through the door in the wall, which one of us had carelessly left open. He didn't see us, but we saw him. And we were afraid because Bassett Oliver knew both of us. He'd met Martin several times in London and in New York. He knew that Martin was no more Marston Greyle than he himself was. So we both shrank behind some shrubs, and Martin went white as death. But Bassett Oliver crossed the lawn never seeing us, entered the turret tower, and went up. Martin said to me 'If Bassett Oliver sees me, there's an end to all this. What's to be done?' But before I could speak or think, we saw Bassett at the top of the tower, making his way round the inside parapet. And suddenly he disappeared!"

Addie's voice had become low and grave during the last few minutes, and she kept her eyes on the table at the end. But she looked up readily enough when Sir Cresswell seized her arm and barked out a question almost in her ear.

"Is that the truth? The real truth?"

"It's the absolute truth," she answered softly, regarding him steadily. "I'm not altogether a bad sort, but I'm telling you the real truth in that. It was a sheer accident; he stepped off the parapet and fell. Martin went into the base of the tower and came back saying he was dead. We were both dazed; we separated. He went off to the house; I went to my father by a roundabout way. We decided to let things take their course. You all know a great deal of what happened then. But later, my husband and Martin began to take certain things into their own hands. I don't quite know how much my father knew of their secrets or how little, but I do know that they determined to make a purse for themselves out of Scarhaven. Martin left certain powers in my husband's hands and went off to London. He was waiting there until Andrius got everything ready for a flight on the *Pike*. Then he was to have set off to Scarhaven to join her crew. But he didn't join, and none of us knew what had become of him until today, when we heard of what had been found at Scarhaven. That explained it; Martin had taken that short cut from the Northborough road through the woods behind the Keep and fallen over the cliff at the Hermit's steps. But that very night, you, Mr. Vickers, Mr. Copplestone, and Miss Greyle nearly stopped everything, and Andrius and Chatfield carried you off. You know what happened after that."

"But," interjected Vickers quickly, "not your share in the last development."

"My share's been to see that the thing was over. If I wanted to save them all, I had to put a stop to it," rejoined Addie with a grim smile. "I tell you, I didn't know what they'd been up to until today. I was in England, wondering what was going on. Yesterday I got a coded message from my husband. When he fetched my father away from you, he forced him to tell where that gold was; then he sent me full instructions to recover it. I did so last night. Never you mind the exact means I took, nor who it was that I got to help. I got the gold, and I took good care to put it where I knew it would be safe. Then this morning I went to meet the two of them at Scarvell's Cut, and I took the upper hand. I got them away from that sail loft safely. I made my husband give me a coded message for the man in charge of the *Pike*, telling him to return at once to Scarhaven; I made my father write a note to Elkin at the bank, telling him to place the gold which I sent with it to the credit of the Greyle Estate. And when all that was done. I got them away. They are gone!"

Vickers, who had never taken his eyes off Addie during her lengthy explanation, gave her a whimsical smile.

"Safely?" he asked.

"I'll defy the police to find them anyway," replied Addie with a quick response of lip and eye. "I don't do things by halves. They are gone. And now I've made a clean breast of it all. The thing's over and done with. There's nothing to prevent Miss Greyle there from coming into her rights; I can prove them, my father can prove them. So is it any use doing what that old gentleman's just craving to do? You all see what he wants; he's dying to hand me over to the police."

Sir Cresswell Oliver rose, glanced at Audrey and her mother, and assumed his old quarter-deck manner.

"Not tonight, I think, Petherton," he said authoritatively. "No, certainly not tonight!"

Some months later, when Audrey Greyle had come into possession of Scarhaven and had married Copplestone in the little church behind her mother's cottage, she and her husband visited a romantic and secluded part of the country. And in the course of their wanderings they came across a very pretty village, wherein lay a charming retreat. It looked so attractive from the road along which they were walking that they halted and peered through its trimly-kept hedge.

And there, seated in the easiest of chairs on the smoothest of lawns, roses about him and newspaper in hand, they saw Peter Chatfield. They looked at him for a long moment; then they looked at each other, smiled pleasantly, and then passed on in silence. But when that village lay behind them, Copplestone gave his wife a sly glance and permitted himself to make one final statement.

"Chatfield!" he mused. "Chatfield, sublimely ungrateful that he isn't in Dartmoor Prison."